'I could find y

'I couldn't ask that of a stranger.'

'If you will allow me an hour of your time to escort you around the main sights of our beautiful city, we may become friends—at *least* friends—and then you would not mind asking favours, would you? We could even make a few stops on the way to pass the word among some of those contacts I mentioned.' His eyes were mocking. 'Unless you are afraid of me?'

Dear Reader

TEN GUINEAS ON LOVE is Alice Thornton's launch in Masquerade, a Georgian romp where the heroine *must* have a husband—you'll be enchanted. And welcome back to Hazel Smith; you'll really enjoy THE GOLDEN PHOENIX rising from the ashes of the 1906 San Francisco earthquake.

Don't forget—see the end pages for next month's treat. . . Enjoy!

The Editor

Hazel Smith was born in Loughborough, but spent her early life in London. She now lives in Thornton Heath, writing around keeping house in an acceptable degree of chaos, and coping with a hectic job and an active son. She has been writing short stories since her teens, before writing historical novels.

THE GOLDEN PHOENIX

Hazel Smith

*First published in Great Britain 1992
by Mills & Boon Limited*

© Hazel Smith 1992

*Australian copyright 1992
Philippine copyright 1992
This edition 1992*

ISBN 0 263 77783 9

*Masquerade is a trademark published by
Mills & Boon Limited, Eton House,
18–24 Paradise Road, Richmond, Surrey, TW9 1SR.*

*Set in 10 on 10½ pt Linotron Times
04-9207-77476*

*Typeset in Great Britain by Centracet, Cambridge
Made and printed in Great Britain*

CHAPTER ONE

THE hawk circled lazily, cruising the high thermals, scanning the land below. It saw the girl on the pinto, knew her as a challenge, and tightened its circle. The rider sat her mount with an ease born of long hours in the saddle, her slightly elongated grey eyes narrowed against the blazing sun, her body carrying a leashed tension as she watched the scrubland below and the hawk above.

It was going to be another of those days, she thought, as the rising sun turned from soft red to the brilliant, dazzling yellow of a deep-stoked furnace. The horse moved restlessly, kicking up small puffs of red dust as it, too, gazed out across that section of the Llano Estacado in Texas. The sky was more white than blue above the plains, and even had there been a cloud it would not have stirred in that vast expanse, and the rider was equally still—but hers was a waiting stillness.

And the jack-rabbit broke cover from the stand of cholla cactus.

In the same instant that the golden bird folded its wings against its body and plummeted in a sixty-mile-per-hour fall towards the earth the girl gave a high-pitched cry and dug in her heels, setting the pinto from a stand to a flat gallop in pursuit. Both raced for the grey-brown rabbit and at that moment the creature felt the vibration of the hoofs and became aware of its danger. With a twist of its spine it raced off at an angle, then jack-knifed and set off for its burrow, twisting and turning in a crazed, suicidal bid for freedom.

The pinto matched it turn for turn, weaving, stopping, turning on another tack, changing course every few seconds, its hoofs striking sparks from the rocks.

5

Suddenly the girl kicked her left foot clear of the stirrup and swung over, Indian fashion, to hang along the side of the horse. The rabbit was tiring and had decided to make one long straight dash to its burrow. The pinto instinctively compensated for the weight change, neck extended, muscles bunched, ears flattened as it sensed the hawk.

With tenths of a second to spare the hawk braked, its body weight slammed to a halt by sudden spread wings as the white cotton blouse of the rider cut across its vision. It twisted in mid-air and soared in one movement, screaming its rage and challenging her right to the prey as, with a cry of jubilation, the girl's fingers closed over the long ears and she swung the jack upwards. For a second she held the animal aloft, brandishing her prize before the hawk's baffled glare as the pinto came to a sliding halt, then, with laughter curving her full lips, she set her prey down within feet of its burrow.

The jack-rabbit froze, disbelieving.

'Go on, stupid,' the girl commanded and the animal bolted to the safety of its home.

Charisse Linton patted the pinto's neck and reached to pull the twitching ears. 'A good run, Chico,' she praised, then, scanning the land to the south, she stiffened. 'Hello. . .what can Lobo want?' And she kicked the pony ahead to meet the approaching rider.

The Indian's normally expressionless features were grave and the deep-set eyes betrayed his concern. 'It's your father, Miss Linton. Just like last time. The doctor is with him now.'

Charisse caught her breath. The last time her father's heart had brought him down the doctor had said that another attack could be his last, but still the indomitable John Linton refused to accept his limitations. Nodding to the man who had been both friend and employee of the family for most of her life, the girl immediately swung her mount around and raced for home.

The rambling, red-tiled adobe hacienda lay silent beneath the heat of the sun, its shutters closed, the servants moving about the rooms on softly sandalled feet, communicating by gestures, glancing fearfully in the direction of the heavily panelled door of the master bedroom if one coughed or a kitchen plate rattled. In that room, on the great oak bed, a man lay with closed eyes, his mane of white hair swept back from the deeply tanned and lined forehead, the shaggy brows, slightly hooked nose and jutting chin giving the impression of a sleeping bird of prey.

Three white candles in the large silver candelabrum threw a soft glow about the spartan room with its dark oak furniture contrasting with the white walls and locally woven Indian rugs. Sitting on a low stool, back to the window-wall, a plump Mexican woman told a rosary, her lips moving soundlessly. All was still.

Suddenly there was a clatter of hoofs on the flagged courtyard outside, the front door banged, there were voices in the hall, then the bedroom door was flung open. Charisse stood there, her loose blouson shirt damp with perspiration, the wide chaperejos over her denims as dusty as the fine-tooled boots. Her white-gold hair was pulled into a large chignon, accentuating the fine bone-structure and cat-like grey eyes, now wide with concern—a concern she knew she must hide for the sake of the man on the bed—and so, drawing a deep breath, she swept into the room, declaring, 'Now don't pretend you are dying, Father. You are simply sulking because Dr Nelson forbade you your brandy and cigars until further notice!'

Instantly the man on the bed opened bright blue eyes and gave a, 'Hrumph! The doctor's a fool!'

Charisse dismissed the servant with a smiling gesture and went to sit on the bedside, regarding her father, head slightly tilted. 'You have suffered another heart attack because you refused to take life easy after the last one six months ago. You won't delegate authority, you consume the better part of a bottle of brandy a day, and at seventy years old still have the wisdom of a child—and a recalcitrant child at that!' She poured a glass of cool water and handed him two pills from a bottle on the bedside cabinet. 'Come on, sit up and take these. Dr Nelson said he was about to give up on you, but I'm a lot tougher. Come on.'

Only half grudgingly the man pulled himself further up on the piled pillows and surrendered to his daughter's bullying, reading the fear and worry in the soft grey eyes that belied her words. 'You're too much like your mother for my comfort,' he complained. 'She was a termagent as well.' But a half-smile betrayed him.

'Being concerned with your welfare doesn't make me a nagging shrew, though you would try the patience of a saint. Poor Dr Nelson has to take a large tequila before he'll even approach you and even the servants we've had for years are terrified of you.'

'So why aren't you?'

'Because I've lived all my life with your bellowing and bad temper. If I were an oak I'd break, if an aspen I'd tremble, but I'm a willow, Father, I bend, and you, Father, are simply a lot of wind, and I'm probably the only one who knows it!' She dropped a kiss on to the leathery cheek and ignored his glare. 'Now, what will you have for lunch, the omelette and creamed chicken?'

'What happened to the steak? That's what happens when you exchange three-thousand head of prime beef for that filthy, inedible black stuff we're sitting on. A man can't find a decent steak!'

'That filthy black stuff, as you call it, has made us more than comfortable and anyway red meat is off the menu for now.' She saw his mutinous expression and smiled, loving him in spite of himself. 'The sooner you get better, the sooner you can go back to your bad old ways.'

'Oh. . .very well!' Then, on a new tack, 'Where were you anyway? You look more like one of our vacqueros—when we had vacqueros—than the lady of the house. You have perfectly good riding skirts and a beauty of a Mexican saddle with all the trimmings that you haven't even looked at.'

'I have no objection to acting the part of a wealthy oil baron's daughter when we have company, and if a group of the ladies at one of our annual *barbacoas* wish to go for a genteel canter then I will obligingly wear hat, gloves and skirt and ride side-saddle.'

He frowned, but the blue eyes were twinkling. 'I know: you can't chase jack-rabbits in a skirt, and that half-broke pinto of yours is only used to an Indian blanket and barely tolerates that scrap of leather that the English call a saddle. I haven't seen you for over two days. You know I don't like you sleeping out alone.'

Charisse took the range-toughened hand. 'I'm safer in the desert than in any city I've been to: at least here the rattlers *warn* you before they attack, which is more than I can say for the two-legged snakes I've met! I spent the whole of last year with Aunt Gemma in England just to please you, but I am far more at home in what she calls "the wilds" than in an English salon or the fashion houses of Doucette and Worth in Paris where she insisted on dragging me.'

'At least you *looked* like a lady when you came back! Your mother would have been proud of you.' The brilliant eyes softened and he gave her hand an abstracted little squeeze. 'Yes. . . I would have liked her to see you in all your finery.'

'You still miss her, don't you? I wish I could remember her.'

'Yes. . .yes I do miss her. You were only three when she died; it doesn't seem all of seventeen years ago, and she only thirty-three.'

'I know it was many years before you allowed me to

ride at all, worrying lest I, too, fell, but accidents do happen, Father. Nothing could have prevented it. You always said Mother was an excellent rider, but even the best can't foresee a gopher hole in late dusk light. Even had *you* been with her it would have been no different.' She did not speak that other name, the name that was no longer mentioned in the house, and was therefore startled when the man admitted,

'Ralph was too young, but the boy had guts even then—a twelve-year-old riding over fifteen miles for help in near dark across the canyonlands at a pace that near killed his horse.'

'Poppa! You haven't spoken of Ralph since. . . since. . .'

'Since I banished him from this house eight years ago. I know.' He turned to stare at the flickering candle-flame as if evading her eyes. 'A brush with death so close to the last gives a man pause for thought—yes, even me. I got to thinking. . .well. . .if things had worked out differently. . .not that I'm one for regrets, mind you. The past is past.' He halted and Charisse held her breath. Then very quietly he confessed, 'I *have* missed Ralph. It would be one helluva waste if I went without telling him so.'

'Oh, Poppa!' And she bent to hug him, unheeding the tears that overspilled, but, immediately regretting his weakness, he pushed her away.

'No need for female carrying on. Not like you. He's gone and that's all there is to it. Unless. . .' the bright eyes held hers '. . .unless he could be found.'

Charisse stared at him, incredulous joy mingling with disbelief. 'Found?'

After that terrible scene eight years before when John Linton—ex-Colonel Linton of five generations of army colonels and majors—had branded his twenty-year-old son a coward for not volunteering to join Teddy Roosevelt's 'Rough Riders' in the Spanish-American War, Ralph's name had been banished too.

Even when a neighbour's boy had been killed during the assault on San Juan Hill on the first of July and the grief-stricken mother had cried to John, 'You should thank God your son never joined!' even then John had stated only,

'I have no son.'

No one, not even Charisse, who loved him, had imagined that the acerbic John Linton had sorely missed the son he loved and been too proud to acknowledge it—until now.

When Ralph had been born it had not occurred to John that, in spite of now being a wealthy rancher, his son would not join the army. He had dreamed and planned of living through his son, watching the boy soar up from the rigid confines of military academy to the highest ranks, as his own father and grandfather had watched him.

Then came the war and to the shocked disbelief of ex-Colonel Linton his son had refused to volunteer, but stated, with quiet resolution, his intention of becoming a doctor. 'I don't want to kill,' he had declared, the bright blue eyes, so like his father's, level and determined. 'I am sorry, Father, but I can't see war as anything but legalised murder. I want to save life, not end it.'

There had been a blazing row that had lasted for three days and almost ended in blows, the outcome of which saw John Linton calling his son a lily-livered coward and vowing that if ever the boy set foot on the ranch again he would have him horse-whipped. That very evening Ralph had bade an emotional farewell to his twelve-year-old sister and left for San Francisco, it being 'as far away from war as I can get'.

Now, Charisse decided, 'I will go myself just as soon as you're on your feet again.'

'No. No time for that.' He waved his hand in a dismissive gesture. 'Nelson told me that the next one would finish me for sure and, since I have absolutely no intention of spending the rest of my life in a wheelchair, I don't know when that will be.' At her expression he reached out to pat the involuntarily clenched fist. 'Now don't look like a gut-shot deer; you knew I'd never make old bones. I'm not a rocking-chair hero. Thanks to this lake of black gold we're apparently sitting on and the dreams of those crazy Germans, Gottlieb Daimler and Carl Benz, back in ninety-three, you will be well provided for and I know you'd not want to see me fretting away in bed. When I go I want to be taking Samson over that five-bar gate at the end of the drive, or with a glass of brandy in my hand and a party in progress.'

Recovered now, Charisse raised a smile. 'Samson is an expensive piece of horseflesh—you'd better make it the party.'

'That's my girl!'

Two days later Charisse began the long and still arduous journey north-west. 'Go to the Gateway Hotel on Nob Hill,' John had instructed. 'It's owned by an old army buddy of mine, George Davis. He gambles like I drink: bets on anything from which piece of sugar a fly will land on to which outsider will romp home at Bay Meadows track, but poker is his first love and a pretty face his second, so he'll take good care of you. San Francisco is no place for a young woman on her own.'

Charisse had laughed at his fears, but to please him carried a tiny snub-nosed forty-one-calibre derringer in her purse—that lethal lady's gun that was more like a squat hand-cannon which, at close quarters, could blow a hole in an attacker as big as a man's fist.

She felt no fear of the unknown; rather, a subdued excitement tingled in her veins. Part of her worried over her father's health, but a more adventurous part welcomed the challenge. She was certain that she would find her brother's name listed in the telephone directory, and, even if he was out of town for any reason, would meet up with him in a day or so. In that time she would explore the legendary City of Hills, the Golden City, the wild and notorious Barbary Coast. Every sense tingled with expectation as she drank in the sights and sounds and scents of the bustling metropolis, as crowded as London and Paris, yet with a strange clarity, an aliveness of its own. San Francisco was a new city in comparison with those others, and its inhabitants were not staid buinessmen or shopkeepers, although both existed. No, this city had been founded by adventurers, pioneers, dreamers, poets, people with impossible visions from every country on earth.

The Gateway Hotel on California Street was not as imposing as the neighbouring wedding-cake mansions of men like Leland Stanford, Collis P. Huntington, Mark Hopkins, or Charles Crocker—the celebrated 'Big Four' of Central Pacific railroads, whose fortunes were at one time in the hundreds of millions—but the white stone edifice, built in the grand French baroque style, certainly rivalled the Fairmont Hotel two blocks away, which was due to be opened within the month.

Eyes wide, Charisse preceded the porter—who had appeared, genie-like, the minute her cab drew up at the door—across the marbled foyer. She took in the slender, fluted columns that supported the high domed ceiling where nymphs and cupids desported, and the curved staircase richly covered in deep blue carpet. . . and there she stopped, gaze riveted to the man who stood there watching her fixedly.

It was almost as if she heard him say, 'Run from me and keep running for I am Danger. I am the personification of all your most atavistic dreams. I am Conquest.'

The aquiline features, haloed by blue-black hair, had an exotically European look—not Mexican, she was certain, but perhaps Spanish, even French, though the deeply tanned skin favoured the former. His stance was deceptively casual as he leaned with one arm on the lower pillar of the marble balustrade, one booted foot crossed negligently over the other, yet it was the relaxation of her old enemy the hawk, holding the upper currents awaiting view of its prey, or the uncoiling sinuousness of a sleek black panther before the charge. Amid the maelstrom of her thoughts came the quote: 'Yond Cassius has a lean and hungry look. . . such men are dangerous'.

Suddenly he smiled, a slow, knowing smile as if, from twenty yards distance, he had read her every thought, and one devil's eyebrow lifted in sardonic query.

Flustered, Charisse felt the heat flood her cheeks and spun away, busying herself with signing in and accepting her key. How *dared* he look at her like that, as if. . .as if every particle of clothing had been stripped from her, melted in the heat of that regard?

'This way, madam,' the boy said, lifting her valise and suitcase.

She had to turn and follow him. The man was gone. Yet his presence remained as she approached the spot where he had stood and she almost expected him to reappear, broad shoulders in the poured-on grey morning suit barring her way. So strong was the feeling that, as she passed on her way to the elevator she was compelled to reach out and touch that marble pillar at the bottom of the staircase—and withdrew her hand as if burned. The marble was warm! How long had he been standing there watching her? Who was he? Was he a guest? Would she see him again? Would he speak. . .? She wouldn't answer!

Heart still erratic, she was unaware of the luxury of her surroundings, the coral and ivory décor, the delicate Louis XIV chairs and chaise-longue carrying forward the French influence to the brocaded four-poster.

Dismissing the boy with a coin, she went to splash some cool water from the jug on the marble-topped wash-stand into the floral hand-painted bowl. Soaking one of the fluffy pink flannels, she dabbed at her cheeks and temples. 'Fool!' she remonstrated aloud. 'You are behaving like a moonstruck teenager! Chances are you will never see him again; after all, you are only here for two or three days. Pull yourself together. While here your whole *raison d'être* is to find Ralph, not wonder what colour a man's eyes are!'

Unpacking the large suitcase that the boy had lifted on to a long padded stool at the foot of the bed, she hung her clothes in the double maplewood wardrobe. Hesitating, she selected a walking dress of palest ice-blue with black velvet trim at hem and cuffs and about the edge of the deep embroidered fichu that fell into points at sides and back. A matching 'ripple-brim' hat held a confection of deeper blue silk flowers with feather 'leaves'. She had purchased both at a London fashion house just prior to her return and knew that wearing them she resembled some porcelain-fragile doll. No one who met this exquisite creature would equate her with Charisse Linton, the oil magnate's high-spirited daughter who rode a half-broke pinto, wore faded denims and boots whenever possible and carried a lethal derringer. Only perhaps the hands betrayed her—square and tanned with short-cut nails and strong wrists—but with a shrug she pulled on a pair of fine kid gloves, hiding the incriminating evidence. 'There!' With a last look in the gilt-edged cheval-glass she gave a nod and, with an air of anticipation, went downstairs.

In the foyer she crossed to ask the clerk for the directory.

'Please allow me,' he smiled helpfully, dazzled by the white-gold and ice-blue vision before him.

'Thank you. I am looking for my brother, Dr Ralph Linton, but I'm afraid I have no idea what part of the city he practises in.'

Scanning the relevant section, the man frowned

perplexedly and shook his head. 'I am sorry, Miss Linton, but there's no one of that name listed. We have a Landon, Lindon, London. . .no. . .no R. Linton.'

'But there *must* be!' Charisse stared at him. She had not for one moment considered that Ralph might not be registered. 'He *must* have a telephone; anyone of any worth has a telephone nowadays. A doctor surely would.'

'One would think so. However, there are those who are. . .shall we say. . .less well-known for a variety of reasons. Some treat the poorer neighbourhoods and therefore would not need one, since their patients obviously would not have. Is it possible that your brother. . .?'

Charisse thought of her brother's almost ascetic Greek-god looks and fastidious taste in clothes and gave a little laugh. 'Possible, but most improbable. It appears I shall need help after all.'

'If I might suggest, Miss Linton, a hired cab that would take you safely about those areas? There is always a remote chance that you might see him out walking, and of course you could instruct the driver to make discreet enquiries for you in certain establishments that a young lady such as yourself would not wish to go. You would at the same time see something of our city and, while you were doing so, I could ask questions on your behalf. One of the staff may know something.'

Charisse gave him a brilliant smile, making him her slave for life. 'How good of you! That is an excellent idea. I shall talk with Mr Davis on my return.'

'Mr Davis?'

'Of course. Your Mr George Davis. He was a close friend of my father's. Will he be available later?'

The clerk accorded her a strange look. 'Mr Davis is no longer here, Miss Linton. He lives over on Franklin Street.'

Charisse frowned. 'I had of course assumed I would meet him in his office.' Then, with a shake of the head, 'It doesn't matter. I may not need his services after all.'

'Do you wish me to have a cab called?'

'No, that's all right. I shall walk for a while.' And, with another smile of thanks, made her way out into the street.

Assailed by the bustle and clatter, she watched from the kerbside, utterly fascinated, as the California Street cable car clanked by, the gripman and conductor almost hidden by the laughing, joking, ebullient passengers who rode the outside step, clinging tightly to the rails, crushing the knees of those sitting more decorously on the wooden benches. As they reached the intersection the signal bell rang out, pulled several times in a gay tintinnabulating melody and Charisse laughed aloud in delight.

'Perfect!' said a voice behind her. 'Just perfect.'

Startled, she turned, the smile still on her lips, and encountered thickly lashed deep green eyes flecked with gold, like the sun glinting on a deep, dark pool almost hidden in a rock fissure. Feeling the breath driven from her body, her smile died, her lips forming a silent, You!

'The softest wind-chimes,' he continued, 'mingled with a bird's song at dawn, your laugh is the loveliest sound I have heard. And if your lips stay in that perfect "O" one moment longer I shall be forced to kiss them.' His voice was a low, seductive purr, with the faintest trace of deep southern molasses and something more. 'Dace LaVelle at your services, Miss Linton.' And smoothly he took her hand and brought it briefly to his lips.

'How. . .how do you know me?' She fought the tremor in her voice and took half a pace away. 'You are a stranger to me.'

'No,' he denied. 'We were never strangers.' But then the white teeth flashed in a smile. 'However, it is true we have never met. The reception clerk sent me after you. It appears we have a mutual acquaintance in George Davis.'

Relief flooded her. 'Oh, you know the owner of the Gateway? He and my father were friends and I was told he would help me.'

'I am sure any man would, but does it have to be Mr Davis?'

'He is the only contact I have. My father and he served together in the army, which is why I am staying at the Gateway. Mr father is very ill and I have come to San Francisco to find my brother who came here eight years ago. It is of the utmost importance that I find him, but my father did not want me staying alone among strangers. Since Mr Davis is the owner, my father knew I would be safe here.'

There was a gleam in the green eyes. 'And so you shall be, Miss Linton, just as safe as you want to be, even though George Davis is no longer the owner of the Gateway. I am.'

CHAPTER TWO

CHARISSE stared into those rare green and gold eyes uncomprehendingly. 'You. . .can't be. . .' she said, taking an involuntary step backwards. A shrill klaxon sounded behind her. She spun and stumbled, not realising how close she had been to the kerb—and was saved by a steely arm that shot out and literally plucked her from the wheels of the black Ford trundling past.

'Easy now!' For a moment she was held against the broad chest and heard a soft laugh in her ear. 'You're right—you aren't safe alone!'

Angrily she pulled free. 'I wouldn't have fallen if you had kept your distance in the first place. I had intended taking a short walk before finding a cab, but in the circumstances I must see Mr Davis without delay and introduce myself. The only reason I booked into the Gateway was in the belief that he was the owner. Since he isn't, I don't know that I should stay.'

'Why not?' He was unsmiling now and there was a slight edge to his words.

'I meant nothing personal, Mr LaVelle——'

'How else am I to take it?'

This was getting out of hand. One did not argue with a complete stranger on a busy thoroughfare after only a few moments of meeting. Straightening her skirt and patting back her hair, she slid a careful step to the side. 'I really can't discuss the matter here, Mr LaVelle. I consider finding my brother, Ralph, of the utmost importance, but it is obviously going to be far more difficult than first anticipated. I am sure Mr Davis will do all he can to help, so I shall obtain his address from Reception and telephone for an appointment.' And was stopped by the lightest touch on her arm.

'Why change your plans? I can take you to meet
Davis, though for a number of reasons I would not be
welcome there myself. I could also, in all probability,
find your brother, having a considerable range of
contacts in both high and low society.'

'I couldn't ask that of a stranger.'

'I told you, we are not strangers, but, if you will
allow me an hour of your time to escort you around
the main sights of our beautiful city, we may even
become friends—at *least* friends—and then you would
not mind asking favours, would you? We could even
make a few stops on the way to pass the word among
some of those contacts I mentioned.' The eyes were
mocking. 'Unless you are afraid of me?'

Stung, she tossed her head, reminding him of a
skittish palomino filly. Yes, he thought, that is what
she is: a thoroughbred palomino, with that sun-golden
skin and the almost-white gold hair. I would bet those
legs that the skirt is moulded against in this wind go on
forever too. He felt the heat in his loins and a hunger
too long suppressed.

Charisse felt that burning stare penetrate her very
soul and, while a part of her wanted to run for cover
like the jack-rabbit beneath the shadow of the hawk,
the more dominant part rose to the challenge. 'No, I'm
not afraid of you, Mr LaVelle. Should I be?'

'Oh, yes.' But his smile took the danger from his
words. 'However, I promised you that you would be as
safe as you wanted to be, so will you trust me in an
open car for an hour or so in broad daylight over
crowded city streets?'

Unable to resist the upward tug of her lips, she
surrendered. 'Put like that, how can I refuse?'

'It is a habit I hope to cultivate in you—not refusing
me. Now, if you will step back into the foyer for just a
minute, I must go up to my room and make arrangements to take time off and then have a car brought
round.'

'You live in the hotel?'

'Since I spend most of my waking hours here, it seemed entirely logical to take the top floor—ten rooms being enough for anyone—and make it a working residence.'

'It doesn't seem very. . .well. . .permanent.' Her thoughts turned to the sun-baked hacienda, possibly built by a lone follower in the footsteps of Coronado, whose only gold was found in his dazzling, gold-plated armour, built over three hundred years ago, a home that would still be standing that long again.

'Nothing is permanent except death,' said Dace, breaking in on her thoughts, 'but it suits my present way of life.'

'I'm sorry. I meant no criticism.'

'None taken. You may tell me about *your* home while we drive.' They had reached the foyer and Dace gestured to a man propping up one of the pillars. 'Jack, I shall be going out for a while. Have a car brought round. I'll go up and tell Mark.' He led Charisse to a comfortable armchair near the reception desk, promising, 'I shall only be a few minutes.' Taking her hand, he held it a moment longer than was socially acceptable, saying for her ears only, 'You, Charisse Linton, will probably be my downfall. I must therefore make quite certain I don't fall in love with you.' And before she could catch her breath he was gone, striding across to the elevators with the long, easy gait of a black panther on the hunt.

Charisse took a deep, steadying breath and wondered at the wisdom of even associating, on any level, with such an obviously expert seducer. The men she knew, hard, rough, oil-men and ranchers' sons with calloused hands and wind-leathered skins, were a million miles distant from this suave, elegantly dressed hotelier, yet she knew instinctively that the spring-coiled steel within Dace LaVelle was equal to any other and it made him seem even more dangerous.

She had almost made up her mind to leave when her gaze was caught by the woman who had entered the foyer and was now crossing to the desk. If Dace reminded her of a hunting panther then this woman had to be a slumberously sensual tigress. She was breath-takingly beautiful with red hair piled in a high pompadour beneath the ultra-fashionable black hat, its ostrich feathers curling over the wide brim. Her voluptuous figure was displayed to advantage in a hip-clinging gown of pale mauve silk with black satin trimmings to the trumpet-shaped trained skirt that rippled as she walked—if that sinuous, hip-swinging perambulation that turned every male *and* female head in the place could be so called.

As she passed Charisse their eyes met in mutual feline assessment, the newcomer's of a clear sky-blue beneath arched brows that lifted a fraction as if in amusement, and the full lips curled. But then she turned to the clerk behind the desk.

'Is Dace in?'

'He is in his suite, Mrs LaVelle, but I don't——'

'Thank you.' And she swept on.

Charisse felt the blood pound in her ears. Mrs LaVelle? How *dared* he? Swinging to her feet, she addressed the man, ice crackling in her voice. 'When Mr LaVelle comes down, *if* Mr LaVelle comes down, advise him that I no longer have need of his services—nor will have at any future date!' Back rigid, she marched out into the busy street and hailed a passing hansom. 'Drive! Anywhere!'

A full fifteen minutes later she gathered together her seething emotions and took in her surroundings. They had reached the outer perimeter of Golden Gate Park and she ordered the cabbie to stop there. Paying him, she made her way across the cool and peaceful lawns of the park, breathing deeply of the pure air blowing in from the sea. 'I'll give him downfall!' she muttered aloud. 'I have heard of married men who are married in name only, philanderers who see any attractive female as fair game in their quest to constantly feed their vanity. I never, ever thought to meet one.' Yet reluctantly she had to acknowledge that he had not appeared like that; something was wrong, but. . . 'Only my judgement of character!' she accepted. 'Oh, well, forget him. I have more important things to do, the main one being to find Ralph and then get home to Father.'

Looking about her, a little shamefaced in case any passer-by had heard this strange woman muttering to herself, she gave a little laugh and calmed down. Drawn to the interior of the Japanese Tea Garden, she consigned Dace LaVelle and his ilk to the devil and spent several minutes wandering among the fairyland of cherry blossom and Japanese maple.

Built for the 1894 International Exhibition, the five-acre garden had literally blossomed under the devoted care of the Hagiwara family, and the delicate magnolia trees, camellias and other exotic blooms created a haven of peace from the bustle of the city.

Returning to the hotel in a lighter mood, she went directly to the desk. 'You said that you could give me the address and telephone number of Mr George Davis. I should like that now, please.'

'Certainly, Miss Linton, but I have a message from Mr LaVelle requesting the immediate pleasure of your company. He said that it was most important.'

'Not to me. The address and number, if you please.'

Obviously unhappy with her cool reply, the clerk wrote the details of the hotel's previous owner on one of the embossed cards and handed it to her, entreating, 'I don't wish to offend, Miss Linton, but Mr LaVelle is the owner of the Gateway now and really does wish to see you. I am sure he could help you with any business you might have had with Mr Davis. He was quite insistent that I apprise you of his wishes.'

Charisse accorded him a sweet smile over gritted

teeth. 'It is only the *hotel* Mr LaVelle controls; I should like dinner in my room this evening, say around seven o'clock.'

Taking a chance, knowing it was not the best of etiquette, Charisse hired another cab to take her to the Franklin Street address. There was, she decided, nothing to lose and, if George Davis had been as good a friend as her father intimated, much to be gained. Within seconds of being admitted to the Queen Anne-style mansion with its soaring towers, conical cupolas and ostentatious ornamentation, Charisse was confronted by a beaming George Davis.

'Come in, Miss Linton, come in! Welcome to San Francisco. I never thought to see John's little girl again. I came out to the ranch about ten, eleven years ago. You had pigtails then.'

At once she took to the still military-looking, though now overweight man with the heavy moustaches in dark contrast to the white hair. 'I apologise for coming without an appointment, but——'

'Nonsense! One doesn't make appointments to see friends. You are lucky I was here, though. I am leaving for Australia next week. I have a brother in Queensland and shall be joining him. Losing the Gateway was the best thing that could possibly have happened to me, though I would choke before I admitted it to that Creole riverboat gambler. But here I am rattling on and you have absolutely no idea what I'm talking about.' He turned to the still hovering butler who had admitted her. 'Pendleton, we will have coffee in the green room. Come, Charisse. May I call you Charisse? I want to hear everything.' And he linked his arm warmly through hers, leading her across the rug-scattered hall.

Charisse's mind was still stumbling over 'losing the Gateway' and 'Creole riverboat gambler'. 'You lost the hotel? I am there at the moment, following Father's suggestion, since he had been under the impression, of course, that you owned it.'

He gave a short bark of laughter. 'So I did. So I did. But your father undoubtedly also told you of my incurable love-hate relationship with Lady Luck. I confess I have won and lost a dozen fortunes in my time, including the Gateway. I met a man over a poker table whom I had already been warned to walk wide circles around. I should have heeded my informants. I knew nothing of the man except he was run out of New Orleans over some fight with the brothers of a Cajun beauty and that he spent most of his time there over the baize on the *Delta Queen*.'

'I am briefly acquainted with Mr Dace LaVelle and nothing about him, especially his dealings with women, would surprise me,' she said tartly.

In the green room—pale jade and gold with a distinctly Chinese influence—her host took a chair and gestured her to one opposite. 'Then you will believe me when I say I consider myself one of the best poker-players in the state, but you don't need skill to beat LaVelle—you need anaesthetic!'

'So you lost the Gateway in a poker game.'

'Seven-card stud to make it more interesting, with jokers wild. There is no fool like an old fool, but, as I say, with hindsight I don't regret it.' The coffee arrived with tiny petits fours and he poured and handed her a cup. 'But that is the least of my interests now, or yours. I want to know how John is and why you have travelled all this way for my help.'

The black lacquered clock ticked on as Charisse told him the whole story and watched the wash of emotions over the kindly face. Finally she finished, 'And so here I am, confronted with searching an unknown city for a brother whom I can only hope I shall recognise and who appears to have disappeared completely.'

The man leaned back in his chair, nodded and scratched at his moustache. 'There is really only one way out. I have had cause over the past two or three years to use the services of a certain Lee Rand, a private investigator who is discretion itself, but who has invaluable contacts in both high and low places. I will call him over right away.'

Charisse remembered similar words from Dace, who also apparently had similarly diverse acquaintances, but now that seeking help from such a man was out of the question she was only too glad to accept it from this kindly stranger, and thanked him profusely.

'Nonsense!' He smiled again. 'My pleasure for John's little girl. I can't put off my leaving, but I can certainly make sure you are in the best hands money can buy.'

He was right, of course. From the moment the man stepped into the room half an hour later Charisse knew that she had found an ally. 'Mr Rand, thank you so much for coming at such short notice.'

The craggy features wore a lived-in appearance, as did his rumpled brown suit and scuffed shoes. The honey-brown eyes held a certain world-weariness of one who had seen the worst that man could inflict on man, yet the smile was gentle and sympathetic. 'When Mr Davis says, "Come right away," I know it means just that.' His eyes complimented her appearance, lingered a second on her mouth, then swung to the man opposite her. 'You should call me more often on this kind of assignment!' And the grin that broke out eradicated ten years from his age.

'Charisse is the daughter of an army friend and came to find a long-lost brother, but I'll let her tell you.'

And once again Charisse related her story.

At the end of it the detective nodded slowly. 'I don't want to be pessimistic, Miss Linton,' he said in a slow, soft drawl, 'but in a city like San Francisco, where the population ebbs and flows with the tide, a person who wants to get lost can generally stay lost.' He studied the miniature of Ralph she had brought with her, then handed it back. 'Nice-looking boy, but he isn't a youngster any longer. He may well be a doctor, though not necessarily; he might have grown a beard, a moustache, even changed his name. From what you have told me the last thing he would want to be associated with are the famous army Lintons.'

Charisse felt her hopes plummet. She had imagined it would be so simple. 'I *must* find him, Mr Rand. For Father's sake I *have* to find him.'

'I will find your brother, Miss Linton,' he promised. 'It may take a while, but I'll find him.'

'I believe you will.' She had put his age at around fifty, but as she rose to shake his hand goodbye she realised he was considerably younger and attractive in a rugged way, more like the men she had been raised with, even to the way his eyes crinkled at the corners when he smiled. 'When shall I see you again?' Somehow it did not come over the way she had meant it and quickly she amended, 'For a progress report and of course your expenses.'

'I shall contact you at the hotel the day after tomorrow to let you know how I'm doing. As for the expenses. . .' He glanced at the other man and received a nod of confirmation. 'I believe they have already been taken care of.' His hand was warmly engulfing hers. 'Try not to worry. Take in some sightseeing. You never know, you may see him yourself, crossing a street, standing on a corner, riding a cable car. I'm a great believer in miracles: they come in all sizes and are a very necessary part of my profession. Trust me.'

'I do,' she reassured him and watched him leave, inexplicably feeling as if a great weight had been lifted from her shoulders. Lee Rand was the kind of man one naturally trusted—with one's very life if necessary. 'I like him,' she admitted.

George gave her a searching look then smiled, well pleased with himself. 'It was obviously mutual. Lee lost his wife five years ago. No children. Nice feller.

Needs a young woman to instil some life into him, even though he is only forty.'

Charisse returned his smile, neither offended nor embarrassed by his obvious matchmaking. 'You sound like my father, but I'm still too possessive of my freedom to consider any commitment. Thank you for all your help, Mr Davis, and for the loan, though of course Father will repay you. I never thought to find a friend so soon. My father will be as grateful as I, I know.'

'You are more than welcome, my dear. You must come to dine with me before I leave. I will also give you my brother's address. I should like to keep in touch now that we have met again. As for the money, well, I'm sure I've owed John far more than that over the years.'

They made a tentative appointment for that Saturday and Charisse left to return to the hotel. She realised, in crossing the foyer, that the image of its arrogant, womanising owner had been put firmly into the background for over an hour, and that of the gentle Lee Rand superimposed. It was a pleasant thought—and a far less dangerous one. Glancing at her watch, she found it to be a few minutes before six-thirty. Just in time to refresh herself and change into a lounging-robe before settling down to a quiet dinner in her room, a quick letter home, and a book of poetry she had brought, before an early night. Her first day in San Francisco had, she admitted, been mentally, if not physically, exhausting.

At seven o'clock precisely she heard the muted rattle of a service trolley in the corridor and a discreet knock. Standing by the window and lost in reverie, she called, 'Come in,' but did not bother to turn, still deep in thoughts of her search for Ralph. 'Thank you, I shan't need anything else this evening.'

'But I do,' a quiet voice stated and, with a gasp, she spun about, peace shattered. 'I need to talk to you.'

Dace LaVelle stood there, dark features almost pagan in the soft light, expression unreadable as he stepped around the laden trolley he had brought.

Charisse's throat went dry. 'We have nothing to say to each other. Now please leave.' She felt the erratic pulse beating there and hid her hands in the deep folds of the robe, clenching them to stop their trembling, reiterating, 'Leave. Now. You would not want the embarrassment of having me scream.'

The mobile mouth barely curved upward. 'You aren't the screaming type. What I have to say can be said in a few minutes, though I had planned to say it over dinner, since I have brought enough for two. I am not leaving, however, until I have said what has to be said, even if it takes all night.' The dark fires in his eyes raked her from head to toe. 'Please tell me, Charisse Linton, that it could take all night!'

CHAPTER THREE

IN A fight-or-flight situation Charisse would invariably take the former course even when, as now, every sense denied its wisdom. Eyes flashing, she crossed to the centre of the room, wiping that infuriating smile from the handsome features with, 'Why, Mr LaVelle? Did your wife lock you out?' and saw the barb go home, but he recovered so quickly that she wondered whether the momentary tightening of the jaw had been imagined.

'No, Melinda would never lock me out, quite the contrary, but now she has no reason to. Many divorced women sometimes choose to retain their married name, Miss Linton, especially if they have a child and more especially if they don't wish to accept the finality of that divorce—although Melinda sometimes chooses to go by the name of Marsh when it suits her. *Now* may we talk?'

Stunned, she allowed him to lead her to the tiny, circular dining-table and seat her on one of the two walnut spoon-back chairs. Still unable to speak, she watched him wheel over the trolley and remove the covers from the silver platters before setting two places at the table. 'A. . .child?'

'His name is Mark; he's seven. Crab mousse?' At her nod he sliced the meringue-like mousse on to plates and placed one before her, continuing, 'However, I did not come here to discuss my life, but yours. I should like to help you find your brother and it would help if I knew more about him—and you.'

Charisse studied her plate, emotions in a whirl. His tone had changed completely since her initial attack and was now gentle, though businesslike, with no trace of his previous seductive purr. 'I don't know, Mr LaVelle. I must tell you that I have already hired a detective through Mr Davis who seems confident that he can find Ralph. . .' She trailed off and Dace finished,

'But two bloodhounds are better than one. You have nothing to lose, Miss Linton, and everything to gain.'

Deciding, she looked up and smiled. 'Thank you, then. I *am* concerned about my father and don't want to stay away any longer than I have to. Time is of the essence just now, so yes, I should be most grateful for your help, Mr LaVelle.'

'Dace. If we are to be friends and working together you must call me Dace.'

She hesitated, then, 'Very well, it will be Dace and Charisse. Now, what do you need to know? I have an old photograph of Ralph but Mr Rand, the detective, didn't seem to think it would be of much use after all these years. I am hoping that even *I* can recognise my brother.'

'Just talk. Tell me all you can about your home and family, you and Ralph. I shall look at the likeness later, but it will help more to know his basic character, his likes and dislikes, what kind of person he is.'

'Oh, Ralph is a beautiful person!' she enthused, then flushed and laughed. 'I shouldn't say that about a man, should I? But he was, in every way.' Eyes shining, she began talking, barely tasting the subtly spiced mousse or the chicken breasts in cream and Madeira sauce that followed, while sipping the light Napa Valley wine, touching tongue to lip with totally innocent sensuality.

All the while Dace studied her, listening to the soft voice rather than to its content, drinking in the golden-peach skin drawn over fine, high bones, noting the changes in the soft grey eyes that mirrored every emotion. His eyes lingered on the full lips that bespoke a passion of which, he was certain, she was quite unaware, and slipped to the tip-tilted though full breasts beneath the light lounging-gown. He felt the deep drumroll of his heart and knew beyond any doubt that before he allowed Charisse Linton to leave San Francisco he would possess her body, if not her soul.

Finally the flow ceased and she gave a little laugh. 'I haven't allowed you a word in edgeways. I don't normally go on like that.'

'I've enjoyed every minute of it,' he said truthfully. 'I'll ring for a boy to clear away and we'll continue in more comfort.' Rising, he went to summon Room Service then came to pull back her chair, bending to breathe in the fresh, floral fragrance of her hair. Leading her to the couch, he sat beside her, only releasing her hand when she blushed and pulled it free, saying,

'You know all about my family, but I know nothing of you and yours, other than that you have a son Mark.'

His eyes darkened and he gave a quick shake of the head. 'Nor need you. Melinda and I are divorced and Mark lives with me here.'

Charisse ignored his brusque reply. 'Mr Davis said that you were once a gambler in New Orleans. I have been down there with my father and have seen the men on the riverboats. It seems a rather hazardous occupation.' She saw his features lighten again.

'It certainly is, but then we are all gamblers at heart. You gambled on coming to San Francisco and finding your brother, and on trusting me.' As he said this last he captured her hand again and turned it palm upward, cradled in his. 'A long lifeline and strong heart-line.' His middle finger moved over the soft mound at the base of her thumb. 'A warm and generous nature.' The voice had once again dropped to that sensual note that vibrated across her senses. '*Are* you warm *and* generous? Could any man be that lucky?'

A discreet tap came at the door and, snatching her hand free, Charisse almost ran to answer it, fuming at

the low chuckle behind her. The waiter came in to
clear the trolley and using his presence as moral
support she said, 'Thank you for listening to me, Dace.
I'm sorry I kept you so long. The meal was delicious
and I am grateful for your offer of help, but I mustn't
detain you further.'

With a smile of complete understanding and a gleam
in his eyes, Dace got to his feet with obvious reluctance. 'I shall make enquiries concerning your brother
at once.'

'Oh, I'm sure the morning will do. Please don't
trouble at this late hour.'

'Most of my contacts are nocturnal anyway.' The
waiter had left and, with a glance at the now closed
door, Dace smiled. 'Shall I call him back?'

'No. . .of course not.'

'So you feel completely safe alone with me in your
room.'

'We have been here for the past hour,' she reminded
him.

'Yes, but then there was a table between us.'

Again Charisse felt that she had been manoeuvred
into a fight-or-flight situation and again reacted instinctively. 'And now there is your word as a gentleman
that I would be as safe as I wished while in your hotel—
of which I'm sure you need no reminder.'

'Touché. You are a formidable challenge, Charisse,
and one I find quite irresistible. Very well, I shall make
a strategic withdrawal for now and return tomorrow.
I'll pick you up at one. I should have made all the
necessary contacts by then and can take you to lunch,
after which I'll show you a little of our city—as I was
about to do the last time you fled so precipitously.'

'I can't allow you to do that; you have a hotel to run
and then there is Mark.'

'I need no reminding of either, but——'

'I'm sorry, I didn't mean——'

'No apology necessary. Both function extremely well

in my absence whereas you, on the other hand, may have some difficulty in a city such as this, where your beauty is a challenge to every male between sixteen and death.'

Charisse felt her breath quicken beneath that intense regard, but forced a smile and light tone. 'Should I wear a heavy veil, do you think?' And she rejoiced in his burst of laughter.

'Heaven forbid! If all I am allowed is the *sight* of you then at least allow me a surfeit of *that* feast.' He took her hand and brought it to his lips. 'Until tomorrow, then.' But his eyes promised much more.

Charisse spent a restless night and after a light breakfast of croissants, preserves and coffee went out into the busy streets. She knew that it would be nothing short of a miracle if she saw her brother, but her character was totally unsuited to sitting back and leaving the search entirely to others. At the junction of California and Powell Streets she braved a five-block ride on the cable car to Union Square. In her talk with George Davis she had heard that not only had the square been the centre of the shopping district since the Civil War, but was also a popular meeting place.

Descending from the cable car at the south-west corner, where Powell crossed Geary, Charisse spent several minutes simply wandering around the palm-lined central green and absorbing the peaceful atmosphere amid the surrounding bustle. She noted a milliner's across the road and decided on impulse to take home a really fashionable hat—she might only wear it once or twice but was feminine enough to know that it would be the envy of all her female acquaintances—yet when she stepped through the door she doubted the wisdom of her decision and almost backed out again.

Melinda LaVelle was sitting before one of the large, gilt-edged mirrors, a pile of hats before her, chatting to an elegantly attired older woman sitting alongside her, and one who obviously knew her well, for as Charisse entered she heard Melinda say, 'Oh, I've no doubt of it, my dear. I can get Dace back any time I crook my little finger.'

The other's laugh held polite doubt, but she nevertheless agreed, 'Of course you could, but then you have been *so* busy and are having *far* too enjoyable a whirl to bother, isn't that right?'

Melinda had glanced up at Charisse's entry and their eyes met in mutual recognition, but with only the slightest nod Melinda turned back to her friend. 'Oh, yes; a non-stop round of parties, which Dace never did enjoy. Rich, my dear, but such a bore.'

'But so devastatingly handsome in a wicked sort of way.'

The manageress had approached Charisse and led her to another mirror, seating her on the delicate gilt chair, exclaiming, 'What perfectly lovely hair madam has! A pale blue or lilac would be perfect for you, or a black—so dramatic!'

'I fear I'm not the dramatic type,' smiled Charisse, only half listening while still unashamedly overhearing the other conversation.

Melinda had settled on a hat in white with egret plumes adorning the brim and to Charisse's disappointment the conversation turned to more mundane matters. Eventually the couple rose, Melinda instructing the manageress, 'Put it on my account,' before turning to leave. As she passed Charisse she gave another nod and a brief, 'Good day.'

Unthinkingly Charisse replied, 'Good day, Mrs LaVelle,' and saw the blue eyes widen in surprise as the woman halted before her.

'You know my name?'

Thinking fast, Charisse said, 'I remember the clerk so addressing you when you came into the Gateway where I am staying,' and saw the other relax.

'Then you might have met my husband. He owns the place.'

This last was said with almost a sneer rather than a note of pride and inexplicably Charisse felt herself bristling. 'I *have* spoken with Mr LaVelle,' she acknowledged. 'In fact he is helping me over a family matter and has proven most kind.'

Melinda gave a light, scornful laugh. 'With respect, my dear, he invariably *is* to attractive women. Like all men, he needs to have his vanity constantly preened. I find it really quite amusing.' So saying, she turned to her friend and, exchanging conspiratorial smiles, they left together.

'Bitch!' stated Charisse and heard the manageress, who had reappeared with three hats, give a choked laugh.

'Madam is perceptive as well as beautiful.'

Ruefully Charisse admitted, 'I'm not usually as offensive. Perhaps a touch of feminine envy: she is an exceptionally beautiful woman.'

'She is, but in ten years' time that voluptuous figure will need a feat of engineering, not stays, to hold it in, whereas, if I may say so, madam's form does not even now need a corset and in that same time will only have added an attractive softening.'

Charisse chuckled. 'Your salesmanship is beyond compare. I really must buy a hat now, mustn't I?'

Twenty minutes later she had ordered not one, but two hat boxes to be delivered to the hotel, in one an exquisite concoction of black and lace and feathers with the tiniest seductive wisp of veil, and in the other an almost masculine short-brimmed top hat, enlivened by a band of velvet and a length of black lacy veiling down the back. Thoughts still with the lovely Melinda and her confident assumption that Dace would fall into her arms any time she so desired, Charisse made her way out of the square and again decided to brave the Powell Street cable car back to California Street.

In her reverie she missed her stop and, alighting hurriedly, started off in what she thought was the way back to the hotel, but soon realised that she had lost all sense of direction. Within minutes she found herself in a different world, one in which golden skins and elongated eyes proliferated, and tiny open-fronted shops sold fruit and vegetables quite unknown to her. Stopping a passer-by, she asked the woman, 'Excuse me, but I am new to——' But, with a shake of the head and stream of incomprehensible language, the woman hurried on. Another did the same.

Feeling no panic but only a strange elation, a thirst for all that was new and different, she wandered on. A strangely sweet scent teased at her nostrils and she stopped at a store, its window hung with smoked pork and chicken, but it was the trays beneath from which the aroma emanated. The fish and meat there were cooking in a variety of sauces and as she watched, fascinated, an old man went in off the street and purchased a bowl of one of the meat dishes. Charisse followed him and approached the elderly, pigtailed storekeeper.

'Do you speak English?'

Nodding and bowing, he affirmed, 'Velly good. Mission boy. Number one English.'

'I should like the directions to California Street, please. I took the cable car too far and now am completely lost.' She hesitated, then, unable to resist, asked, 'But first may I have some of that? It smells delicious.'

The man gave a strangely high-pitched laugh. 'Good! Good! You try. Some and some.' Into a bowl he put a small spoonful of rice and over it poured a spoonful from each of three deep trays. 'You like. You see.'

'It smells out of this world.' Then, with a laugh, 'But I can hardly carry it back to the hotel like this.'

'You eat here. Much honour for my humble home. Come. This way. This way.'

Parting a curtain made of tiny pieces of bamboo strung on cord, he led her into a back room and deftly set a mat, chopsticks, and, with a quick glance, added a spoon, on to a tiny round, ornately carved wooden table.

'I can't possibly. . .!' Charisse exclaimed embarrassedly, realising that this was indeed his own home.

'Please. Honour all mine.'

He left with another bow to attend the shop and Charisse ate the honeyed pork and the slices of duck in oyster sauce with mushrooms and water chestnuts. Finally he returned with a tiny cup of aromatic tea and Charisse sat back with a sigh. 'That was the best food I have tasted in a long time. I really must come again, perhaps one evening.'

A strange expression crossed the high-boned broad features. 'You are very kind, but you only come daytime like now. Little China good for daytime. Many tourists come. But not for lady alone at night. You bring along husband night-time and then only Grant Avenue, not side-streets.'

'I shall remember that,' she smiled, certain that he was over-reacting. The people she had passed seemed like any other inhabitants of a busy city, the only difference being in the colour of their skins. Giving a mental shrug and reiterating her thanks, she rose to go. 'I really must get back now. I am supposed to be meeting someone for lunch in an hour, though I must admit that I am already quite full. I am so grateful for your kind hospitality. Will you please tell me how much I owe you for the food, then direct me back to California Street?'

'No charge.'

'Oh, but——'

'Honour all mine. Please. California only four blocks

that way, then you turn right. Humble apologies, no cabs come into Little China.'

Thanking him, she made her way outside, stopping for a moment on the pavement to take a note of the shop name, vowing to return and thank the hospitable Chinese properly, in generous trade.

Suddenly she was slammed against the wall of the shop by a blow to the back and her purse was torn from her hand. Lightning crashed behind her eyes as her forehead hit the brick wall and with a moan she lost consciousness as the young thief raced off into the crowd and disappeared.

A faint ringing in her ears and a strange, sickly sweet scent brought her to wakefulness. She gave a groan and opened her eyes, first seeing the tinkling brass windbells in the doorway, then the smoking joss-sticks on a carved side-table. At once the face of her previous host swam into view and a glass of cool water was held to her lips.

'A thousand apologies. A terrible thing.'

'My. . .bag. . .'

'Regrettably vanished with the evil one. I put out word. Maybe find, but no money. A terrible thing. Great dishonour. Stranger to city may not come again.'

Carefully Charisse sat up, finding herself in a small back room adjacent to the one in which she had eaten. Lifting her fingers to her face, she winced as she felt the rising bruise where her forehead had hit the wall. 'I must get back to my hotel.'

'I send for husband. I send son of Number Two son at once.'

'I. . . I have no husband.'

'You alone San Francisco? No one to come?'

'Yes and no.' Then hesitantly, 'There is someone. The owner of the Gateway hotel whom I was to meet for lunch. He should be at the hotel by now. Would it be too much to ask. . .?'

'Oh, no! Great honour. Least can do to apologise

for my countryman.' Within minutes he had summoned a young, fresh-faced teenager and half an hour after that Dace LaVelle's broad frame filled the doorway.

At his expression Charisse warned, 'Don't you dare say "I told you so"!' and saw his relieved smile.

He crossed to lower himself on one knee beside her, and his gentle fingers came up to turn her face first one way then the other. 'You'll live. I figure you've learned your lesson. I have the car outside, but they've probably stripped off the wheels by now.'

'No, sir!' the alarmed Chinese promised. 'I go see. You take time. I make sure car she all safe.'

'You shouldn't tease him; he had enough of a fright with me,' Charisse reprimanded, allowing him to lift her to her feet.

'Who was teasing? I know this part of the world, believe me. Now, are you going to accept my protection?'

'I really think I must.'

His deep gaze roved over her face and with no smile he said, 'A bodyguard is normally paid for his services, is he not?'

'You know I've no money,' she replied, but already her pulse had quickened.

'I'm a thirsty man, Charisse, not a poor one. I would take your lips, not your gold.'

'You're no gentleman!'

'That's true. Well? Will you pay, or take your chances with others who may be even thirstier than I? That hair of yours is like a shining banner of war in this neighbourhood.'

Charisse felt the colour rise to her cheeks. 'One kiss, then, since you leave me little choice.'

His lips brushed her proffered cheek, then swooped downwards to capture her mouth. The kiss took her breath away, its barely leashed passion forcing her lips apart, his tongue tracing the sweetness of her inner lips, brushing against her teeth and, as she opened her mouth to protest, slipping between them to explore the damp walls of her mouth, sliding over her own tongue and tasting the smoothness there.

Panicking, fighting the waves of heat his kiss ignited, she brought up both hands and tugged sharply at his hair, wrenching his head upwards and away from her. Trembling with fury and a far deeper emotion than she dared acknowledge, she brought her hand up to crack against his cheek, but found it caught before it made contact and held in a vice-like grip.

'Oh, no, my sweet lady,' he mocked, holding her easily. 'I took only my due. Now leave well alone and take my arm lest you slip on the sidewalk. I'd not wish further damage to that peach-blossom skin: it will take a day or so to repair that already suffered. Stop glaring at me, Texas, and take my arm.'

Throwing him a venomous look, she ignored the proffered arm and preceded him outside to where a nervous Chinese stood guard on the gleaming Mercedes.

Laughing softly, Dace helped her up, asking, 'Will you take lunch now or retreat to your suite? You really aren't badly hurt and that bruise needs only an application of ice, which I am sure the restaurant I had in mind will provide while we are awaiting our meal.' And when she still said nothing he added, 'I have put word out on your brother and hope to call on one more man, a doctor himself, this evening. Don't you want to hear all about my fascinating morning?'

Charisse had to smile in spite of herself. 'Blackmailer! Of course I do. Very well, then; I'll go to lunch with you.'

'And sightseeing afterwards?'

'Don't deal more cards than you can hold, gambler.'

He laughed, eyes taking up the challenge. 'I never do, Texas,' he assured her, swinging the car off into an entirely new direction and heading north towards Fisherman's Wharf.

Feasting on fresh cracked crab—cooked on the wharfside to a deep terracotta in boiling cauldrons—and the crisp local sourdough bread, washed down with a quantity of Napa Valley wine, Charisse cautiously lowered her guard, admitting, 'That was delicious, even though after eating a bowl of heaven-knows-what in the Chinaman's shop I thought myself full.'

Dace shook his head in exasperation. 'You really are an incredible person, you know. Most women I know would never have strayed into Chinatown alone in the first instance, and then to make friends with some unknown Chinese and accept a bowl of strange food in his back room when, for all you know, he could have been a white slaver, or worse, with every intention of luring you there the moment he saw you.'

'This is no time to make such jokes!'

'Believe me, I wasn't. From now on, Charisse Linton, you will have an escort or chaperon at all times.'

'I'm not a child,' she bristled, 'and am quite accustomed to being out alone; even last year, visiting my aunt in London, I never had anyone fuss as much as you.' Then she gave him a captivating upward glance, head slightly tilted. 'Apart from which, I *can* take care of myself. I even thought to transfer *this* from my purse to my skirt pocket.' And she laid the derringer on the table between them.

Dace exploded quietly. 'Ye Gods, woman, put that thing away! Don't *think* of using it, not for one moment. Any *real* attacker confronted with that would more than likely take it off you and ram it down your throat! You're no killer, Charisse, and that toy is useless unless you're as close to your assailant as you are to me.'

'That was the general idea,' she defended hotly, lowering her voice as heads turned. 'Since you men only seem to have one thing on your mind, close contact would appear to be the one position that I could guarantee!'

Anger mingled with concern and an admiration for her courage. 'Not all men are potential rapists, Charisse, and most could not ever contemplate it, in any circumstances. In my experience such men who do fall into two distinct categories: the man who has been goaded beyond his limits by a tease, and the sick animals that deserve shooting like the rabid dogs they are. You wouldn't stand a chance against either. The former is likely to back-hand his victim first out of sheer frustrated rage, and the latter generally hunt in packs anyway. Now put that toy away and when we get back to the hotel leave it in a drawer until your return home. Now let's change the subject and find a lighter topic.'

Charisse obligingly returned the pistol to her pocket and allowed him to steer the conversation into safer channels, but knew that, vulnerable or not, she would still feel more confident if the derringer remained with her.

CHAPTER FOUR

EARLY the following afternoon Lee Rand called Charisse from the foyer and the moment she appeared he hurried over, a smile lighting the craggily handsome features, taking her outstretched hand between both of his. 'Now, don't get your hopes up, Miss Linton, but I may possibly have a lead.'

Over the sudden leap of her heart she had time to observe that his tie was an inch off-centre, and for some inexplicable reason she wanted to straighten it. 'Tell me. I'm ready to go.'

'One of my acquaintances says a doctor who is a dead ringer for Ralph has a successful practice out on Geary just north of the park. It's quite a way, but I have an ancient beaten-up Ford outside which is embarrassing the doorman and I hope won't embarrass you too much.'

Charisse linked her hand through his arm. 'The doorman obviously has no appreciation of a fine antique. Let's go.' Watching him from the corner of her eye as they crossed the foyer, Charisse had to admit to herself, It is so. . .comfortable with him, so easy. It's as if I've known him all my life. Even as the car trundled west along the busy road, and Lee had to swerve a couple of times to avoid over-exuberant drivers in new and gleaming brass-festooned vehicles, conversation was warm and gently flowing. He spoke of his dead wife with no show of grief or catch to his voice, but his quiet, 'Somehow the stars seemed less bright without her,' spoke volumes.

Her excitement and hope grew as they reached their destination—a double-fronted house with large five-section bow-windows ornately decorated in the Italian style. 'Oh, yes; this is just the sort of place I could imagine Ralph being in.'

The plaque outside advertised Dr R. L. Webb and for a moment her heart plummeted, but then Lee said, 'Don't despair yet. We knew he might have changed his name. It could easily be interpreted as Ralph Linton Webb—as in, "O, what a tangled web we weave. . .".' And, at her surprised look, 'Not all private investigators spend their waking hours in seedy bars. Me? I get through a mess of books.'

'Could it be?' She seized his hand, willing him to say yes.

He coloured a little beneath the tan and brought his free hand to cover hers, engulfing it. 'Yes, it could be, but we won't find out if we remain here.' Then, almost as an afterthought, 'Such strength in such tiny hands.'

Embarrassedly Charisse snatched her hand free. 'I don't have the hands of a lady, that's for sure,' she said and went to turn away, but was stopped by a firm grip on her arm.

'Yes, you do. My mother spent her whole life on a farm in Oklahoma, working alongside my father every daylight hour. Her skin was like leather and her hands pure rawhide.' He smiled, the honey-brown eyes soft with memory. 'But no one on this earth could be more gentle with a lamb or a baby. I never heard her raise her voice or say ill of anyone and she would ride miles to help a neighbour in trouble. She was a Christian who never drank nor swore—not even when my brother and I raised Cain—and she spent every day loving and giving with everything that was in her. She was more of a lady than any I've met since, and that includes my Amy, who had a ferocious temper when roused.' A half-rueful laugh brought him out of the past and he apologised, 'I do get carried away at times—not often and not with many people I know. You must have cast *some* sort of spell to draw me out like that, Miss Linton.'

'It's called instant friendship. Let's go and meet this Dr Webb, and pray to whichever God is listening.'

In the light and airy waiting-room a young nurse informed them, 'Yes, Dr Webb is free now. Please go right on in.'

'Go ahead,' Lee urged, 'I'll wait here,' and was warmed by her smile of gratitude.

Taking a deep breath, Charisse tapped on the panelled door and entered, then halted, pulse and hopes racing. The back of a blond head, slim build, long pianist's fingers resting on the window from which he surveyed the street below. 'Ralph?' At her voice he turned, smiling, yet with a tiny frown drawing in his brows—and her heart fell. It could have been his twin, but it was not Ralph Linton. 'I'm. . . I'm sorry.'

Quickly the man came forward, taking in the pale features and suddenly tear-filled eyes. 'Sit down. Please. What is wrong? How may I help, Miss. . . Miss. . .?'

'Linton. Charisse Linton.' Swiftly she brushed the back of her hand across her eyes. 'You can't, I'm afraid. Foolish of me to get so upset when it's really only the first failure.'

'Forgive me; I don't——'

'No. My fault. You see, I am looking for a long-lost brother, whom I believe to be a doctor here in San Francisco. The private investigator I hired had news that a doctor bearing Ralph's description practised here. You *are* like my brother, Dr Webb, very much so——'

'But I'm not him. I'm sorry, too, Miss Linton.' He went to a cabinet and poured a finger of brandy into a small glass. 'Here, take this. Purely medicinal, I assure you.' And when she took a tiny sip, 'That's no way to take medicine.' So with a grimace she drank it down, coughed, and felt immediately better as the fiery liquid burned a path to her stomach. 'There! Already your colour is returning.'

'Thank you. I must be going now. I'm sorry I took up your time.'

'I was having an exceedingly quiet morning anyway, which has now been brightened considerably.' He led her to the door and as they shook hands said, 'I sincerely hope you find your brother, Miss Linton.'

'I have to. Goodbye, Dr Webb, and thank you again.' To a hovering Lee she gave a shake of the head. 'Take me back now, please.'

Once in the old car he asked, 'Why don't you come back to my office with me first? There may be other news and it will save time if you're already there.'

Charisse gave a sigh, but then shook off her disappointment and agreed, 'Of course; I have nothing else to do with my time and you are my main hope.'

'But not your only one?'

'The owner of the Gateway has offered to help.'

A slight smile twitched at the corners of his mouth. 'Mr Davis had told me a little of Mr LaVelle, and it's my guess he will have quite as many contacts as I have and just as varied. He isn't, by all accounts, your average hotelier.'

'You could say that. He has a chequered past, to say the least, and isn't an easy man to be with.' She remembered that kiss and felt the colour rise to her face, so changed the subject rapidly.

Lee Rand had also seen that soft wash of colour suffuse the lovely features and felt the slightest twinge in the region of his heart, so he, too, gladly accepted a conversational piece that was far distant from the man George Davis had said possessed 'the mind of an abacus, the morals of an alley-cat and the smile of a shark'.

The Rand Detective Agency occupied two small rooms on the second floor of a Market Street conversion. The room into which Lee showed Charisse was overflowing with books, papers and an assortment of legal paraphernalia which spread across every horizontal surface. 'I'm not the tidiest of people,' he admitted, stating the obvious with a candid grin, 'but I do know where everything is, believe it or not. I tried employing a secretary last year. Within a month the place was pristine. . .and I couldn't find a thing. When she started sewing on my buttons and straightening my tie I had to let her go.'

Charisse had to smile, remembering her own impulse to do just that. 'Regrettably, Mr Rand, you tend to have that effect on the average female.'

He threw her a lop-sided grin and went to dump the contents of one of the two over-stuffed and over-used wing-back chairs on to the floor. 'Please sit down while I sort through my messages.'

'Who takes those for you?'

He had the grace to look embarrassed. 'The caretaker's wife, who used to be a stenographer and has absolutely no curiosity at all.' He had been flipping through a small sheaf of papers left to one side of the piled desk, then turned back one and looked up, eyes alight. 'We have it! A man who actually knew your brother. Here!'

Seizing the proffered note, Charisse eagerly read, 'Ralph Linton known. See Clay Tarrent,' and an apartment address on Sutter. 'Let's go!' she cried.

Lee caught her excitement and nodded. 'It isn't that far, but we'll take the car in case the man has a firm location for us. Keep your fingers crossed. The net is closing in.'

Hurrying to the car, they drove along Market Street and then north to Sutter, pulling up outside a seedy-looking apartment block. Charisse smiled ruefully. 'Not exactly the *crème de la crème*.'

'Few of my contacts are.'

On the second floor Lee knocked at a door on which paint was a mere memory and called, 'Mr Tarrant? My name is Lee Rand.'

The door opened a crack, revealing an eye and half a face. 'You the detective?'

Lee stepped back a pace, assailed by a lethal combination of sweat, garlic and beer. 'Yes. I've brought Miss Linton, Dr Linton's sister, with me.'

The door was opened wide to reveal a large, pot-bellied individual with lank brown hair and sweat-stained vest tucked into greasy trousers. 'You'd better come in, then. Old Bill said you'd pay me.'

As an aside to Charisse, Lee explained, 'Bill is a tramp who frequents the waterfront, but he has the eyes of a hawk.' To the man before him he agreed, 'Two dollars now and five more if your information checks out. Twenty if it leads us to Ralph Linton.'

A grimy hand was extended and the two dollars vanished into a pocket. 'The man you want used to work around here, but that was over a year ago. He called himself Dr Ralph Leonard then, but that don't mean to say he still does.'

'Did you know him personally?' Charisse put in eagerly.

'Met a few times, but didn't cotton on to him. He told me if I didn't quit my bourbon and beer I'd not live out another ten years—an' me only forty and in my prime!'

Charisse looked between him and the craggily handsome and rangily built Lee Rand, also forty, and gave an almost imperceptible nod. She had judged Tarrent to be a man in his mid-sixties! 'My brother was never known for his tact,' she sympathised, but, delving into her purse, produced the faded photograph of Ralph which she had taken from her dresser that morning. 'I'm afraid this is many years old but it's the best we have.'

Tarrent studied it briefly then gave an unhesitating nod. 'That's him. Course he's grown a beard since, but he's still as skinny as two sticks and with them sharp eyes—bright blue as I recall—that went right through you.'

'Do you know the address of his old practice?' Lee questioned, but the other shook his head.

'Didn't have a practice proper. Used to come and go around the down-'n'-outs here and on the Barbary Coast. Respected, he was. Don't know where his office was, if he had one. You might try the hospital——'

'I have,' cut in Lee before Charisse could allow her hopes to rise. 'No luck. If this Ralph Linton is one of the practising Samaritans that operate by word of mouth, we have a rough road before us.' Without thought he reached and gave Charisse's hand an encouraging squeeze. 'We'll find him.' They left and once again in the street he asked, 'Do you want me to take you back to the Gateway?'

'No. . .no, I think I'll walk a while, thank you.'

Reading her depression, he again took her hand. 'Miss Linton. . . Charisse. . . I know how you feel, believe me. We *will* find your brother—maybe not today, nor even tomorrow, but *one* tomorrow we'll find him, I promise you.' He saw the courage behind the threatening tears in the eyes turned up to his and reiterated, 'I promise.' At that moment he would have promised her the earth, sun, moon and stars, had he a chance of delivering them. There was a strength beneath the almost tragic vulnerability that captured his heart and caused his blood to pound. Silently he remonstrated with himself, Don't be a fool, Rand! You are twice her age. You're a battered old wreck who's been alone far too long and this girl just happened to be in the right place at the right time to have your loneliness hit you square between the eyes.

'You're staring,' Charisse said softly and again saw that appealing boyish flush.

'Sorry. Bad habit.'

'Oh, I didn't mind! I didn't mind at all.' Then, on impulse, 'Are you inundated with work this afternoon?'

'None that can't be put aside for an hour or four.'

'When I first came to the city I found a wonderfully peaceful place called the Japanese Tea Garden in a great park. Do you know the place? Would you take me there again, just for an hour?' A dimple touched the corner of her mouth. 'After all, I *am* a valued client, aren't I?'

'You don't know the half of it! Very well, the park it is.'

It already being mid-afternoon, the grey-white mist was rolling in from the Pacific and sifting silently over the lush green lawns of the park, and strollers were making their way homeward, but Charisse drew up her collar and plunged her hands deep into the tiny flat muff she had brought. 'It's exhilarating, isn't it, yet somehow mysterious at the same time, like a fairyland?'

Lee laughed at her fancies. 'It's hard to imagine this as miles of sand dunes just over thirty-five years ago.'

Charisse pouted prettily. 'Nothing mysterious in desert unless one is a sheikh with a great palace and an army of servants.'

'Complete with harem and white horse? You *are* a romantic!'

'Don't you ever fantasise? Dream up situations and how you'd like to react to them? Stopping a runaway horse or rescuing a damsel in distress from the rogue twice your size?'

'Sure I do: there's little else to do on an all-night stake-out, but my fantasies are a bit more down to earth than yours, like winning a million dollars! Look, there's the conservatory. We'll go there first: it has always been a favourite place of mine. You talk of mystery. . .in there you can quite easily imagine you are in some deep, dark jungle—complete with orchids. I heard that it was brought here all the way from England nearly thirty years ago. Can you imagine such a journey around the Cape by boat and some poor insurance man walking a tightrope until it arrived safe and sound?'

Charisse tilted her head at him, eyes sparkling. 'How quickly you move around—one minute in a dense orchid jungle and the next in a dusty insurance office. You do have quite an imagination!'

'For a detective?' They had entered the tropical world of the Amazon, with exotic ferns and exquisite orchids. 'I'm an Oklahoma farm boy by nature and one who could never afford books in my youth. Once I escaped to the big city I devoured every written word I could lay my hands on, so now I'm an educated Oklahoma farm boy. I used to dream of places like this and now I can come here whenever the mood takes me.' He breathed in the warm, damp air. 'You almost wait for the scream of a jaguar or cry of a parrot.' With a shamefaced grin he moved on. 'You must think I'm a complete jackass—to stay with the animal kingdom.'

'I have a fondness for jackasses, especially intelligent, warm-hearted and exceedingly imaginative ones,' she assured him, linking her arm through his.

He drank in the delicate planes and curves of the smiling face turned up to his and felt that the sun was spinning around him personally, but already she was strolling on, leading him over to a label, then on to touch a flower, and he knew that her words had been only those one would say in friendly social chatter. Mentally kicking himself into shape, he put aside the game of 'let's pretend'—before his imagination *really* took off!

From the conservatory they walked across the lawns to another world, a world of singing bamboo and a serenity that could watch the stones grow. Charisse halted by a pool where a slender willow bent to regard its reflection in the water, rustling its leaves as a young girl might shake her long hair into a more becoming image. A tiny arched bridge spanned the water, leading from nowhere to nowhere, yet complete in just being.

'Charisse. . .'

She turned from her contemplation of the view, comfortable with the transition. 'Yes, Lee?'

'Do you think that just for a moment you could forget why you're here, pretend we're just two people taking an afternoon's stroll through the park? Could you perhaps take this minute—only this one—as a time *out* of time?'

She grew still, watching him. 'I might. Why?' He was close, very close, so close that she could see individual eyelashes tipped with gold surrounding the suddenly serious honey-brown eyes, see the texture of his skin and the tiny lines on his lower lip as he moved even closer. At the very last moment she closed her eyes and felt his mouth cover hers, gently, lightly, with neither passion nor possessiveness.

For several seconds he savoured the contours of her lips, tongue tasting, teeth nibbling, yet so lightly that it was almost a dream image, part of the fantasy world they inhabited. Then he raised his head, saying quietly, 'You see? It can be done.'

Dazedly Charisse looked up into the smiling regard, aware that he had not held her, nor touched her in any way with his hands, yet she felt as if she had been enfolded in a deep, warm embrace. 'Lee. . . I——' And broke off, startled, as the earth suddenly jerked, as if in spasm beneath her feet. As her shocked gaze flew to his face there was another tremor, fiercer this time, throwing her against him. For a moment only she clung to him, needing the strong arms about her, but then she heard his chuckle, his mouth against her temple, reassuring,

'It's only a shaker. If you lived here you'd get used to them in time.'

She pulled away, annoyed by her own timidity, and

forced a light laugh. 'That was some kiss! Do they always have such an effect?'

'You should have experienced the one I gave to my number one mistress in my previous incarnation as Procurator of Pompeii!' But his easy smile hid more serious thoughts, brought to light by his saying, 'These tremors are becoming more frequent of late—it was the same before the previous quake, apparently. The city doesn't need another October sixty-five; it has become too large by far.' He gave a brief shake of the head, clearing it of dark thoughts. 'But this is the here and now and I think, for both our sakes, I ought to take you back to your hotel. This place has put a hex on me.'

Charisse wrinkled her nose at him, but made no reply and turned back in the direction of the car, once there only saying, 'Thank you, Lee. I needed someone to relieve me of the load I am carrying, just for a while. I can take it back now.'

'Any time, Charisse; you know that.'

They drove back to the Gateway in comparative silence, each needing to take stock of unkempt thoughts. Charisse could not deny that she found the rugged detective attractive, but only as a friend. His kiss had warmed and calmed her, but had not moved her one fraction as much as the earth-moving, mouth-to-mouth, heart-to-heart, soul-searing embrace of Dace LaVelle.

For Lee Rand the choice was far simpler. Should he walk away from this case and assign it to another—or surrender to the inevitable and fall in love with a woman whom he could never keep? If he did his job badly and did not find her brother, she would leave and seek other help; and if he did his job well, then she and her brother would leave the city anyway. 'Heads you win, tails I lose!' he murmured. 'But I guess it's still worth it.'

'What is, Lee?'

THE GOLDEN PHOENIX 55

He pulled up before the Gateway and came to help her alight. 'Knowing you. I'll see you again soon.'

'Make it very soon. Thank you again for this afternoon.' She waited for him to suggest dinner and when he did not she turned away with a little wave, not seeing the bleakness in his eyes or the hand that tightened whitely on the car door.

But another saw that tell-tale gesture before Lee returned to his vehicle and drove off, for as Charisse started up the steps to the great glass doors Dace appeared at the top and came to meet her. 'Your Mr Rand doesn't look too happy. Is he not having the speedy success he had hoped for?'

Charisse looked up at him searchingly, detecting a hint of sarcasm in his tone. 'We had both hoped for a speedy success, Dace, and I'm sure Lee was as disappointed as I that neither of this afternoon's leads were positive.'

He had reached the same step and with a complete change of tone apologised. 'I'm sorry. It can't be easy for you.'

'It isn't. Even apart from wanting to see Ralph after all these years, I'm naturally worried over my father. He promised faithfully to take things easy until I got back, but that's like trying to harness a tornado. The sooner both Ralph and I get home to him, the more chance there is of Ralph, being a doctor, being able to help him both morally and medically.' But then she brightened. 'There is always tomorrow. We went to the park, to the conservatory and the Japanese Tea Gardens to alleviate our depression: it's a beautiful place to lose oneself in and find even temporary forgetfulness.'

'And did it bring that?'

Remembering, a tiny smile curved her mouth. 'Yes.'

Dace caught that smile and the softening of her eyes and deliberately changed the subject, for reasons too deep to bring to the surface not wanting her to dwell on thoughts of Lee Rand. 'Were you there when we caught the tremor?' he asked, and saw, by the faintest tint of rose on the peach of her skin and the quickly averted profile, that he had not changed the subject at all.

But she merely said, 'Yes. I shouldn't want to experience a worse one. Lee said there was a major one in sixty-five.'

Dace nodded. 'I heard talk of it. A fair demolition job by all accounts. It would be worse now with buildings like this—they weren't half as tall then, but with the city the size and shape it is the only way *to* build is straight up. The brick buildings downtown may be all right—at least they are supposed to be fireproof—but most of the city—especially around the Mission District and south of Market, as you've seen—are mostly flimsy wood structures that are real tinderbox material.'

'But what has that to do with a quake?'

'Fire will always follow. Overturned cooking pots, broken ranges, severed electricity cables, any one of a dozen different causes will start it. Chief Sullivan himself has tried to get the powers-that-be to increase his budget, but our Mayor Schmitz isn't known for lining the pockets of others. No, the city would go through hell if a real shaker hit us.'*

'Doesn't it worry you?'

He smiled and shook his head. 'If it did I wouldn't be here. It's all a gamble, isn't it? Right now, however, I'd like to take you to dinner and discuss more interesting topics.'

'Such as?' She had not meant to sound coquettish but that was the way it emerged and she could have bitten her tongue at the gleam in his eye as he stepped closer.

---

* To the Reader: Mayor Schmitz was later indicted for taking bribes.

'You. Then me. Then perhaps you and me.'

In spite of herself she laughed. 'You never give up, do you?'

'Life's too short to waste on good intentions. One must take the moment and wring every ounce of life out of it. I have a business colleague to see now, but I'll come for you at eight.'

'I haven't yet agreed to go with you.'

'But you will. Wear the blue dress I first saw you in—it makes me feel like slaying dragons and I'm in the mood to slay a dragon or two.' Before she could speak he made a short bow and left her there, taking the remaining steps two at a time, striding off down the hill.

'Dragons indeed!' muttered Charisse, but she was smiling as she made her way into the hotel.

CHAPTER FIVE

AT EIGHT o'clock precisely Dace rapped on Charisse's door and when she opened it, immediately ready to leave, he gave a shake of the head.

'Don't you know you're supposed to keep a gentleman waiting? A quarter of an hour is quite acceptable, though twenty minutes more common. I do approve wholeheartedly of your choice of costume, however.'

At her gesture he entered, dropping the silk top hat on to a chair. He was dressed in a black double-breasted tail-coat which accentuated the broad shoulders, with poured-on trousers that barely held their razor crease over muscular thighs, and a snowy white shirt that threw the deeply tanned skin into sharp contrast. He was, Charisse reflected, a sleekly magnificent animal, and she had no intention of becoming his next prey.

'*Your* choice of costume,' she corrected, going to the mirror for an infinitesimal adjustment to her hat. 'And I don't believe in such silly social games that are designed only to build the lady's self-esteem and lower the gentleman's. My own doesn't need building and I'm sure yours could not be lowered, so why don't we snap our fingers at all such useless posing and enjoy the evening?' She gave him an arch look. 'Apart from which, having you prowling my rooms while I completed my *toilette* would not only be socially unacceptable, but potentially dangerous, and I can't imagine you twirling your thumbs in the foyer of your own hotel.'

White teeth were bared in a wide smile. 'You're really quite a woman, Charisse Linton, but I've said that before. I may experience a variety of emotions

when with you, but never boredom. Very well, with
what shall I tempt your palate this evening? French?
Italian? Spanish? Chinese? We have them all.'

Picking up her purse and gloves, she said, 'I'll leave
it to your undoubtedly knowledgeable taste,' and, with
a teasing smile, 'I'm only a simple rancher's daughter,
after all!'

'Never simple and the way you look right now would
shame the most *haute* of *coutures*,' he replied gallantly.
'There isn't woman in the city to touch you and no man
who won't envy me. Maybe I'll simply parade you
about the street as a rare *objet d'art* and not feed you
at all.'

'Then I shall expire on you within the hour and I'm
certain you have other plans for me than an early
demise.' Then, as that devil's eyebrow lifted wickedly,
'So where will you take me? I have never known such
a cosmopolitan city; not even when passing through
New York did I experience such a variety of race,
creed, and colour.'

'You name it, we have it,' he laughed, leading her
out. 'From descendants of the Spanish hidalgos who
founded the tiny settlement they called Yerba Buena
in 1776 to the brash business tycoons who own it today,
and everything in between. The Forty-Niners who
came from almost everywhere, and later a few
Frenchmen who were washed out by a veritable tidal
wave of Italians, though a few set up restaurants in the
Tenderloin District with food downstairs and quite
another cuisine above.'

'I shouldn't know what you're talking about,' grinned
Charisse, utterly fascinated. 'Go on. Who came next?'

'The Irish who built the first railroads—or kissed the
blarney-stone and went into politics—and of course
the Germans with their hardworking, emotionless
industry and, totally opposite, the negroes escaped
from slavery. The Jews slipped in almost unnoticed—
not all wear funny hats and long black coats—and took

over a fair amount of the business district. I guess the real discrimination is against the Chinese, originally brought as forced labour for the railroads and then driven into the ghetto they have made uniquely their own, as you've seen, although the Japanese are almost equally despised—though I have found them an honest and hardworking race on the whole. Of course every kind of transient river rat appears on the Barbary Coast: Russians, Lascars, Hawaiians, Kanakas, Blacks, Greeks, Filipinos and every other nationality that has access to the sea. All of which is why you *must* not venture out alone.'

Charisse shook her head in denial. 'I appreciate that I shouldn't venture out at night—heaven knows, I've heard the shouts and general rowdiness even in this district—but surely as long as I keep clear of China-town and the area you call the Barbary Coast I'll be safe enough during the day.'

The smile never reached his eyes. 'The city has no closing laws, so you get drunks twenty-four hours a day, seven days a week, and that's just the start. Nob Hill is well named for the nabobs who own it, but still it lies only just west of Chinatown and barely south of Italian North Beach that spills over north to the wharf. Even fashionable Union Square carries much of the human refuse from the slums south of Market Street, not to mention certain establishments on Maiden Lane, just off the Square, which, although not as bawdy as of old, are equally as attractive to men of. . .lesser taste, shall we say?'

Again Charisse shook her head. 'You seem to have effectively eliminated all but the Gateway itself and of course I have only *your* word that I am safe here!'

'Do I detect a note of challenge there, or simply a request for me to reiterate my original promise that you would be as safe as you wished?'

The lift doors opened and they moved into the close

confines, where Dace put it into motion before turning to face her, his very size dominating.

Moving to stand with her back against the wall, Charisse said, 'I wouldn't dream of challenging a man who would enjoy it so much. I was merely commenting that I must take the word of someone I hardly know and one who already has proved somewhat less than totally trustworthy.' But she was smiling as she said it and he moved closer, putting one hand on the wall beside her head, trapping her in the corner.

'I'm never sure with you which reputation I should live up to—protector or seducer. You know, your eyes are the colour of early morning mists on the bayous, but they are distinctly cat-shaped. What kind of bayou cat are you, Charisse Linton?'

'One with claws, Dace.'

A soft laugh. 'I don't doubt it, but I swear I'll have you purring for me one day—or night.'

They had reached the ground floor and she pushed his arm aside. 'Don't bet on it,' she retorted, and walked passed him, feeling the breath of his laugh fan her cheek.

He took her to a fashionably discreet French restaurant where they were led to a table to one side of the softly playing quartet.

'Will you order for me?' Charisse asked, admitting, 'I've no knowledge of either the language or the food, though I'm willing to try anything. This city has already given me a taste for adventure.'

'So I've observed, and I'm glad to be a part of it. I like this place: the waiters aren't as condescending as some but, for the most part, are Americans with fake accents to appeal to the clientele, though don't admit I told you or Freddie could be most embarrassed.'

'Freddie?'

'The owner, Fred Brown—or François Le Brun to you—a London cockney who started as kitchen washer-up in New York when he first emigrated here twenty odd years ago, graduated to assistant chef and finally came west as chef here. Made a good friend of the owner to the degree that he inherited on the man's death. Ah, here he is now.'

The portly, beaming man who approached looked every inch the affluent, dapper Frenchman, with sleeked-back Macassared hair, twirled moustache and elegant black suit. 'Monsieur LaVelle!' he cried, extending a beringed hand. 'An *honneur* indeed!' The twinkling eyes lingered on Charisse's face. 'And your lady, she is *ravissante*.'

'I think so. Miss Linton is a guest at the Gateway, a Texan whom I've persuaded to taste your unrivalled cuisine.'

The man's gold-plated smile widened. 'You are too, too kind, *monsieur*. . .but truthful. I shall personally choose your meal, a delectation, a gastronomic delight, a taste of paradise, and of course the champagne, for such a beautiful lady, is on the house.' With a low bow he hurried away, gesturing coded messages to waiters, kissing his fingertips at a diamond-encrusted dowager and gesticulating widely before disappearing through the swing-doors at the back of the room.

'Some Fred Brown!' laughed Charisse. 'I would never have guessed in a million years. The accent was as thick as pea soup—I would have sworn he was just off the boat. Is he another of your contacts?'

'Yes and no. I have put a fair amount of trade his way through recommendation at the hotel when our guests wanted a change from our own dining-room. Then, too, it was a favourite of Melinda's in our happier days.'

Charisse searched his face for some emotion and, finding none, asked, 'But you brought me here. I would have thought you'd prefer to go elsewhere, having such mixed memories.'

A half-smile. 'They serve the best French cuisine in San Francisco and I've a fondness for French fare.'

'And you never settle for second-best.'

The eyes were smoked jade as they settled on her mouth. 'Never.'

'*Have* you never?'

'You're trying to side-track me.'

'Am I succeeding?'

He laughed, and the hunger that her beauty aroused each time they met evaporated just a little as his mind went back. 'I guess you have. I made a personal promise when I left New Orleans that whatever or whomever I took for my own, for however brief a time, would always be the best I could find and, if I couldn't afford it, I would wait until I could.' He reached to run a finger along the wrist that was resting on the table. 'Of course some things are beyond price, but it doesn't prevent me from trying for them.'

Voice husky, she had to ask, 'And how often do you succeed?'

The finger moved to insinuate itself into the curled hand, rubbing gently over her palm. 'Always.'

Quickly she pulled free and clasped her hands in her lap, but was saved from replying by the arrival of an ice bucket containing the bottle of Veuve Clicquot and another waiter bearing an exquisitely decorated *saumon mayonnaise*. Exclaiming over the dish, Charisse caught a ripple from the other patrons and, looking past Dace, froze momentarily before saying, 'It appears that this is still one of Melinda's favourite restaurants.'

With a frown Dace glanced over his shoulder and the frown deepened as his mind raged, Why did she have to appear this night of all nights? His second thought was, Why does she have to be so damned desirable still? He had to acknowledge that, in spite of all she had done to him, Melinda could still coil his loins into red-hot snakes—his and, by the look of them, every other man's in the room.

Melinda stood for a moment in the doorway, waiting for her escort to hand his top hat and coat to the check girl, while the long-lashed blue eyes assessed the room. She was dressed entirely in black, but rather than resembling mourning wear it was the total antithesis of it. The silk dress moulded itself to her body in the 'mermaid' fashion, flaring only at the knees, proclaiming to the world that there was nothing but Melinda beneath, and there was shock and horror on every female face—as there was naked lust on every male one. Even the tiny veiled hat was not worn fashionably atop the high-piled red hair, but pinned to one side and slightly forward so that the scrap of lace that passed for a veil drifted wickedly over one eye. She saw Dace and the full lips curved into a smile—that died as Dace turned back immediately to his meal without acknowledging her.

Quickly Charisse said, 'We don't have to stay if you'd rather not.' For she had seen, as Melinda could not, the tell-tale muscle that had leapt in Dace's jaw and the split-second flare in his eyes before he had returned to his contemplation of the salmon.

'Not at all. I am set to enjoy a good meal and that is precisely what I shall do.' He smiled, though it did not quite reach his eyes. 'It's a small town and the circle we move in even smaller. Melinda and I are bound to meet. She won't make a scene in public, so we can forget her. . .unless her presence here makes you uncomfortable, in which case we can certainly leave?'

Charisse helped herself to the fish, giving her time to make a decision, but then shook her head. 'No, I've no reason to feel uncomfortable; it's poor François who is looking decidedly awkward, trying to find a table for them that is in a prime position for a valued customer yet at a distance from our own. Ah! There! He has put them by the window over to our right.'

Dace glanced over to where she had indicated and a frown again marred the handsome features. 'Fool woman!' And, at Charisse's enquiring brow, 'The man with her, apart from being old enough to be her father, is Calvin Hughes-Weston: Hughes Mercantile and Weston Freight.'

'Is that old money or new?'

A brief twist of the lips. 'Positively ancient. I've had the unpleasant experience of playing poker with him once or twice. Like many of what passes for the upper class in America—the greenback aristocracy, not to be confused with the English or European genuine article that has a thousand years and more advantage—he has an in-built ability, with his unfailing *bonhomie* and the hide of a rhino, to raise the hackles of almost everyone he meets. Combined with an equal ability to sink a couple of bottles of bourbon a day, it makes him a more than somewhat undesirable character.'

Trying not to sound bitchy, Charisse observed, 'Melinda doesn't seem to think so.'

Again that mirthless half-smile. 'Melinda could never resist the gravitational pull of an open wallet.' Then he looked into her eyes and the smile widened and grew warm. 'But I didn't come here to talk of cabbages and king-makers, I came to talk of all your yesterdays and at least a few of your tomorrows. Tell me more of Texas and whether the horns of a longhorn are really ten feet wide as I've heard.'

Charisse's eyes sparkled. 'Probably someone telling you Texas tales, though I have seen a six-foot spread on more than one occasion. Mind you,' she continued with mock seriousness, 'we do have some wonderful creatures in Texas. There's the famous jackalope, a cross between a jack-rabbit and an antelope—looks like a three-foot-high rabbit with horns.' He was really smiling now. 'And then, of course, there is the wagon-wheel rattler. When he sees a good meal off aways he takes his tail between his teeth, rolls into a perfect circle and just bowls off after it like a hoop—they say he can reach twenty miles an hour and more.'

Dace's laugh turned heads, but he did not care and that too showed as he reached out his hand across the table. 'You *are* priceless!'

Flushed, Charisse hedged, 'More salmon?'

'I'll keep my appetite for the other courses, temptress.'

Charisse soon realised that it was a wise move as the salmon was followed by four other courses, each painstakingly presented and each one more mouthwatering than the last. Even when, at her enquiring eye, Dace advised, 'Frog's legs,' she unhesitatingly nibbled at the delicate, battered objects on her plate and pronounced them delicious.

As the meal progressed she could not help but sneak glances towards the table at which Melinda and her escort were seated. Mercantile and Freight was obviously living up to his reputation and was already well into his third bottle of wine. Melinda was looking decidedly irritated and Charisse could almost feel the electricity crackling between them. Finally she asked Dace, 'Do you think Melinda will be all right? Mr Obnoxious is getting through the wine as if he has just emerged from the desert.' But before he could answer the situation resolved itself.

Calvin made the mistake of leaning across the table and, with a leer, made some comment, pursuing his proposition by touching one ripe breast with his fingertip. Melinda's chair crashed back as she rose, scorn mingling with fury as she took up her plate of trout mousse and tipped the entire contents over his head before storming out, magnificent in her rage.

Instantly waiters flocked to the rescue, flapping napkins, dabbing at face, hair and suit until François took over, producing a damp flannel and towel with murmured apologies and platitudes, though barely able to contain his approval of the action. Calvin shook them all off with raised hands and a laugh that was only a little forced, declaring to the gaping assembly,

'I'll say it with roses next time!' and raising a relieved laugh as conversation recommenced. Reeling only slightly, he started to leave, instructing François, 'Call a cab,' in tones that one would use to the lowest minion.

Dace murmured, 'I almost feel sorry for him—almost,' but then cursed beneath his breath as the man weaved towards their table, grinning broadly.

'Hey, LaVelle, did you see that? Your ex is a real barracuda when she's riled, isn't she? I love a fighting female.' The red-veined eyes settled on Charisse and, addressing Dace, he continued, 'If your taste runs true, I'll take on your present li'l filly any time she, too, decides to change riders. *Any* time.'

Charisse felt the colour rise to her face, but there was ice crackling in her words as she stated, 'Perhaps you should ask me. As a guest in Mr LaVelle's hotel I am unacquainted with *his* taste, but I know my own. . . and you couldn't be further from it. . .at *any* price!'

Dace had risen and towered over the elderly roué, crowding him. 'I believe you owe Miss Linton an apology,' he suggested quietly and, as drunk as he was, Calvin could not mistake the menace in the words or the expression in the eyes that had darkened the gold-flecked emerald fire.

With a placatory gesture, warding off the broad frame, he turned and accorded Charisse a low bow. 'Sincerely sorry, beautiful lady. Sincerely sorry. Had a glass too many.'

'Several, I'd imagine,' Charisse corrected tartly, 'but I'll accept your apology. Now, if you don't mind, we'd like to finish our meal.'

He nodded several times slowly. 'I hope we meet again, beautiful Miss Linton. I shall leave now.' And, so saying, he weaved carefully out.

'What a repulsive individual!' Charisse exclaimed.

'Yes, though generally harmless enough.' Dace

resumed his seat as the dessert trolley was wheeled forward. 'I'm sorry you had to experience his particular brand of charm.'

'We get the type in Texas, too, especially among the new oil barons who think their wealth cloaks them with irresistibility. Unfortunately there are also enough so-called ladies to convince them they are right. I prefer the honest-to-goodness cowboys who have no side at all and can be pleased by the slightest extra attention.' To the hovering waiter she said, 'Just some fresh fruit, please.'

Dace had never until this moment wished to be a cowboy, and felt annoyed at the wash of emotion that he refused to acknowledge as jealousy. 'The next question might be, how often and to how many has this . . .extra attention been awarded? Or you could simply tell me to go to the devil.'

She paused in her selection from the super-abundance of choice in the wicker basket of fruit and gave him a long look before returning to her task. 'I should tell you to go to the devil, but I think I'm a little late for that, so I shall just say not often and not many.'

Dissatisfied, he pursued, 'But enough to make you certain of your taste in the male of the species.'

Carefully Charisse placed a banana and a large peach on her plate then smiled up at him with that tiny tilt of the head that sent his pulse racing and declared softly, 'Yes.'

A totally uncharitable thought crossed Dace's mind—he would welcome the opportunity to be left alone with the largest of her dozen or so suitors for just five minutes, but all he said was, 'I think I shall take the sorbet.'

A little smile, more inside than out, and Charisse dissected the peach with the curved knife provided, giving it her undivided attention, knowing that she had his, and put a small segment into her mouth. 'Delectable.'

'So are you.'

'Tell me more about San Francisco.'

With a resigned sigh he took her on a verbal tour of the city, but his eyes rarely left her as she finished the peach.

'You aren't eating your sorbet; it will get cold!'

He took an obliging spoonful, watching the precise way in which she peeled the banana, then cut it in half and lifted one part to her mouth. As he saw her lips fit perfectly over the end of the fruit a torrent—no, a tidal wave—of erotic fantasy deluged him. Instantly—and painfully—he was aroused. He bit back a groan and pushed his napkin hard into his lap.

'Are you all right?' she asked anxiously. 'You've turned quite pale.'

'Yes,' he croaked, 'yes, I'm fine,' silently cursing his rampaging hormones, which had not betrayed him quite so thoroughly since his teens. Glad that the meal was not quite at an end, certain that he would not have been able to make it to the door without the whole restaurant being aware of his discomfort, he lingered over the sorbet and attempted to continue his dissertation, keeping his gaze fixed to the untasted dessert.

Eventually Charisse suggested, 'If you have finished mashing your sorbet into liquid we could call for the bill,' and her eyes were laughing at him.

At that point he could cheerfully have strangled her!

Outside in the cool night air Dace felt that he had just been physically and mentally steamrollered. It was not a condition he was accustomed to, nor one that apparently he had any control over, and the lady who had caused it was innocently suggesting, 'It's such a lovely night; shall we walk? It can only be a mile to the hotel,' already moving ahead and throwing a smile over her shoulder.

'Why not?' groaned Dace, quite unable to give her a reason for not doing so, and started after her on rubbery legs.

Charisse was right: it *was* a perfect night, crisp and clear with a buttermilk moon and a heavenful of stars. A night made for romance. A night made for men like Dace LaVelle, and it took him all of a dozen paces to realise it.

'Wait!' he called and, when she halted, added, 'We don't have to return to the hotel just yet, do we? We could take the car up to Mount Tamalpais and watch the city lights, like candles on a birthday cake, going out below us. It puts the whole roistering, wheeling and dealing mess into perfect perspective and certainly isn't a view you'll find in Texas.' He saw her hesitation and softly challenged, 'Surely a woman who ventures into Chinatown alone isn't afraid of a drive along a moonlit mountain with the very person who has appointed himself her protector?'

'Something tells me that on a night such as this I may well feel safer *out* of your protection.' She smiled. 'You are as much of a protector as Tamalpais is a mountain—as high and wide as the occasion warrants.'

Dace was unaccustomed to females vacillating—charmingly or otherwise—especially in the middle of the sidewalk, and reasoned he had two choices. He could reach out, drag her into his arms and kiss her in such a way as to preclude any and all argument, or he could use reverse psychology.

'You are right, of course,' he agreed, affecting a shrug. 'I am definitely untrustworthy. No woman of any sophistication would be alone with me for a minute in such a place. I'll take you back to your suite where you can write home about your narrow escape.'

Charisse considered his proposition. 'I should guess there must be a great number of unsophisticated women in San Francisco, then, and more than a few who *couldn't* write home even if they wanted to, which I doubt. Is there a special spot on your local mountain reserved for you, full and crescent moons optional?'

'You'll never know unless you come.'

She came to stand before him, looking up into the Pandean, night-shadowed face. 'I must be all kinds of a fool and I may hate myself tomorrow.'

'I guarantee you won't.' And *then* he judged it the right time to kiss her, but, with the battle already won, merely bent to brush his lips lightly over hers, touching a kiss to each corner of the now smiling mouth and dropping a final kiss on the tip of her nose. 'Your carriage awaits.'

'It *is* beautiful!' Charisse breathed as, finally, they reached the peak of Tamalpais, having taken the meandering road upwards at dreamer's pace. 'I never realised there were so many lights in the city: it's as if a whole bucketful of glow-worms has been spilled over a black velvet blanket!'

'In competition with the diamond-studded blanket above,' he said against her hair as they stood together, she standing in front of him, his hands on her shoulders. The cool breeze brought the fresh floral scent of her hair to mingle with the night's scents about them and he breathed it in deeply.

Charisse felt the warm hands slip down to her arms and then up again, stroking seductively. Part of her wanted to lean back against the broad chest, part fought against succumbing, as so many others must have, to the magic of the night. She resisted, stepping forward, away from him, and going to a wooden seat near the edge. 'Is this your spot? The bench that has a plaque commemorating Dace LaVelle's hundredth conquest?'

'No,' he differed easily. 'They don't give you one for the first hundred.'

'Modesty personified!' She sat down, smoothing her skirt, spreading it a little so that when he joined her he would have to sit a foot away.

Dace smiled at the manoeuvre and promptly went to

sit on the wooden arm, his own arm resting on the back, fingers touching her shoulder, leg swinging negligently, calf against her knee. 'Now,' he smiled, 'you can either move nervously away or relax, lean back and enjoy the view.'

'You are incorrigible!' But she did not move away.

'*Quite* encourageable.'

'Come and sit beside me so that I can look at you when I'm talking.'

'You can do so now.'

'Only if I tilt my head back—so—and rest it against your arm—so.' She smiled up at him, feeling perfectly—and illogically—safe. 'But if I do that you will kiss me again and I don't want you to do so.' And the moment before his head lowered she turned away, leaning forward a little, saying, 'For I've a feeling you are accustomed to such games.'

'Games?' When she did not answer he rose and went to sit beside her, taking her hand.

Charisse withdrew the captive. 'Verbal chess if you like. Opening moves are made in accordance with well-practised rules. A pawn is sacrificed, perhaps then a knight. . .however you spell it. The battle moves into more serious ground until eventually the queen is cornered and is taken.'

'Or surrenders.'

'No chess-piece surrenders, Dace—it is either sacrificed or is taken, and then mate and checkmate.'

'I like that word.'

'I'm sure you do.'

'However, I don't see the delightful pursuit and capture of a woman as a battle between opponents, but rather as the acquisition of a beautiful *object d'art* or piece of exquisitely carved antique furniture: something to be watched over, cared for, displayed in perfect surroundings, touched often, caressed in appreciation.'

Charisse felt that deep velvet voice vibrating along

every nerve-ending and recognised such strategy. She wondered how many woman had surrendered either to the incredible striking handsomeness of the man, or to that voice. 'Your life is so full of such. . .pieces that they can mean very little to you after a while.'

He caught the questioning behind the lightly mocking tone and it struck a chord in him, so that quite seriously he answered, 'Each one meant something at the time; none lasted, not even Melinda—surely the most beautiful of my collection. You could last, Charisse; you could outlast them all.'

Half angrily she gave herself a mental shake and rose to her feet. 'I've no doubt, but I have no intention of becoming a temporary part of your bedroom furniture, Dace, so will you please take me back now? I have seen the view from your mountain, but, whether on a mountain or pedestal, I don't belong at such a height. I'm a plains woman, Dace, and always will be. You can put me in any surroundings you like and festoon me with diamonds or tinsel—it's all the same to me—but, like the plains, at the heart I still belong only to myself. I *am* Texas, Dace, through and through.'

'Well!' And there was both admiration and determination in the soft exclamation. 'I have never aimed so high, it seems—to conquer, to possess the whole of Texas—but I could never pass by such a challenge or I'd not be the gambler I am. *Now* I shall take you back, for I need to plan my strategy and the very prize I am playing for is, in itself, the greatest distraction of the game.'

Charisse regarded him appraisingly. 'You don't think you might be aiming a little *too* high this time, gambler? I mean. . .the *whole* of Texas?'

Dace chuckled and reached to touch her cheek with the back of his fingers. 'To the peak of every hill and depth of each valley, every length and breadth of sun-kissed plain, every inch of lush woodland.'

He could not see her blush in the moonlight but knew it was there when she spun away and in a strangled voice demanded, 'Enough! Take me back now. This minute!'

CHAPTER SIX

CHARISSE made her way back through the foyer late the following afternoon from another long day vainly searching the streets of the city, combining both sightseeing and her seemingly endless search for Ralph. She imagined she had enquired of at least a hundred people, in shops, offices, on the streets—'Do you know a Dr Ralph Leonard or Linton?'—but her brother seemed as elusive as Baroness Orczy's pimpernel. At least, she reasoned, she knew the parts of the city she should *not* venture alone, and had undoubtedly seen more than most casual tourists, *and* a fair number of residents, all of whom moved within strictly confined circles.

As she picked up the key from the clerk at the reception desk, she was almost brushed aside by a thin, pale-faced, middle-aged man who, with a brusque apology, demanded of the clerk, 'I must reach Mr LaVelle. Do you know where he is?'

The other shook his head apologetically. 'No, Mr Tate, but the manager may.'

'Well, send for him at once and then a runner for Mr LaVelle's doctor; young Mark isn't at all well. Some kind of stomach upset. Could even be food poisoning for all I know. I understand nothing of children's illnesses, I'm only the boy's tutor.' He gave a shudder and reached for a snowy handkerchief which he waved before his thin, hooked nose. 'I couldn't even clean the child up. That sort of thing quite turns my stomach. Why doesn't he have a nanny? The doctor will have to see to it. I just couldn't! He really should have a nanny; all the best households do. . .not that one could call that a household, not by any stretch of the imagination. I feel quite ill.'

Unhesitatingly Charisse said, 'Please let me go to him. I am an acquaintance of Mr LaVelle's and until you find him I'm sure I can calm his son and at least make him comfortable until the doctor arrives.'

The man's pallid features registered infinite relief. 'Madam, I would be forever in your debt. Sickness is not my forte.' He handed her a key. 'This will open the outer door and you can——'

'Aren't you coming up to introduce me? After all, I am a complete stranger.'

'Oh, I'm certain it will be all right. The child will go to anyone. I feel quite ill myself and must take some air. Please forgive me. The bellboy can show you the way and the manager can send a messenger for Mr LaVelle.'

Charisse watched in incredulous disbelief as he hurried off, then caught the clerk's eye mirroring her own anger. 'What an unfeeling boor!'

'Mr Tate hasn't been employed for very long: the previous tutor emigrated, though he wasn't with us very long either. Good tutors are as rare as gold out west, even in the twentieth century. I'll call the bellboy to take you up, miss.'

'No, I can find my way. Call the doctor immediately. If it *is* food poisoning all haste is vital.' And without waiting to see him carry out the task she ran for the lift and within minutes had let herself into the main hall that separated the top floor from the rest of the hotel.

Looking neither to right nor left, she went into the first door and crossed the deeply piled carpet of the living-room towards the partially open door of a small room, to the side from which emerged the heartrending sound of a child's tired sobs, pushed the door wide, then halted in the doorway, anger and pity washing over her.

Mark LaVelle had been left with only a hand-towel soaked in water beside him. He was now curled into a tight foetal ball on the floor of what served as a tiny schoolroom and crying in a frightened, lonely way that tore at her heart. He had been sick and had attempted in vain to clean both himself and the carpet, but the sickly-sweet smell filled the room.

'Oh, Mark! My poor love! How could he leave you like this?'

He looked up, blinking rapidly, his face deathly white in stark contrast to the raven curls of his father and Melinda's brilliant blue eyes. 'Who are you?'

'My name is Charisse. I'm a friend of your daddy's and I'm going to help you. We've sent for the doctor, so you will soon feel better, but there are certain things we must do first.' Crossing to kneel beside him, she put her hand across his forehead, finding it cold and clammy. 'Does it hurt badly? Is it a sharp pain like a knife or a dull, steady pain like a red-hot ball?'

'It. . .it's like a big hand grabbing at me; then it lets go and then it comes again. I've been sick twice. I'm sorry. I couldn't help it.'

'It's a good thing you were.' And she heaved an internal sigh of relief, knowing that it could well have saved his life. 'I'm going to get something to clean you up with and then we'll get you to bed, but first let's just wash your face, and you must drink a lot of water—as much as you can.' She ran into the kitchen and filled a jug of cold water, pouring some into a short tumbler, urging, 'Here, Mark, honey, drink this,' and held the damp head while he swallowed bravely. 'Tell me what you ate last and when. Did you eat here or in the city somewhere?'

He finished the glass and she poured another. 'I. . . I don't remember. . .' Then, ashamed of the lie, 'Frankie said it was all right. We. . .we picked some mushrooms for a picnic. Frankie's my almost-best friend, though he's nearly ten.'

'Mushrooms? Oh, merciful lord! How many? How long ago?'

Another spasm hit him and he doubled up with a cry

and, regardless of the state he was in, she held him tightly in comfort until it passed. 'Where *is* that doctor? Why doesn't he come? Come on, Mark, you must get some more water down you and you must try to be sick again.'

'I can't!'

Leaving him briefly, she went to bring more towels from the bathroom, one soaked under the tap, and a china bowl. The spasm had passed and she was able to remove the boy's sweater and shirt, then his stained trousers. Wrapping him in one of the large towels, she bathed his face and head. 'I'm sorry, sweetheart, but I must do this. I'm going to put my finger into your mouth and try to make you sick.' She smiled into the frightened eyes with a reassurance she was far from feeling. 'Just don't bite me!'

A moment later Mark doubled up over the bowl, retching pitifully. Again Charisse cleansed him and forced him to drink more water. He was halfway down the glass when the door opened and a white-haired man in black suit and carrying a Gladstone bag entered. 'I'm Dr Benjamin,' he introduced, not even glancing at her, his attention concentrated wholly on the child in her arms. Bending on to one knee, he took a pulse, raised an eyelid, felt the neck and forehead. 'How long has he been like this?'

'I've been here less than fifteen minutes, so. . .about a half-hour, at a guess. He says that he ate some mushrooms that he and a friend gathered on a picnic. He has been sick at least three times and had three glasses of water.'

Mark was breathing more easily now, but was still frightened, more of being punished than of the symptoms he did not understand. 'They were real mushrooms, not toadstools,' he told them in a shaky voice, looking from one to the other, willing them to believe. 'Frankie said we had to cook them with a silver coin in the pot and if it went a funny colour they were poisonous; but it didn't, so we ate them. I didn't like the taste so I only ate three or four: Frankie ate the rest.'

The doctor and Charisse exchanged looks. Carefully keeping the horror from her voice, Charisse asked, 'What's Frankie's whole name, Mark, and where does he live?'

As the boy gave the name and address, near to tears again, the doctor rose to his feet, grim-faced. 'These damned superstitions! That particular old wives' tale causes more tragedies in a year than I care to count.' He rummaged in his bag and brought out a bottle of milky liquid. 'There is nothing more I can do here. Mark will be fine, thanks to your timely arrival and his being sick. Put him to bed and keep him warm. When he has calmed a little give him a teaspoonful of this in a glass of water and another in an hour's time.' Again their eyes met. 'I have another patient to call on; I pray I am in time.'

'So do I. Thank you, Dr Benjamin.'

The doctor left and Charisse turned to Mark with a smile. 'To bed with you, young man. Where are your night things and which bedroom is yours?'

'Am I going to die?'

'Good heavens, no. You heard the doctor. You're going to be just fine. But you could have been very, very ill had you eaten more. You must never, *ever* eat *anything* that hasn't been prepared and cooked by either the hotel staff or your own father. Promise me.'

A very small voice promised. 'When is Daddy coming?'

Tucking him into his narrow bed, Charisse assured him, 'Soon. Do you want me to go downstairs and find out or stay here and wait with you? Here, drink this medicine; it will take the last of the pain away.'

The pains had subsided almost completely and he was able to straighten in the bed and swallow the antacid mixture. 'I'd like to see Daddy. Will *you* go and get him and bring him back? I know he is very busy making lots of money, but if *you* asked him I just *know* he would come. It's not that I am frightened. . . well. . .not much. . .but I would like Daddy to tell me I'm all right.'

Charisse smoothed back the still damp hair. 'I promise you he will. I'll be back very soon.' She dropped a kiss on his forehead before going briefly to her room to change out of the ruined dress then hurrying downstairs, demanding of the clerk, 'Where *is* Mr LaVelle? Why isn't he here?'

The manager emerged from the rear room, features strained. 'How is the boy?'

'He will be fine, but it could have been worse, much worse. He wants his father and his father he shall have; now, where *is* he?'

The manager bit his lip, vacillating. 'If the child is all right surely——'

'Surely nothing!' Charisse exploded. 'He isn't "the boy", "the child". His name is Mark and he is frightened and very sick and no one will make him feel better but his father, who should never have allowed a seven-year-old to go to an unsupervised picnic with a friend little older in the first instance—and a friend who at this moment in time may be fighting for his life, or have lost the fight, thanks to LaVelle's indifference. He may well be too busy making money, but I demand to know where this wheeler-dealer business meeting is. I told Mark that I would bring back his father and so I shall.'

The manager looked shocked. 'Forgive me, Miss Linton, I didn't realise. Mr LaVelle is only a block away. An exclusive and closed game for exceedingly high stakes that he attends every Friday evening. He is always back in time to put the boy. . . Mark to bed.'

Charisse could not believe her ears. 'He's playing poker? His son could have been at death's door and you didn't want to disturb Mr Dace LaVelle at a *card* game!'

'Please——'

Her voice was glacial as she enunciated clearly and concisely, 'Give—me—that—address.' And when it was scribbled down she spun and walked out, her rage building as she made her way up the hill.

A heavy, waiting silence lay over the room. Even the sounds from the street were muffled by thick blue velvet curtains. Finally one of the men around the baize-topped table said, 'I'll stay and raise three.'

There was a collective stir from the other five players and with a sigh the man to his left shook his head and flipped his cards face down. 'Too rich for me.' The man next to him smiled, pushed over enough chips to stay in the game, but did not raise the stakes, as did the fourth player.

Dace LaVelle's face was totally expressionless as he placed his chips on the pile in the centre, then selected two more from one of the stacks at his hand and said quietly, 'And two.'

There was a sound that was a cross between a moan and a whimper from the man to his left as he threw in his hand. They were playing for units of one hundred dollars. The pot already stood at over fifty thousand and the price of admission was now nine hundred dollars. 'Me too,' admitted his neighbour and folded.

Dace looked across at the last man left and permitted the faintest smile to touch his lips. . .and at that precise moment there was a commotion outside, the door flew open and Charisse Linton stormed in, followed by a red-faced guard who begged, 'Sorry, gentlemen. The lady threatened to shoot me if I stopped her from seeing Mr LaVelle here.'

At once all eyes were riveted on the woman replacing the derringer in her purse and, seeing that there was no reason to delay now, she immediately said to Dace,

'I apologise for interrupting your game, but Mark has food poisoning; he is ill and needs you. I'm sure these gentlemen will forgive you.'

'How serious?'

'The worst is over, no thanks to the tutor who left him in his own vomit on the floor. Had I not been in the foyer I don't know what would have happened. I'll tell you on the way. Dr Benjamin has left and Mark's alone.'

Dace had paled, but then turned back to his opponent. 'Shall we finish this quickly?'

'Of course.' With a quick glance at Dace's cards—three kings and an ace—and his own nine, ten, Jack and Queen of hearts, knowing that his concealed eight made it an incredible straight, he gambled on the odds that Dace had only three of a kind. 'I'll take the pot, my friend, and if you're in any doubt I'll raise you another five.'

There was a gasp from the dealer, but that turned into open disbelief as Dace nodded. 'And five more. I said I wanted this over quickly.'

'It—it *can't* be!' his victim stammered, eyes bulging. 'It's impossible!'

'So call my bluff—if it is one.'

But the man's hands were shaking and with a curse he called, revealing his straight.

Dace's smile was enigmatic. 'Very good. . .' he said, and, as the other moved with a laugh of relief to rake in the pot, 'But not quite good enough,' turning over his downcard to reveal another ace. Not three of a kind but a full house and, since they were playing five card stud, at odds against an initial deal of seven hundred to one. Dace rose and turned to Charisse. '*Now* we can go.'

'Don't forget your winnings,' she said sarcastically. 'After all, you weren't bothered about quitting the game immediately, even for Mark, so don't let me hurry you now.'

Before he could reply one of the other players also
pushed back his chair and rose to his feet, a belligerent
expression darkening features that bespoke a long
acquaintanceship with the brandy bottle. 'Yes, Mr
LaVelle, why hurry? If *my* son was ill I'd be gone by
now. On the other hand, if he wasn't and this was a
set-up between me and a lady friend, I'd be acting
much as you are now.'

An incredulous gasp torn from Charisse was echoed
by the other players. Only Dace remained impassive
and only one who knew him would have noticed that
the gold-flecked green eyes had darkened to deep
emerald. 'What are you trying to say, Mr Turner?'

Turner was too angry for caution: the afternoon had
almost bankrupted him. 'Perfect timing, that's what
I'm saying. Your lady friend charges in and while we're
looking at her you replace your downcard with——'
Which was as far as he got before Dace hit him,
pivoting with his whole body weight behind the blow
to the stomach and, as his victim doubled up, following
with a crashing upper-cut to the chin. Turner went
down like a pole-axed steer and stayed there.

'Anyone else unhappy about my cards?'

The dealer spoke for all those remaining. 'I've never
known you to cheat, Mr LaVelle, and I'd stake my
reputation on your never doing so. We changed from
draw poker to stud to beat you, but your luck even
outweighs your skill. You go see your son and I'll cash
in your chips and have your money brought to the
hotel.'

'Thanks, Red.' He turned to Charisse. 'Let's go.'
With a half-bow he opened the door for her, but once
the door closed behind them he spun on her with
glittering eyes. 'Don't *ever* accuse me, even by impli-
cation, of neglecting my son. Not ever. Do you
understand?'

Before she could speak he turned on his heel and
started out of the building at a long pace too fast for

her to match other than by running, and within minutes had disappeared into the Gateway far ahead of her. 'Boor! Pig!' At the hotel she was torn between returning to her room and awaiting news or going directly to Mark and facing the possibility of Dace ordering her to leave. With a lift of the chin she made her way again to the top floor and knocked on the large double doors.

'It's open.'

This time, as she crossed the main living-room, she had time to notice the luxury of her surroundings. An essentially masculine domain, the room still held touches of a softer nature: delicate Parianware on the what-not in the corner, a large onyx horse rearing from a marble-topped table, and a collection of jade net-sukes—probably worth a fortune, she thought—in a walnut-inlaid display cabinet. A restless seascape on one wall echoed the greens, turquoises, and golds of the room and possibly, she wondered, the restlessness of its owner's heart. Pushing such thought from her mind, she approached Mark's bedroom.

Dace was sitting on the bedside, jacket discarded on the bedpost and the broad back bent attentively over the boy lying beneath the covers. Without turning he said, 'He's still over-pale. Did Benjamin say he would return?'

'No, but I'm sure he will.' She did not know whether to hover in the doorway or approach, but Mark solved her dilemma by holding out his hand.

'Hello, Charisse. I'm glad you brought Daddy back like you promised. I feel a lot better now he's here.'

Charisse went to kneel at the bedside and take the hot little hand. 'Of course you do.'

'How is Frankie?'

She swallowed hard. 'I don't know, Mark. Dr Benjamin went to see him straight from here. He'll let us know as soon as he can, I'm sure.'

At the tone in her voice Dace frowned. 'Frankie? Is he sick too?'

'May I see you for a moment, Dace? We'll be right back, Mark.'

He rose from the bed and lifted her to her feet. It must have been an oversight, she reasoned, that he forgot to release her hand when they reached the living-room and he turned her to face him. 'First allow me to apologise for my previous anger. I would have indeed left the game at once, had I thought it warranted, but, since you had indicated the danger was past and that the doctor had come and gone, I had to weigh the loss of over fifty thousand dollars against the comfort that an extra five minutes would have given Mark. I make no excuse for my choice. Now tell me of Frankie?'

Pulling her hand free, Charisse told him, 'You shouldn't have let them picnic alone. Frankie's only ten, for heaven's sake!'

'I didn't know they were alone. What kind of father do you think I am. . .? No, you've already answered that! Frankie's sister was supposed to have taken them. She's married with a baby of her own. Now tell me the rest.'

She did so, sparing him no detail, and saw his face turn grey and his fists clench. He said nothing, but spun away, walked three fast paces, whipped around and strode back again, fighting for control. Finally he asked, 'Will you stay with Mark until I get back—twenty minutes at the most?'

'Of course; as long as you wish.'

But at that moment, with a sharp rap on the door, Dr Benjamin entered. His face told the whole story and even before he shook his head Charisse had folded weakly into a chair with a soft, 'Oh, no!'

'I'm sorry. His mother told me that he admitted eating a fair-sized plateful, more out of bravado than because he enjoyed them. I've given her a heavy opiate and she's sleeping. There are friends with her now.'

Voice tight, Dace asked, 'And the sister? The

woman whose fault this is? Tell me where *she* was before I get my hands on her.'

Again the doctor gave a sigh and a shake of the head. 'They did indeed go to the woods together but the toddler became fractious and demanding. Not wanting to spoil the boys' outing, she told them to play for an hour while she took the baby to her mother's. Unfortunately the mother was out. The boys became hungry and restless and decided to fix themselves some lunch, but didn't want to break into the lunch basket for fear of being reprimanded.'

'But surely when she returned. . .' Charisse cried.

The doctor's lips thinned. 'Unfortunately when she *did* return she immediately began quizzing them as to what they had been up to and whether they had eaten any berries or anything. Too scared to own up, they denied having done so, but said they weren't hungry for lunch and too tired to play for much longer. Your son, Mr LaVelle, had only eaten a little of the toad-stools, so was still peckish and ate some bread and cheese, washed down with a quantity of milk. The other boy had nothing.' He spread his hands in a gesture of deep mental weariness. 'Frankie died fifteen minutes ago, not recovering from the coma he was in when I arrived. Your son, sir, is a miraculously lucky boy. I'll go in to him now and check on his condition, but I'm certain he will be perfectly well. Do you wish me to tell him of his friend or would you prefer to?'

Dace did not answer.

Charisse looked up at him and her heart turned over, for his eyes held all the horrors of the pit. And she had accused him of indifference! 'Dace?'

'What? Oh. . .yes. Yes, if you would, doctor.' The words seemed to rouse him and, striding over to the sideboard, he poured a large measure of bourbon into a cut-crystal glass, downing it in one gulp, then, crossing to stare sightlessly out of the window, he ground out, 'It could have been Mark!'

Charisse hurried to him and put a comforting hand over his arm, feeling the muscles bunch beneath the fine linen shirt. 'It was a terrible accident, Dace, but it was no one's fault. You can't be with him all of the time. He'll never do such a thing again, but he is a boy and, unless you imprison him, there will be other accidents, other near misses, as he grows.'

'I know, but the knowledge doesn't help. It doesn't help at all.' They heard the sound of quiet sobs from the next room and the man turned towards it. 'At least I'm here this time to comfort him.' His expression was apologetic. 'You probably saved his life, Charisse, and all I did was shout at you.'

'We both misunderstood. Go to him, Dace. I won't keep you, but perhaps I could see him later or if it's inconvenient. . .'

'Don't leave. . .not for a while.'

Green eyes met grey. 'I'll stay for as long as you need me.' And somehow she knew that she had made some kind of commitment.

The doctor had left, saying that all would be fine, but leaving the bottle of medicine and a sleeping draught. Dace had comforted Mark over the loss of his friend, and Charisse had bade the boy goodnight with a promise to see him the following day. Nothing but the ticking of the clock on the marble fireplace disturbed the quietness of the living-room as Dace and Charisse sat in a strangely waiting silence, he in a high wing-back chair by the fire and she at one end of the facing couch.

Finally he said, 'Not many women would have done what you did for a stranger's child—none that I know. Most would have sent for the doctor and a maid.'

'I like children.'

A quick, searching look. 'Do you? Melinda never did.'

'I'm sorry.'

'Don't be. Mark told me he made a mess of your gown; I shall replace it of course.'

'There's no need; it wasn't new.'

A half-smile lifted one corner of the firm mouth. 'A woman who refuses a new dress?'

'I have little use for such at home. Most of my clothes have to withstand hard riding and ranch life; I'm not one to play the oil baron's daughter when the ranch and the plains please me more.' She remembered the milliner's and smiled. 'However, I did weaken and purchase a quite inappropriate hat when I saw——' She pulled up sharply, but realised that already she had said too much to stop, so finished, 'Your wife was at the milliner's with a friend.'

It did not have the reaction she expected as he merely shrugged and said, 'Ex-wife. I assume the friend was a male?'

'No, an elder woman.' Then, with unquenchable female curiosity, she added, 'She is very beautiful,' and this time earned a harsh laugh.

'Oh, yes, she is that if nothing else!'

'You must have loved her once. There is, after all, Mark.'

'Mark,' he mused softly. 'Yes, there is Mark and I guess for that one sacrifice on her part I shall forgive her almost anything.' His glance took in the involuntary stiffening of her frame and again came that self-mocking twist of the lips. 'Forgive her, yes. Live with her? Never again.'

'Do you want to talk about it, or shall we talk of more pleasant matters?'

'There's little to tell. Like most men who become cuckolds in spite of all efforts to the contrary, I suppose I didn't want to know. She possessed enough beauty, charm, wit, elegance, social poise to content any man, but Melinda was never, would never be, content with any one man. She needed all men, every man she met. No one could have been enough for her and in my vanity I did not believe it until the truth hit me between the eyes. You see, like many vain women, Melinda kept a list of her conquests—more than a list, a detailed diary.'

'Oh, Dace!' But Charisse's whisper was never heard as, in a strangely remote voice, he began talking, as if he had needed this moment for years.

As he talked on, staring into the fire, hands loosely clasped in his lap as if his words no longer caused the pain that his heart revealed, Charisse heard, between the words, a tale of anger and rejection, betrayal and treachery. She heard of a woman who had shamed her parents by eloping with a wealthy, though weak young lawyer only to throw him aside when the handsome— and above all wealthier—hotelier appeared. She saw, as if with her own eyes, the vanity that resented the growth of a child in her womb after a pregnancy had been the only way to capture her man, and the fury at not being able to obtain a miscarriage or abortion once that marriage was a *fait accompli*. 'I told her I would strangle her with my own hands if she harmed our child,' Dace stated quietly and, like Melinda, Charisse believed him.

He talked on, exposing only the surface scars caused by Melinda's last affair and final leaving with the devastatingly handsome, though selfish and shallow, hotel pianist, taking several thousand dollars of Dace's money from the safe. The following two years were spanned in a few sentences—his devotion and growing love for his son unmentioned, but blindingly apparent in every word and gesture. At last it was finished, the flood turned to a trickle, then dried up and ceased, as he ended, 'So now she is back in San Francisco, living in a variety of hotels and throwing her net again to capture whichever poor fish is rich enough and foolish enough to become entangled in it. With hindsight I can admire her technique.' And Charisse knew that he had bared his soul.

'Thank you, Dace. Thank you for telling me.'

He shrugged, though she felt it was contrived. 'You wanted to know. Why not? The rest of the city has already forgotten the story: it's too familiar a one to hold the interest for long.' He rose and came to sit beside her on the couch. 'This isn't my usual conversational gambit when alone with a beautiful woman. Melinda is a female piranha and one I would rather forget.'

Charisse retrieved the hand he had reached for, knowing that there was still too much unsaid for any lasting relationship between them, knowing too that friendship was not what the dangerously handsome Creole had in mind. 'I should be leaving.'

'You should,' he agreed, 'but *must* you?' He leaned forward a little, his knee touching hers, and one hand came to rest along the back of the couch behind her head. 'It's much too early to be thinking of sleep.' She noticed he did not use the word 'bed' but it hung between them. 'I could order a late supper—some champagne.' The panther-like purr held a challenge as his fingers slipped down to barely touch the nape of her neck and Charisse fought the sensual somnolence that turned her limbs to liquid.

'I must go.'

Dace searched the soul mirrored in her eyes and felt the sure knowledge deep inside. 'Very well.' He read the surprise she tried in vain to hide at his easy capitulation and hid a smile, thinking, Oh, yes, Charisse Linton! You *are* that transparent. You wear your innocence like a suit of armour, but I have the heat to melt even the toughest steel. You'll see! Aloud he said, 'I shall look forward to a long and lonely evening, then.'

Momentary panic quelled, she could smile. 'I doubt that. San Francisco is full of beautiful women and the greater majority, I'm sure, more than eager to share that champagne. . .at least the champagne.' She rose and turned to the door. 'I shall come to see Mark tomorrow.'

'Only Mark?' He too had risen, and took her arm, escorting her to the door. 'I'm devastated.' But he merely lifted the very tips of her fingers to his lips. 'Have a pleasant evening, Charisse.' Then, as he opened the door, 'Thank you for all you did for Mark.'

'You're welcome.'

He was close, very close. 'Dream of me, Texas.' And before she knew it she had been put gently outside and the door closed behind her. Inexplicably she felt disorientated, wondering why he had not kissed her— exactly as he had known she would!

CHAPTER SEVEN

THE following ten days passed all too quickly for
Charisse. Each day she went out into the streets,
quartering every section of town—the reputable ones
on foot and the others in a closed cab—and each
evening she visited Mark. The tutor had been summar-
ily dismissed and, as an angry and unforgiving Dace
had made certain that no family of substance would
employ him, had left the city. Between Charisse and
Mark was formed a warm, close bond that she knew
she would miss deeply when she returned home. She
wrote to her father daily of her progress—or lack of
it—and mentioned only in passing a long afternoon
with Lee Rand, riding in Muir Woods 'to capture lost
youth', and a theatre evening with Dace. She did not
mention that Lee had kissed her again, gently, sweetly,
with a laughing apology for totally severing employer-
employee relations—or that Dace had not.

That Saturday Dace had accepted an invitation to a
ball at the Haas-Lilienthal house on Franklin Street
and asked Charisse to accompany him. When she
exclaimed over the impossibility of finding a ball dress
in only three days he had even 'magicked' a seamstress
seemingly out of the air who could achieve such a
miracle, since, 'I virtually set her up in business, paying
Melinda's endless bills.'

'Do you know a hairdresser, too?' she asked
worriedly. 'This will hardly be the kind of ball I am
accustomed to.' And that, too, was accomplished, so it
was with some trepidation underlying a growing excitement that Charisse awaited Saturday evening.

* * *

The strikingly beautiful Eastlake-style house of William Haas was as legendary as the family's hospitality down the years, its strange assortment of geometric additions, the triangular gables, multitudinous windows, and Queen Anne tower with its high, conical peak making it a landmark. That evening the chandeliered ballroom was ablaze with light and the sound of music and laughter filtered into the street below.

The seamstress had indeed achieved a miracle and Charisse twirled before the mirror in her room, attempting in vain to keep the glow from her eyes. 'It's perfect! Just perfect!' Then, hesitantly, 'Not too décolletée?'

'Madam has the figure to take such a neckline.'

Charisse again questioned and was reassured and it was only when both seamstress and hairdresser had departed that she whirled in a dream of disbelief, knowing that she had never looked as beautiful.

The dress was of midnight-blue chiffon over silk so that while the top layers of the huge skirt floated and billowed the underskirt rustled provocatively with every movement. The bodice barely skimmed her shoulders before plunging into a deeply scooped neckline above which the full curve of her breasts rose tantalisingly, and the sleeves—a single layer of chiffon in the demi-gigot style—allowed the skin tone to glow through. On the silk of the bodice and the underskirt intricate embroidery in silver thread created a constellation of stars and crescent moons that shone through the chiffon as through night clouds. It was the very substance that dreams were made of. Her hair had been left loose with only the sides swept upward into a coronet of cascading curls, held by a star-studded velvet band contrasting with the white-gold hair seemingly held so loosely that it begged to be pulled free.

Only for one moment, as she entered the ballroom on Dace's arm and an incredulous hush fell, then was immediately lost in the resumed babble, did she feel

nervous. Then, even knowing that the conversation, as
well as all eyes that she passed, were concentrated on
her and the fairy-tale dress, she floated through on a
bubble of elation. 'I never knew I could feel so
wonderful!' she whispered to her partner, blushing a
little at the confession.

Dace covered the fingers resting lightly on his arm
with his other hand. 'You wear an entire galaxy of stars
and still it pales beside your own beauty.' Then, in a
lighter tone to hide the catch in his throat, 'I am the
envy of every man here and you have just made your
seamstress a very wealthy woman. Shall we dance?' He
then immediately swung her into the dipping, whirling
throng.

Charisse felt her breath taken away, felt that she was
wheeling and soaring like a night bird in the midnight
sky of her gown. She was aware only of the spread
fingers at her waist, the firm hand enfolding hers and
guiding her through the other dancers as though they
were non-existent. No words were necessary between
them as they moved in perfect unison and it was only
when the waltz ended and reluctantly Charisse floated
back to earth that she breathed, 'If I believed in
reincarnation I'd know we had danced together in
some previous life.'

She expected him to laugh, but quite seriously he
said, 'I have never held a woman who melted into me
as you do,' and there was a strange inflexion in his tone
and a puzzlement in the dark eyes. But then, with an
almost imperceptible shake of his head, as if to rid
himself of disquieting thoughts, he said, 'As grand an
affair as this is, it still doesn't compare, in my estima-
tion, with the balls of Comus I used to attend with my
father in New Orleans. He was a master in that élite
and oldest of Houses and as such earned a special
attention at the famous Creole balls, which appealed
to my youthful vanity, since much of that attention
rubbed off on me.'

'As did the flocks of beautiful Creole maidens, no doubt,' she smiled teasingly.

'They are,' he admitted, 'probably some of the most exceptional creatures I have ever seen and quite famous in the south, rivalling even the creamy magnolia octoroons, which is saying something.'

'And there I was thinking your taste ran to blondes!'

He laughed, drawing her again into the next waltz. 'My taste runs to any young and beautiful woman, from the whitest alabaster blonde to the darkest brunette and all shades between. Apart from a good poker game I find the fairest sex the one thing certain to relieve any moment of temporary ennui.'

Charisse knew that he was baiting her, but refused to rise to it, reciprocating, 'You are lucky. I find the male of the species the one thing certain to *cause* it!'

'*Touché!*' He swung her around expertly, then reversed so quickly that her feet almost left the ground. 'I can see I must beware of being too predictable: the last thing I would wish is to bore you, even for an instant.'

Charisse allowed herself to surrender completely to his dominant lead, following instinctively, as if they were melded together. 'Oh, I don't think there is much chance of that.'

A lively polka followed and, without allowing her breath, he spun her into that. A feeling of exhilaration swept through her, as breathlessly joyful as when riding her pinto, Chico, down a steep-sided canyon trail, and she laughed aloud.

Dace felt his heart swell at that uninhibited display of sheer exuberance. He had never known a woman with so many facets to her character, and doubted he would ever meet another. He had seen her silent and thoughtful, tender and loving with Mark, courageous, and even magnificently angry. Now she was like a child on a carousel, eyes no longer like bayou mist, but sparkling with the almost blue-grey of a sun-kissed sea on a summer's day, lips slightly parted with her quickened breath—eminently kissable. God, how he wanted her! It was like a ball of fire in his loins. No! This must stop—especially in such company!

'Enough!' he cried, leading her out to the edge of the floor. 'I have obviously spent far too long at the tables and not half long enough in decent exercise. I must be getting old.'

Charisse, too, had blamed her breathlessness on the pace of the dance, but, looking up into that burning gaze that totally belied his flippant words, knew that they were both making excuses and attempted to lighten the air between them. 'I doubt that you will *ever* grow old. I, on the other hand, will become a plump matron with skin leathered by the Texan wind and eyes lined by the sun, so you had best enjoy me while you may.' Again his answer threw her off balance.

'I should never see the change. I think I shall always see you as you are tonight in that dress.' He pulled himself up sharply and in quite a different voice offered, 'I'll bring you some punch.'

'Thank you.' She watched the broad shoulders cleave a path through the crowd and wondered at his words. She had expected flippancy or, more typically, a provocative challenge, but his answer had been strangely brooding.

A waft of heavy perfume caught at her nostrils a moment before a familiar voice exclaimed, 'Well, if it isn't the rancher's daughter!' and she turned to meet the cool stare of Melinda Marsh.

Her first reaction was, did Dace know? Had he planned this? 'I'm flattered you bothered to make enquiries,' she answered with as cool a smile, hiding her uncertainty. The woman was certainly beautiful, she had to acknowledge; how could Dace, or any man, resist her?

'I didn't,' the other said bluntly. 'But when the same

woman visits the room of one of the city's most prominent and infamous citizens every evening for over a week, staff talk, and one would have to be quite deaf to ignore the sound of the grapevine—in this city more like a firebell than wind-chimes. I knew you were coming this evening—don't forget we share the same dressmaker—and thought it would prove amusing to accept the invitation.'

'She has excelled herself,' Charisse complimented generously. 'Your dress is stunning.'

The crimsoned lips that matched the silk sheath parted in a baring of feline fangs. 'Thank you. Her diversity never ceases to amaze me, though I would have thought she would put you in virginal white rather than half-mourning: she is usually more perceptive. Had any other colour been more appropriate, I am certain Dace would have lost interest by now.'

Charisse refrained from curling her fingers into claws. 'You really think so? Is that why you are in scarlet?' She did not add, And why Dace *has* lost interest.

The blow was reflected in the blue eyes, but Melinda gave a throaty laugh. 'I simply decided to wear Dace's favourite colour and of a style appropriate to rekindling old flames.' Her eyes had gone past Charisse and she smiled. 'But Dace can wait. I see another old flame who believes himself happily engaged to be married. I can call on Dace any time I see fit, but I don't have a key to that particular house. . .yet.'

'I am learning a great deal about city dwellers,' Charisse stated quietly. 'Where I come from rattle-snakes crawl on their belly.'

Melinda's laugh was completely unaffected as her brilliant gaze swung back to the girl beside her. 'Oh, I can do that too. . .with quite devastating results! Ask Dace!' And with a flicker of her fingers she deliberately turned her back and slid sinuously off through the crowd towards the next unfortunate victim.

Dace appeared a bare minute later carrying two punch-cups, took one look at her face and demanded, 'What is it? What has happened?'

Charisse took one of the filled cups, drew a deep breath and drained it, ignoring his exclamation. 'Nothing that won't be put right by our leaving—immediately.'

'But——'

'At once, Dace!' she whispered fiercely. 'Or I leave alone.'

Wordlessly he took her arm and steered her towards the door, not even daring to seek out his host and extend his thanks and farewells. Selecting one of the cabs lined up at the pavement, he helped her in, gave the driver the address, even though it was a bare five minutes away, then turned to regard the mutinously averted profile. 'Now suppose you tell me what in Hades caused that little explosion?'

'Did you know Melinda would be there this evening? Is that why you invited me? Did you also invite me to visit Mark each evening knowing that she still has a key to your rooms and would have put the only possible interpretation on my presence had she found me there? What kind of power games are you playing, Dace?'

Tightly he said, 'I have all the power I need, Charisse, and don't need to play games with it. Again you have elected yourself judge, jury and executioner without giving the accused a hearing. I wonder why such a violent reaction this time?' And when she refused to answer he continued, 'Melinda Marsh certainly deserves her name. Like a marsh she can appear sweet and inviting on the surface, but is black and treacherous beneath. I've seen both sides of her character, don't forget, but for what we once were and for giving me Mark I still pay her a not inconsiderable allowance. This is usually done once a month in my rooms rather than in my office, and at that time she usually has a few words with Mark, at my suggestion, not hers.

There was a time when things were different between us, very different; I won't deny that.'

'So that's what she meant by re-kindling old flames.'

'There is nothing but ashes between us now. If I had known she was coming tonight I would not have invited you. We would have gone elsewhere, for your sake, not hers. Neither did I know she still had a key to my rooms; she has always knocked on her previous visits. I demanded she hand her keys over when the divorce became absolute. However, it will be a simple matter to have the locks changed if it concerns you.'

'Why should it concern me? I shall be gone soon and you may continue your life as you please. I should not have agreed to come to visit Mark from the first, not in your rooms, knowing how staff gossip.'

The cab had reached the hotel and Dace swung down, paid the cabbie and helped Charisse to the ground. 'I wouldn't want you to stop seeing Mark. If you prefer it he can visit you; it's only two floors down.' He took her elbow and led her up the steps and across the foyer. 'I'll see you to your room——'

'And then return to the ball?' she enquired before she could stop herself.

They were close together in the quilted interior of the elevator and she had nowhere to turn as he gripped her arm. 'Don't bait me, Charisse. If I had wanted to remain at the ball I would have done so. Whatever I choose to do I generally do, regardless of outside influence or opinion.' The lift stopped and he led her out and along the corridor, retaining his firm grip, and she wondered whether there would be bruises there the following day. 'As you continually remind me, you are a transient, passing through my life, and can therefore hardly expect me to turn it upside-down to accommodate your feminine jealousies.'

'Jealousy?' She dug in her heels, bringing him to a halt, reiterating, 'Jealousy?' The grey eyes resembled a thundercloud behind which lightning flashed. 'What you choose to do and with whom is of supreme indifference to me, *Mr* LaVelle. As for your over-weight, over-decorated, over-sexed ex-wife, I wish you both all happiness. You *deserve* each other!' She wrenched her arm free and ran the last few yards to her door, fumbling desperately in her purse for the key, fitting it into the lock with shaking fingers.

'Oh, no, you don't!' He almost swung her off her feet as he pulled her around and hard against him, but the anger died as he met the wide eyes, tear-washed half in anger, half in acknowledgement of that very jealousy she had denied. Softly he said, 'I can't let you go like this, Charisse.' One hand captured her hair, forcing her face upwards as his mouth descended, covering hers, moving over it in almost painful plunder, crushing the breath from her.

At first she fought him, but then, as the kiss deep-ened and lengthened—tongue thrusting inward, teeth closing over her lower lip—the hands that beat at his back stilled, then slipped upwards. With a soft, despair-ing sigh she felt the silky curls at the back of his neck as one hand caressed there and the other splayed over the corded shoulder muscles. Senses reeling, she arched into the length of him, the heat of his thighs, the desire in his loins scalding her. 'No!' Suddenly afraid, she pulled her head away. 'No, Dace.' And she was released, yet still held loosely within the circle of his arms. Both were breathing heavily.

'I don't need you, nor ever will,' he stated quietly, holding her gaze. 'But I want you and always will. Let me come in, Charisse.'

'No.' But it emerged a whisper. Only when the arm about her began to tighten and she recognised the predatory gleam in his eyes, only then did her resolve strengthen. 'No,' she repeated and, afraid of herself more than of him, dragged free and ran into her room, slamming the door. Weakly she leaned against it until she heard his footsteps receding down the corridor and then went shakily to fold into the armchair, cursing herself for her weakness. 'I *won't* be another passing fancy for a day or a week,' she vowed. 'I won't be a poor substitute for Melinda, not while there is that look in his eyes whenever he speaks of her. Even if I weren't going home soon, he isn't worth fighting for.' But the tears of frustrated rage that flooded her eyes and caused her to hurl her fan at the closed door gave the words the lie.

The following afternoon, after Charisse had stubbornly refused to answer all calls, two dozen yellow roses were delivered. 'On a Sunday? In April?' she exclaimed in disbelief. The gold-edged embossed card answered, 'Easier by far to empty my greenhouse than to reproduce the spun gold of your hair.' No signature given. None needed.

Then on Monday morning came a sharp double knock unlike those previous and a voice called, 'Miss Linton. . . Charisse, it's Lee Rand.'

Running to answer it, Charisse immediately saw the ill-concealed excitement in the craggy features. 'It's Ralph! You have found him! Come in. No. We'll go at once. I'll get my coat.'

'Calm down,' he laughed, stepping inside. 'I have his address, but he may well be out on calls at this time of the day.'

'Then we'll wait there for him. We can, can't we?'

He could refuse her nothing. 'All day and overnight if you wish. Yes, I guess you might say we have found him at last.'

Sensitive to his feelings, she said, 'I don't know what I would have done without you, Lee. I'll be eternally grateful, as will my father. Perhaps you could accompany us back and let him tell you himself.'

Lee was more practical and, tempting as the invitation was, knew that it could only serve to prolong the pain of parting. 'No, I think not.' He helped her on with her coat and gave a rueful grin. 'I'd be lost in your

world, far more than you are in mine, but thanks for
the offer.'

'But you were a farm boy, you told me so yourself.
We don't exactly have a farm, but country folks are
country folks whatever the location.'

He led her out and down the corridor. 'I wouldn't
call a massive hacienda on an oil baron's land the home
of country folks, baby doll. No, I don't think I'd fit at
all.'

'I thought you would want to. . .to make our friendship last as long as you could,' she said bewilderedly, a
little hurt by his firm refusal. 'I thought you liked me.'

They had reached the lift and he turned her to face
him, eyes revealing all. 'I'm in love with you,
Charisse—an unrequited love, but love for all that.'

'Oh, Lee, I never knew! I'm sorry.'

Again that lop-sided grin. 'Me too, believe me. Now
let's go and pick up your brother at the rainbow's end.'

There was a silence between them as they drove
south into the seedy and mean streets of the Mission
District. For Lee, every block nearer his quarry was
another granite slab over his heart; for Charisse, the
end of her quest brought both joy and sorrow, and a
curious kind of longing, a temptation to send her
brother home and stay, at least for a while, in the city
on the bay.

They pulled up before a dilapidated tenement, little
different from its neighbours, and exchanged looks.
Lee read the half-fearful wondering in hers and asked,
'Do you want me to go in and bring him out? The
landlord wasn't in earlier, but may be now. If Ralph is
out I might pursuade him to let us go up and leave a
message.'

Forcing down the racing of her heart, Charisse shook
her head. 'No, I'll come with you. Are you. . .are you
absolutely certain?'

'Yes, Charisse, I am. This time I am. The man in
apartment 3B answers to the description of your

brother, beard *et al*, and is a Dr Ralph Leonard.' Then
gently, 'Come on, honey, don't stop trusting me now.'
He took her hand to help her down and felt her fingers
curl tightly about his, retaining hold as they made their
way inside.

The landlord was a sleepy, unshaven scarecrow of
indeterminate origin, who slowly pulled himself to his
feet at the sight of a lady and rubbed a hand over his
jaw. 'Doc Leonard lives here, that's fer sure, but he
bin an' gone outa town fer a few days. . .mebbe a
week.'

Lee put a strong arm about Charisse's waist as she
swayed against him. So near, yet so far!

'Please,' she begged. 'I am Dr Leonard's sister. Our
father is ill and I must take my brother home to see
him. Can we leave a message in his room to call me the
minute he returns? It really is most urgent.'

The man hesitated, scratching his chin, but then gave
a decisive nod. 'Guess that's all right. You *could* be his
sister. Same colouring.' With a gesture at Lee, he
asked, 'This your husband?'

'Unfortunately no,' denied Lee before she could
answer. 'Lee Rand Detective Agency.' And he pulled
out his card. 'I'd be obliged if you would take us up,
Mr. . .'

'Zuchowski. Call me Zeke; everyone else does. OK.
Follow me. No fancy elevators, but I guess you could
say the walk'll do you good. That's what Doc says
anyway. More healthy to walk. Nice kid, your brother.'

'Yes, I think so.'

The apartment consisted of a living-dining room with
a tiny cooking area in one corner, a bedroom and
bathroom. All was in immaculate order, almost anti-
septically clean, but when Charisse compared it to the
huge, lavishly furnished rooms at the hacienda she
could have wept. 'Has my brother lived here long?'

Again Zeke scratched at the stubble on his chin with
broken fingernails. 'Reckon about three years now.'

His sharp eyes took in the quality of her clothing and heard the educated tones and he gave a nod. 'It mayn't be what he come from, ma'am, but it suits where he's at now. Doc Leonard treats the folks hereabouts all times of the day or night. Most folks don't got them new-fangled telephones; they just come a'runnin', and the doc is right here for them.'

Charisse smiled. 'That sort of sacrifice sounds just like Ralph.' She looked towards the partly open window. 'Aren't you afraid of burglars?'

The man gave a snort of laughter. 'In *this* neighbourhood? No, missy; if a burglar broke into most of these houses he'd feel so sorry for them, he'd leave a donation. No, the doc always leaves the window open. Says fresh air is healthy. Not that I go for that thinking, but who'm I to argue?'

Wanting to be on his way, Lee produced a small notepad and pencil from his pocket, handing them to Charisse. 'Here, write a couple of lines telling Ralph where to contact you and then I'll take you back. There's nothing more we can do until his return.'

'You're right, of course, and the waiting will be far easier now.' She took the paper to the little round dining table and scribbled a few lines.

Ralph, Father is very ill and asking for you. I am at the Gateway Hotel on California Street. Please, *please* come at once. All love, Charisse.

'There!' she said, placing the note carefully at the centre of the table. 'He is bound to see that the moment he walks through the door. Very well, let's go back now.' She turned to Lee with shining eyes. 'I'm so very grateful to you.'

He smiled that endearing sideways smile and touched her cheek, then, in embarrassment at his own emotion, effected a broad 'Okie' drawl. 'Shoot, ma'am, weren't nuthin' at all!'

They moved out into the corridor and the landlord

pulled the door shut behind them with a bang. . .and the cross-draught it caused with the open window wafted that precious scrap of paper off the table and into the fireplace—to drift gently on to the other papers crumpled for lighting.

CHAPTER EIGHT

THE following morning dawned sunny and clear, with an unseasonably warm breeze coming in from the bay. Charisse revelled in the warmth of her bed for a full hour past her self-imposed time of eight o'clock, but then rose and threw back the curtains, letting the sunlight wash over her. 'San Francisco, I love you!' she breathed. 'I am going to miss you so much when I leave. Of course that has absolutely nothing to do with Dace LaVelle, or the sweet and gentle Lee, who took me on a wonderfully long ramble around the city. It can't be, because I have found Ralph and soon we'll all be together again as a real family. I feel. . . I feel like soaring and it can only be some kind of wondrous affliction that turns all humans into lotus-eaters on arrival.' She laughed at her fancies and went to dress. She must see Dace—he had been out last night when she returned—and tell him of her wonderful news.

Dace saw by the glow that surrounded her as she hurried across the foyer to greet him that her previous day had been fruitful at last, and was irritated by the lurch his heart gave. She would be leaving, then—he had known that from the moment she arrived. He had known, too, that she could be seduced with the same ease of any other, that the very way she moved, the tilt of her head, the look in her eyes, bespoke a passion of which she was quite unaware. He had determined to unleash that passion, to teach her what it was to be a woman. Now, seeing her cross to meet him, grey eyes sparkling, he knew that his conquest would have to be soon, possibly today. And what then? Firmly he put that thought aside. She was a woman, just a woman, as fickle and shallow and treacherous as any other—a toy, a beautiful body to bring a few hours of pleasure. But his usual logic did not seem to work when applied to Charisse. No logic did, and that bothered him.

'Dace, I'm so glad I found you! I have wonderful news!'

'That can only mean you've found Ralph.'

'Yes. . .no. . .not quite. We have his address and I have seen the apartment where he lives. We left a note, but he is away for a few days. I know he'll come to me the minute he gets back. I don't know whether to laugh or cry, I'm so happy.'

He held up a hand in mock agitation. 'Please, dear madam, don't cry. It would quite ruin my reputation!'

She had to laugh. 'I'm sorry; I am acting like a fool. I just wanted to tell you that you don't have to waste any more time on me and can tell all your contacts that everything is all right now. However, I really do appreciate all you, and they, have done. Be glad for me, Dace.'

'I *am* glad for you; I just wish it had been through *my* endeavours that you had that look in your eyes. . . or *is* it just finding Ralph that has done it?' He noted the tell-tale flush and his previous liking for Lee Rand took an ice-cold shower. 'Well!' he said, unable to keep the sarcasm from his tone. 'It appears our Mr Rand has excelled himself in his close attention to his client's needs.'

Charisse stiffened. 'Lee Rand has been kindness itself at a time when I needed that. Apart from being a first-class private investigator—as has been proved— he has also proved a good friend, nothing more, so you can take that glower off your face. Either way, it has absolutely nothing to do with you *what* relationship, if any, there is between Lee and me.' She regretted the sting in her words and laid a hand on his arm. 'Don't let's quarrel, least of all over Lee. I'm going to relax and enjoy the next few days. It will be my last week here and I won't allow you to detract from that.'

Dace searched her eyes and the strange ache gnawing
at him, like a hunger that could only be related to a
starving wolf savaging a dry bone, eased fractionally.
He had met Lee Rand once or twice in the past on a
purely business level and both liked and respected the
man. But this was not business and Dace LaVelle was
not the kind of man who would tolerate competition.
He firmly leashed the wolf within and gave it the
buttermilk voice that had seduced Red Riding Hood.
'Quite the contrary,' he purred. 'I had intended making
your last week not only memorable, but quite
unforgettable.'

'I. . .' Her heart beat out 'retreat', but she ignored
the tattoo. What harm could come of it? Again that
drumroll. She knew all too well the answer to that
question. 'That's very good of you, but——'

'That's what I had in mind: to be good to you. . .for
you.' His voice dropped to that now familiar note that
vibrated along every nerve. 'I don't want to lose you,
Charisse. When you go home I want it to be quite
impossible for you to stay there. I want you to see me
in every dream, until you make that dream a reality
and return to San Francisco.'

'What are you saying, Dace?'

A lean hand came up to brush back a lock of hair
that had escaped. 'Not here in a crowded foyer and not
yet.' The dark eyes promised another time and place,
a magic place. But then, sensing her hesitation—like a
half-broke filly that longed for, yet feared the master's
caress—he deliberately lightened the mood and took a
teasing tone. 'First I shall whisk you away to Cliff
House for an early lunch, lure you into a false sense of
security with lobster, quicken your pulse with quail's
eggs in mushroom mousse nests, and tantalise your
taste-buds with a sensual Sauterne.'

Charisse felt the smile tugging at her mouth. 'Or at
the very least attain my attention with alliteration!'

'Madam, you mock me!'

The laughter was a trill of sheer delight. 'Now would I do a thing like that? Very well, I surrender. I shall allow myself to be abducted. Cliff House, you say?'

'Out along the toll road towards Point Lobos. Adolph Sutro's gingerbread castle—complete with witches'-hat turret at each corner—built around ten years ago; a most fashionable venue for luncheon. Your carriage awaits.'

On the short drive the conversation was easy and casual. Charisse told him more of her home and he revealed a little of his life in New Orleans, though only the incidents that would entertain and amuse. 'Like the night Skeeter Bannou and I went 'gator hunting in a pirogue—a kind of low, dug-out canoe to you uneducated types—with one lantern between us and a pair of ancient rifles that should have been left on whichever civil war battlefield they were discovered on.'

He glanced at her half-believing smile and answered it. 'It's the truth——'

'The whole truth and nothing but the truth.' She giggled deliciously. 'Go on. Now tell me you captured a monster of the deep by hand.'

He clapped a hand to his brow. 'You have ruined my punch line! Well, almost. We were both well saturated with the devil's brew—corn likker: White Lightning— so it was only by a miracle that we were able to stay in the craft at all. Within twenty minutes I was completely lost and Skeeter almost paralytic, when out of the blackness, beyond that circle of light, appeared two great yellow orbs. "Shoot!" shouted Skeeter, and immediately dropped the lantern into the bayou and reached for his gun. At that point all hell broke loose. The lantern was lost, both guns went off, and that great bull 'gator charged the canoe.'

He stopped and Charisse, almost bouncing in the seat, cried, 'Go on! Go on!'

He threw her a laughing look. 'Not much more to tell. Both guns had found their mark and, although we didn't know it at the time, it was a very dead 'gator that clamped its jaws into the side of the pirogue. We all ended up in the water, some idiot with my voice screaming, "I got him! I got him!" and both arms wrapped tight about the brute that resembled a rodeo bull, and Skeeter doing a fair impression of a bird trying to get back into the pirogue.' The chuckle was totally self-deprecatory. 'Well, I did say we were both flying pretty high! Come dawn, we found our way ashore—all three of us—and earned the kind of reputation only drunken fools and four-star generals deserve.'

Charisse shook her head in laughing amazement. Even if only half the story was true it said much about the man at her side, and was completely at odds with the portrait of a suave riverboat gambler or the present immaculately attired hotelier.

Over lunch, not lobster or quail's eggs but a San Franciscan springtime delicacy, the delectable capretto—suckling kid—a dish that Charisse immediately recognised as a more lightly spiced version of the Mexican cabrito, he allowed her to talk on. She told him of the annual *barbacoas* they would have at the hacienda, with people coming from miles around to join in the celebrations, a horse race being the final event with a three-mile track staked out in a suicidal pattern of U-turns and chicanes.

Only occasionally did he listen to her words, just enough to answer intelligently, but it was the light, mellifluous tones that washed over him. Her face glowed in the candle-light from the centre-piece, its dancing shadows accentuating the soft hollows and curves there, and making the grey eyes deeply mysterious. When he himself spoke he watched the way she ate her food and was utterly fascinated by the action of taking food from her fork between pearly teeth without disturbing the light salve that glossed her lips.

'You are staring,' she accused, flushing a little beneath the scrutiny.

'You make it difficult not to.'

'The. . .meat is. . .excellent. I think I prefer it to the hotter cabrito.'

'You don't like hot things?' he softly challenged.

His voice was seductively suggestive and she felt her dress being slowly licked off with his eyes. Denying the effect he had on her—even with the table between them—she tossed her head a little, again reminding him of a skittish palomino. 'I can take them or leave them. Everything to its appropriate time and place, don't you agree?' she replied, daring him not to.

'I am a poker player, Charisse. I never observe the rules if it means the difference between winning or losing. . .and I don't often lose.'

Her eyes flashed at the challenge though her voice was as deceptively sweet as her smile. 'Then you had best stick to poker, *Mr* LaVelle,' she retorted, and deliberately changed the subject, hating his low chuckle.

From Cliff House they walked north towards Point Lobos, obtaining a clearer view of the Californian sea-lions playing follow-my-leader in the thundering surf. Charisse wondered aloud at the creatures' apparent suicidal tendencies as they rode the great breakers that threw them high on to the rocks, where they turned only to plunge once more into that grey-white cauldron.

'They love the challenge, the life-or-death gamble,' Dace answered musingly. 'I can understand that. The quicksilver that runs in your veins when you know there is a chance you may win, the slow building of the volcano that explodes inside you when you know you *have* won. The icy dread when the cards are stacked against you and the stubborn pride that prevents you from folding, hoping beyond hope, as those sleek surfers out there hope, that the wave you are riding won't let you down, won't allow you to crash on to the rocks.' He turned to find her wide eyes pinned to his face and finished quietly, 'Yes, I am a gambler, Charisse. Whatever else I am in life, I am first and foremost a gambler.'

'Not I,' she stated firmly, continuing along the cliff-top. 'I want a home like the hacienda that will last forever, not one that can be lost on the turn of a card.' And she saw the barb go home. 'I want a family, comfort, security—all the things you disdain.' She smiled, though it never quite reached her eyes. 'I am having a wonderful day and I'm truly grateful for your time, but I think it is just as well we are only passing acquaintants, don't you? I should hate either one of us to begin questioning our values.'

He returned the smile easily. 'I'm too much of a lost cause for that. However. . .' He gave her a long, raking sideways assessment. 'I am willing to be converted if *you* would care to take the gamble.'

'Sorry. As I said, I'm no gambler.' Then she cried, 'Oh, look! Poor thing!' as a small black and white bird, caught in the high up-current by the cliffs, was whipped helplessly over their heads and hurled into a bush.

At once they ran to it and Dace bent to gather the stunned creature into his hands. Gentle fingers probed for injury and spread the delicate wings as the tiny claws clung tightly in shock to his finger. 'It's a young sandpiper, way off course. It looks as though the wing is broken.' He went to sit on the stone wall, holding the bird close and sheltering it from the wind until he felt the erratic heartbeat steady, stroking it to calm its shock and fear. 'We'll take it back to the Gateway.'

Charisse found herself mesmerised by the long fore-finger that stroked the tiny back and felt a shiver go down her spine. When that finger moved to caress the soft, downy breast she experienced a moment of pure empathy and, with a quick, involuntary gasp, her hand rose to spread over the place where his finger rested on the bird.

Dace looked up at the sound, saw the hand, looked into her eyes, and read her thoughts—every one. 'A poor substitute,' he said softly. He rose, and as a feeling of inexplicable panic washed over her Charisse took a pace backwards, but all he did was hold out the bird to her. 'This orphan of the storm isn't the only one blown out of its territory by winds of change. You can keep each other company on the way back.' He withdrew a large white linen handkerchief from his pocket and wrapped it gently but firmly around the bird, binding its wings to its side.

Carefully keeping her eyes on the sandpiper, Charisse approached to take it from him, cursing the weakness of a moment before, a weakness that the man's very presence created. She knew that he was an expert seducer and she should have been on her guard, should have been able to laugh off that dangerous virility. Yet as he transferred the bird to her and his hands engulfed hers in the action she felt the trembling deep inside and, worse, knew that he had felt it too. Raising her eyes to his, she affirmed, 'It's not that I'm afraid of you,' and saw the quirk of one devil's eyebrow.

'You should be.' But then he withdrew with a smile. 'However, at this moment your priority is the sandpiper and mine is to deliver you both safely. We can bind the wing and then. . .' He stopped, gave a small, enigmatic smile as a thought struck him, a moment of sheer inspiration. 'And then re-locate him somewhere safer, a sandpiper's paradise.'

Intrigued, Charisse gave him a questioning look. 'A beach?'

'Miles of beach and a surfeit of sea-birds, including sandpipers, and only just over a hundred and twenty miles from here.'

He had said it in a casual, conversational tone so that it took a second for Charisse to absorb it—then she stopped dead. 'A hundred and twenty miles?'

'To the south.'

'A. . .hundred. . .and twenty miles?'

'A mere speck in the distance of the stars. It is a tiny dream village called Carmel. I know a man with a place just south of there, a reclusive artist who retreated there when fame and fortune passed him by in the big city. He was the one who did those two seascapes in the foyer, but I was one of the very élite clientele who appreciated him.'

They had almost reached the car before Charisse's spinning mind came to rest. 'You would drive a hundred miles and more just to re-locate a sandpiper? Not even *you* could be that crazy.'

He handed her carefully up into the car, settling her skirts so that she could rest the bird in her lap. 'Not I, *we*, and we would take the train—pure luxury—to Carmel and hire a gig for the rest of the way.'

'No. No, Dace. Definitely not.'

'Wouldn't you like to see some of the most magnificent scenery in the whole of America? Doesn't a cliff-top picnic overlooking giant rollers crashing on to great black rocks appeal to the wild spirit in you? Or a hidden strip of beach secluded from the waves and unknown by any but the gulls, where we could even paddle if you were that adventurous? Wouldn't you like the chance of seeing whales playing tag, or gulls hovering motionless for minutes on end couched on air cushions?'

'Dace, stop!'

'Coward!'

'You know I'm not,' she objected. Everything in her cried out against her decision and she had to explain, 'Of course I would love to see all that, but. . .but it wouldn't be right.' Even then she knew it for the lie it was; whatever society might say, it *was* right, wonderfully, completely right, to accompany this perfect stranger—this far from perfect stranger—anywhere he might lead.

Dace started the car and drove a hundred yards down the road without speaking, then he said quietly, 'In spite of what I said earlier, you really have no need to fear me, you know. We could take Mark with us. We could put a splint on the bird's wing at the hotel, find a box and some packing, and all four of us could be at Buck's place before nightfall. The house is a rambling series of joined timber sheds in appearance, an ugliness that seems to blend in completely with the landscape as if formed by nature itself. There are rooms for everyone: Buck likes to spread himself.'

'A recluse would hardly welcome three unexpected visitors.' By her very words both knew that she had capitulated, though was not ready to admit it. 'Either way, and even with Mark there, I couldn't consider spending the night in a house with two bachelors.' And she was startled by his laugh.

'Buck Sellick is cruising around his mid-seventies—I don't think he would give you much of a problem. So that leaves me.'

'Yes.'

He shot her an amused look. 'All right. I shall probably hate myself for saying this, and you must take my word for it that it is entirely out of character, but I suppose you could always share a room with Mark. . . *and* the damned bird if it would make you feel safer!'

Charisse gave a gurgle of laughter, knowing even before he spoke that she had already surrendered to this chameleon-like character who could turn from devil's advocate to Peter Pan in the space of seconds. Pretending to give the matter serious consideration, she admitted, 'The bird *would* make all the difference,' and rejoiced in his answering laughter.

At the Gateway Dace had the effrontery to summon an eminent veterinarian to splint the bird's wing, not with wood but a fine thread of bone that was virtually weightless and afforded the least impediment to the mending of the bone beneath. 'Money has its occasional uses,' he smiled.

In the meantime the kitchen had been ordered to prepare a hamper for the long journey, an afternoon tea of thinly sliced chicken and ham, cheeses, tossed salad, fresh baked rolls with butter and preserves, a bottle of chilled wine and a flask of lemonade for Mark, as well as a basket of fruit.

'It's a feast!' exclaimed Charisse delightedly.

Mark took his attention from the sandpiper, now nestling quietly in a small box with finely shredded paper cushioning it, and gave her a wide grin. 'You should have been with us when Daddy took me to stay with Uncle Buck last fall. Uncle Buck cooked a whole chicken for us and we took it out on to the beach and tore it apart with our fingers. It was the most I have ever eaten and the most fun I have ever had!'

'Heathen!' stated his father. 'Charisse doesn't want to hear of a grubby beach urchin with greasy chin and sandy paws.'

'Quite the contrary,' Charisse denied, slanting a teasing look up at him. 'I'd love to hear about *both* urchins with greasy chins and sandy paws.' And as she turned aside she murmured, 'Certainly no more surprising than wrestling alligators at midnight!' She had come to the conclusion that there was very little about this many-faceted man that could surprise her and with Mark chattering on she could study him as he moved about the room, but found the view disturbing and rose abruptly from the armchair she had curled into. 'I must get changed and pack some overnight things.'

Dace met that half-defensive, half-challenging look and smiled. 'Pack something with ribbons and lace on,' he ordered softly. 'Then at least I can dream!' And he chuckled as, with an exasperated shake of the head, she flounced out.

*   *   *

In spite of her reservations, Charisse found both the journey and the tiny hamlet of Carmel enchanting. The wild and rugged coastline of Monterrey was all that Dace had promised and she was impatient to see it in full daylight. Apart from the mission of San Carlos Borromeo de Rio Carmelo, the second oldest in the chain of twenty-one Franciscan missions in California, Carmel itself had an air of Englishness about it that reminded her of her visit to that country the previous year. 'I love it!' she enthused. 'May we explore tomorrow before we return?'

'Your slightest wish is my command and pleasure,' rejoined Dace gallantly. 'But first we must settle in and see what a raid on Buck's larder yields for supper.'

Buck Sellick was the complete antithesis of all that one would expect an artist to be. Charisse, who had half imagined an elderly, frail and reclusive ascetic, gently wielding brush and palette, realised that, knowing Dace LaVelle, she should have known better. From the first moment that the giant figure with massive snowy white beard and mane erupted from the huge front door and bellowed, 'Dace LaVelle, you reprobate! Welcome!' she gained the distinct impression that she faced a Texas longhorn on the rampage.

'Hello, Buck. Can you take three and a bit weekenders?'

'Surely can if your lady is one of the three. *She is gorgeous*! Dare you introduce us?'

With a laugh, as much at Charisse's dazed expression as his host's manner, Dace made the introductions and Charisse saw her tentatively extended hand disappear into the great paw. 'Take it easy, Buck,' Dace ordered. 'We've already one broken bone aboard. We brought a young sandpiper with a broken wing for you.'

With obvious reluctance, the giant released Charisse's hand and turned to Mark, who was carrying the box with the sandpiper. 'Mark. How are you surviving in that overcrowded, brick-built jungle? Let's have a look at your patient and you can tell me about it.' He led them into the large square, airy room that served as living and dining-room and, sweeping a pile of sketches from a heavy redwood table, set the box down, instructing over his shoulder, 'Make yourselves at home. Dace, you know where the kitchen is. I ate earlier and you take pot luck.'

'Can you cook, Charisse, as well as look beautiful?' Dace asked.

'I'm no French chef.'

'That's all right. Buck's food is more likely to be peasant than pheasant. I'll show you where everything is and then you can fix us something while I sort out the sleeping arrangements.' At Buck's snort of laughter he corrected the man's assumptions of nocturnal wanderings with, 'Charisse and Mark can share the room he and I slept in last fall. . . Oh, yes, and the bird!' And the eyes that caught Charisse's held pure devilry. 'This way.'

Buck shook his head as the man disappeared through a far door. 'There's none so queer as folks! I tell you, Moonbeam, a man could lose his mind trying to put that face and body of yours on canvas, but I'd not trade places with old Dace for all the tea in China.'

She knew she shouldn't ask, but. . . 'Why?'

'Well, I'd only stand to lose my mind in the painting of it. Dace there stands to sell his soul to the devil for the possessing of it.'

'Mr Sellick!' And, crimson-cheeked, she fled into the kitchen after Dace, hearing the boom of laughter following her.

CHAPTER NINE

BUCK SELLICK'S words returned again and again to Charisse's waking dreams as she tossed and turned in the soft, high bed. 'Sell his soul to the devil for the possessing of it.' Possessing. Possession. Being possessed by Dace. Being taken, conquered, possessed. She had been kissed by Dace and the very memory of it caused her lips to burn, and she bit them to keep the burning sensation as raw and as fiery as her thoughts. But what would it be like to. . .to. . .? Her innocence was a barrier to imagination, even though she had a rancher's daughter's knowledge of horses and cattle and the vaguest idea of the male anatomy from the children of the servants who often played with naked abandon in the nearby creek. But Dace. What was Dace like? How would he look? How would he act? The perspiration broke out on her body beneath the white lawn nightdress—complete with ribbon and lace trimmings.

'Stop it!' she remonstrated aloud, then glanced over guiltily as Mark turned, with a mutter, in the bed against the far wall. In silence she finished, Change direction, Charisse, you fool, or your imagination will run riot. He is only a man and in no way marriage material, so forget it!

But forgetting was far from easy, and even less so the following morning when, having given up on sleep, she rose at dawn and, throwing on a warm wrap, crept out of the house, disturbed by a rhythmic thudding noise.

The air was tingly, crisp and cool with the tang of sea-salt and the scent of wild flowers and grasses carried on it. Charisse inhaled deeply through her nostrils and gave a shiver of pleasure. Having heard the clink of glasses and Buck's booming laughter long after she had retired, she assumed that both he and Dace would be sleeping off sore heads—there were certainly stentorian snores coming from one of the rooms—but, rounding a corner of the house in pursuit of the noise, she realised that, once again, she had been completely wrong about Dace LaVelle.

Stripped to the waist, he was chopping logs for Buck's great stone fireplace, wielding the long-handled axe with easy, sweeping strokes. Charisse stared, fascinated, feeling her throat go dry and, even in the crisp sea breeze, the heat course through her veins. Dace had his back to her and the rippling shoulder muscles and corded arms moved in perfect unison as he stretched, twisted and dipped and stretched upward again at the peak of his swing. The flat planes of his buttocks tightened and relaxed, the bulging thighs and rounded calves standing in sharp relief, encased in light linen trousers. A fine sheen of perspiration glossed the coppery skin and for one wild, crazy moment Charisse wondered what it would taste like, how it would feel to lap at that salty back, over one shoulder, and in tiny, tasting licks move across the broad chest and. . . and. . . A tiny sound emerged from her throat at the image.

Dace heard it and turned. The image intensified. The broad expanse of chest with its coiled pectorals held a sprinkling of curling black hair that spread in an inverted triangle from between the dark nipples down the board-flat abdomen to vanish into the belted trousers. She found herself unable to move and in her churning mind she heard, Run from me; never stop running.

Dace leaned the axe against the woodpile and crossed to stop three feet from her. He did not speak, looking into the wide grey eyes, reading the conflict, the fear—not of him but of herself—the hunger, the longing for things of which she was unaware. 'Come here,' he commanded softly.

Mesmerised, heart pounding, Charisse took two small steps forward, against all will closing the gap, staring up at him.

His hands came up under her arms so that his palms were against the sides of her breasts and he lifted her on to her toes, pulling her against him. 'Now kiss me.'

'I. . .' But as her mouth opened in timid protest his mouth descended, his tongue gaining access between her parted teeth, not passionately, not possessively, but with a calculated sexual expertise that took her breath away. Of their own volition her arms came up and her fingers splayed over the taut back muscles. She felt his hands shift their grip as that kiss went on, one hand moving back and down to cup one soft buttock beneath the layers of gown and nightdress, the other slipping around one breast only slightly, his thumb teasing the peak.

Charisse felt a throbbing heat radiate up from her stomach and lower, felt the weakness in her limbs, and she melted against him. Wasn't this how it was meant to be? Wasn't this why she had really come? Then, without warning, the grip moved again, her upper arms were taken and she was put away. She stared at him uncomprehendingly, confused at the hardness of his features.

'Get inside and get dressed,' he ordered, then, as she hesitated, 'Unless you want to be taken here and now on the cliff-top?' He saw the answer in her eyes even as she began to back away, her eyes denying her retreat, the innocent longing belying the clenched hand that went in trembling impotence to her breast. 'Go!' he commanded harshly, then, knowing he had to send her out of reach before his hard-won control snapped, he drew in a deep breath and affected a bored southern drawl. 'I like a challenge, Texas, and frankly you aren't one. Now be a good girl and fix us some breakfast!' He read the shock, the lightning flash of disbelief, the shame, the sudden, brilliant tears, all in the split second before she spun and raced back towards the house. Instant remorse hit him. 'Wait!'

She turned at the door, one hand on the frame, breasts heaving with her emotion. 'Get your own breakfast, you conceited bastard; I'm packing and leaving!'

'Wait!' Before she had reached the bedroom door she was caught by the arm and swung about. 'I'm sorry. Before God, I'm sorry!'

'*Let—me—go*!'

'I *had* to make you leave. If you had stayed one more minute. . .one second longer. . .don't you see?' A fraction of the tension went out of her but still her frame was rigid, her arms taut beneath his grip. 'Charisse, I want you. I want you so much that it's like a stoked furnace inside me that never goes out, doesn't diminish in intensity even when you aren't near. Yes, I was playing with your emotions out there at first and yes, I knew—we both knew—that you wanted me. You want me as much as I want you, you can't deny it.'

'No.' It was a murmured denial, the pain of his initial rejection overlying her objection.

Dace released her, but only to bring his hands to cup her face, and there was no smile in the gold-flecked eyes that stared into hers. 'Woman, you have more passion in you than I think *either* of us believes possible. I want to be the one to release that, but not on a wind-swept cliff-top.'

'Please let me go.'

He did so with reluctance. 'Don't pack.'

'I have to get dressed and then I'll think on it.' Refusing to look at him or hear more, she went into the still dark room and closed the door firmly behind her. She felt drained, as if every emotion within her had been played out and there was nothing left. Her body ached, though she had been through no physical activity, and her throat felt parched. Her eyes stung as if from a day under the harsh Texas sun and she lifted her hands to a pounding head. Was knowing Dace LaVelle really worth all this? she questioned, dressing with little thought of what she pulled on.

Mark stirred and with a sigh she went to pull back the curtains, glad of the distraction. The morning light flooded the room. 'Come on, sleepyhead.'

He yawned widely and stretched with the total abandonment of a puppy, then screwed up his face against the sunlight and opened his eyes, rubbing at them with clenched fists. Sitting up, he gave her a wide smile. 'Morning, Charisse. Isn't it wonderful? We have a whole day with Buck. We can build sand-castles, chase sea-birds, find pebbles that look like animals— all sorts of things.'

Charisse found it within her to return the bright smile, realising that it would be quite impossible for her to deprive him of such a day simply to assuage her wounded pride. She had thrown herself at Dace like some wanton and, for whatever reason, he had rejected her advances. She should be grateful, not burning with shame at her action. . .perhaps a little of both, she acknowledged. 'Yes, Mark,' she decided, 'we'll have a great day. Do you know, not only have I never built a sand-castle, but I have never been on a beach? We don't have such things in north-west Texas. So you hurry and get dressed and we'll see what Mr Sellick has for breakfast.'

'You have to call him Buck. Everyone calls him Buck. He told you to last night, remember?'

'We'll see.' She tilted her head as Buck's booming tones came from beyond the door. 'He seems to be up and about now. I'll see what I can do about breakfast while you wash and dress.' Going into the living-room, she saw her host pouring a generous measure of whisky into a glass. 'Is that breakfast, Mr Sellick, or can I fix you something more substantial?'

'Buck. . . I told you, it's Buck. Hair of the dog, this, and no, thanks. Dace is doing the cooking. He just volunteered. I reckon that makes you one of those emancipated suffragette females that figures she is equal to all men, does it? Funny, you don't look like one.'

At his grin she could not take offence, but felt the need to make a point and shook her head. 'No, I'm not, Buck, not at all. Before we struck oil, and that was not so long ago, I was a cattleman's daughter. I ran the ranch, since Momma was dead, did the accounts, helped with the round-up when we were short-handed, tended an assortment of broken bones and bruises, and generally organised the whole she-bang. I can trap game, hunt down, shoot, skin, and cook anything on four legs, then come home to change and attend a full-dress ball. I can put up preserves and pickles in the morning and break a horse in the afternoon. I can talk recipes or rifles. No, Buck, I wouldn't want to be equal to *any* man. . .why should I lower *my* standards?'

His roar of laughter brought Dace from the kitchen and Buck wiped his eyes, still laughing. 'You've got a feisty one here, m'boy. I like her, I surely do.'

Dace's eyes were wary as they met Charisse's. 'I'm learning,' he said carefully.

Mark had emerged from the bedroom and Charisse put an arm loosely about his slender shoulders. 'Mark is going to teach me how to build a sand-castle,' she advised, answering Dace's unasked question, and saw the relief flame in his eyes.

'I am glad. Well, breakfast is ready if you are. I hope you're hungry. I can never resist Buck's food store: after the meals at the Gateway it's good to find *real* food.'

The plates he set on the table were piled high with slabs of gammon, fluffy scrambled eggs, thin and crispy fried potato slices, lamb cutlets and tomatoes, sliced and reduced to a soft purée. Charisse stared. 'Are you certain you haven't forgotten anything? Dace, this is enough for an army!'

Buck patted her arm. 'You eat up, now. A few more pounds wouldn't go amiss on you.' His gaze was frankly appreciative, but then, on a completely different tack, he asked, 'You reckon on wearing that outfit to the beach?'

Charisse looked down at her fashionable, slightly trained watered silk morning dress that she had packed to impress Dace's 'elderly gentleman', and gave a rueful smile. 'It isn't exactly the most appropriate thing, is it? I have a skirt and blouse, but I'm afraid they are equally unsuitable—I don't think chiffon and sea spray would go well together, and the skirt is of pale grey, not even a decent sand colour. No, it will have to be this.' Glancing at Mark's suddenly crestfallen face, she reassured him, 'I'm certainly not going to miss the chance to build my first sand-castle.'

Buck nodded approval. 'Not many females I can think of would get that mussed up—glad to see you can get your priorities right.' His quizzical gaze raked over her. 'Yep, you're all right. I wouldn't suggest it to most fancy females, but. . .'

'Suggest what?' Charisse encouraged, intrigued as he allowed the sentence to hang in the air.

'Well, there's a young lad that comes up here every week or two, just for a morning. He has it in his mind to be another Van Gogh—all thick bright colours and wild strokes, not bad either—and has got it into his head that I can teach him a thing or two. In return for lessons he tidies my sketches and moves the dust around. He keeps some old shirts and work trousers in the robe cupboard in the room Dace is in now. He's much of a height as you and skinny as a reed. Of course you'd need a belt to cinch in the pants, but the shirt should be OK—a sight better looking on you than on him, I'd guess.'

'I couldn't!'

'Why not? There's only us three and the gulls to see you, and if you had a mind to get your feet wet the clothes wouldn't matter none at all.'

'Please, Charisse!' begged Mark, eyes alight. 'You would be *so* much more comfortable and we wouldn't mind a bit. It would be like. . .like having one of my real friends along. Oh, not that you're *not* a real friend, but you would look like a boy, wouldn't you?'

She refused to meet Dace's eyes. 'I somehow don't think so, but it does make a lot of sense.' Remembering how she enjoyed her rides out from the hacienda wearing shirt and denims, she finally nodded. 'Very well, but the very first person that laughs, I get changed back immediately.'

When she emerged a few minutes later a stunned Dace reflected that the last thing he wanted to do was laugh. What he felt was anything but amusement. What he experienced was a wave of pure, unadulterated lust.

The white shirt had lost most of its buttons and only a length of cord laced it together over the full breasts beneath the silky chemisette top she had retained. The white cotton trousers encircled a handspan waist and, made for a boy's slender hips, fitted like a second skin over the more softly rounded curves of the woman, and ended just below the knees, revealing delicately formed calves, racehorse-slender ankles and tiny feet slipped into rope sandals a size too large. 'I can't wear these!'

Mark hopped from one foot to the other and clapped his hands. 'You look like a pirate! You look great, Charisse! Oh, don't change. No one is laughing. You're not, are you, Uncle Buck?'

'Looks pretty good to me.'

'You aren't, are you, Daddy?'

There was a long silence as green eyes met grey. Finally he said, 'No, I'm not laughing.'

'One word,' she warned softly. 'Just one word.' And left the rest unsaid, not needed.

'Oh, hurry!' urged Mark, tugging at her hand, and with one look at Dace she allowed herself to be pulled outside.

Buck tugged at his beard. 'Jeez! If I was thirty years younger. . . Hell, if I was *ten* years younger!'

Dace remained unsmiling, eyes on the still open door that revealed Charisse and Mark heading towards the steeply stepped track that led to the tiny beach. 'She is leaving within the week,' he said almost to himself.

Buck accorded him a long, searching look. 'Got it bad, haven't you, boy?'

'What?' A false laugh. 'The man with so many notches in his gun it's practically unusable?' His crudery fooled neither of them and he subsided with a sheepish grin. 'Shut up, Buck! I'll do the dishes then join them.'

'Forget the dishes. I wouldn't want to deprive you of one minute of your time left with her; you're going to need it!'

With a feinted punch to the stomach, Dace passed his friend on the way out, muttering to himself, 'After that jackass remark earlier you may well be right!'

By the time he reached the strip of beach Charisse and Mark were already absorbed in their play and for several minutes he stood in the shadows at the base of the cliff, observing them. A slight frown drew his brows together as he saw the way Mark pushed and tugged at her with an easy familiarity that he had shown to no other, and how Charisse swept him off his feet to tumble on to the sand as they fought for possession of a piece of driftwood they had found on the shoreline. Their laughter was carried to him on the inshore wind, gay, carefree—something Dace could barely remember. Yet there was more, and Dace's frown deepened. Charisse was treating his son as if. . .as if. . . 'No!' he denied aloud, forcing the thought into the dark recesses of his mind, and strode forward. 'Well, you two, whose log is it anyway?'

'Mine!' they claimed in unison, turning bright, laughing eyes upwards from their sprawled position on the sand.

'Charisse is the *most* fun!' Mark cried. 'And it's not a log, it's a sea-lion.'

'A sleeping hawk,' argued Charisse. 'Well, Dace? Are you going to stand there looking disapproving, or are you going to join us?'

Dace forced his attention from the curve of hip and thigh. 'It's a dolphin, anyone can see that. But right now I think I need more sobering up to do. We raised more than one jug last night and I seem to be having some trouble in concentrating. . .on driftwood. I'd best take a dip.'

'You can't! It's freezing!' Charisse protested.

'Precisely!'

'I beg your pardon?' But already he had turned and raced down to the shoreline, took three strides in, then leapt, cleaving the water and swimming out to sea with long, even strokes. 'But he still has his shirt and trousers on!'

'Of course he has.' Mark giggled. 'You might *look* like a boy, but you are still a lady, Charisse, and gentlemen don't wander around in the buff when there are ladies present. That's what Daddy told me when I came out of the bath and the maid was serving tea in the living-room.'

Charisse barely paid attention. Dace had swum in a curving half-circle and had now risen from the surf like the Greek god Poseidon, shirt and trousers clinging to him, almost transparent, as he came up the beach towards them. Voice husky, she admonished, 'You'll freeze to death.'

'Then you'll have to warm me.' And all the beneficial effects of the icy water dissolved into steam. 'Sorry.'

A faint smile. 'Forgiven.' Gazes locked. She reached

up and took his hand, drawing him down on the sand
beside her. A heavy lock of the sable hair had fallen
across his forehead and she was compelled to brush it
back.

'Your hand is trembling.'

Her fingers drifted over the jaw-line, then down his
neck to his shoulder. 'You are, too.'

'The cold water.'

'Of course.'

Mark stared from one to the other in puzzlement
and growing impatience. 'What about the sand-castle?'
he asked, tearing them apart.

'Sure, son,' Dace agreed, ruffling the boy's hair.
'Let's go into the construction industry.'

'Oh, Daddy, you're funny! I don't ever want today
to end! Here is where the moat will be and the front
door.'

Dace smoothed a large sweep of sand and Charisse
watched the strong, spread fingers. 'You look as though
you've done this before,' she commented, desperately
attempting to divert her thoughts.

'A couple of times. It's the nearest most of us come
to creating the castle in our minds.' He looked up,
studying her profile as she piled up the sides of the
mound, patting it smooth. 'When I was a kid I used to
have a particular place in our immaculately laundered
gardens that was uniquely my own. It was a great live
oak that had been partially blasted in two by a lightning
bolt in one of the freak summer storms that hit the
delta on occasion. It had fallen, yet was still held by a
fractured section of trunk, and created a cave of
branches and leaves that, for some reason, no one ever
bothered to clear. I would sit in that green cave for
hours on end re-shaping the world.' He gave a self-
mocking smile. 'You must appreciate that I was very
young, of an age at which one believes in such
miracles.'

Charisse halted in her task and sat back on her heels,

not looking at him but at a sand crab that, with dogged determination, was attempting to scale the sandy walls. 'One doesn't have to be so very young to believe in trying for a better world, one just has to start smaller, with one's own corner of it, and work outwards.'

Dace reached and picked up the struggling crab, setting it on the peak of the hill. 'We all have visions of Atlantis.' But then he removed it again and set it on a path towards the rippling water's edge. 'We invariably settle for the best cave or mud hut our puny strength allows.' His hand covered hers. 'But very occasionally Atlantis sends an emissary above the waves just to prove it is still there. A mermaid in torn blouse and sandy trousers with the gold of Atlantean treasure in her hair and the deep grey depths in her eyes.'

'I. . . I think I had better go back to the house. . . The. . .lunch. . .'

'Buck will attend to it.'

'No.' She wrenched herself away, breaking the spell. 'Mark, Daddy will stay to help you with your castle while he dries off. I must go and talk to Buck.'

'Will you come back later?'

'Perhaps.' Then, seeing the disappointment in his eyes, 'Yes, of course I shall. I must see it finished.' She rose and brushed her sandy fingers against the trouser legs. 'I wouldn't want the tide to wash it away before I had seen it.'

Dace paid careful attention to the sand an inch to the side of the bare, perfectly formed foot. 'The tide doesn't come up this far.'

Charisse definitely did not notice the way the damp wavy hair clung to his neck, or that the lock of hair had again fallen forward over his forehead. 'Why, then. . . it could last forever.'

He looked up. The word 'forever' spun in an incandescent bubble between them.

'The. . .lunch!' With a quick, helpless gesture, she turned and ran back up the beach.

Mark gave his father a grin. 'Aren't ladies funny? I know Charisse was having the most fun time, but just now it looked as though she was going to cry. That doesn't make any sense, does it?'

Dace turned his attention from the figure climbing the cliff steps. 'No, Mark,' he agreed musingly. 'But then. . .ladies don't *have* to make sense. They just have to. . .be.'

CHAPTER TEN

'IT WAS a beautiful sand-castle,' assured Charisse for the hundredth time as she tucked the sleepy Mark into his own bed at the Gateway. 'And it was a perfect weekend, but now you really must sleep.' She dropped a kiss on the soft cheek and was rewarded by a hug and rather wet kiss in return. 'Goodnight, darling.'

'See you tomorrow and tomorrow and tomorrow.'

'Go to sleep, trouble.' She turned away to see the shadowy figure of Dace filling the doorway. He came into the room to bid Mark goodnight and Charisse returned to the other room. 'It was a long journey back,' she said when he reappeared and closed the door. Then, with a catch in her voice, she added, 'I shall miss him terribly.'

'Likewise.' His tone was neutral, but his taut features betrayed him.

'We left far too late. I like Buck.'

'He seemed pretty taken with you, too. It is a pity you won't see each other again: it's a long haul from Texas.'

She swallowed hard. 'I made it once.' Then quickly she told him, 'I must go. Goodnight, Dace, and thank you.'

'You're welcome, Texas.' He came to brush one forefinger along her lipline. 'I'll see you in the morning.'

'You still have a hotel to run,' she reminded him and, when he would have spoken, 'No, the afternoon, after lunch.'

'Do I have a choice?'

'No,' she replied lightly, reaching for the door-handle. 'You could well be addictive, Dace LaVelle,

and I have no intention of succumbing. Goodnight.'
And quickly she let herself out, hurrying down the
corridor to the elevator, knowing that already the drug
had taken effect.

Dace closed the door behind her with a smile. 'You
just don't know, lady,' he promised. 'You just don't
know!'

Charisse slept in late, the fresh sea air and the strenu-
ous weekend acting as an opiate, but when eventually
she awoke she was completely refreshed with an air of
expectation. 'So much!' she whispered. 'So much to
do; so much that is new and different; so much beauty.
The sea, the earth, the way the very air seems to
breathe life into you. How can anyone *not* be a
Californian?' The thought instantly sobered her. 'Fool!
Poppa is in Texas. Your home is in Texas. All your
friends, people you have known all your life. Come on,
Charisse! It's only a temporary magic. In a few days
Ralph will come and we shall take the next train
home—to Texas.'

She rose and changed into a pale lemon walking
dress that made her golden hair appear even brighter.
Piling her hair into a high puffed bouffant, she set one
of her new hats, the black one with the veil, atop it and
gave her mirror image a satisfied nod. 'You'll do. Now
. . .let's explore. Carefully this time. Be prepared for
anything and don't think of Dace LaVelle at all.'

But that proved more difficult than imagined and, by
the third pair of broad shoulders walking before her
and the fourth head of black hair waved just so that
caused her heart to leap, she stopped dead in her tracks
and declared, 'Enough!' Turning about, she caught the
Market Street cable car and alighted outside the Rand
Detective Agency. Making her way to the second floor,
she rapped and entered. 'Lee, will you please have
lunch with me?'

He came from behind the high-piled desk with a

wide smile of surprised welcome. 'I'd be delighted to. To what do I owe this unexpected pleasure?'

'I was exploring and happened to be passing,' she lied. 'I thought of you delving into dusty case histories and decided to take you away from it all—at least for an hour. Where shall we go?'

Leading her with one hand beneath her elbow and locking the door carefully behind him, he decided, 'Where I can show you off. That dress is. . .' He stopped and turned her to face him gently. 'You know, Charisse, I have always enjoyed being a detective.'

She laughed, puzzled. 'So?'

'Well. . .' That lop-sided grin she loved—almost loved. 'Suddenly I feel an overwhelming ambition to be a poet or a composer or artist. How can I describe you otherwise?'

'Oh, Lee!'

'Hey, don't look like that! I'm a durned good detective and even if I was the best poet in the world I probably couldn't do you justice. Be that as it may, I still like the dress.'

Charisse kissed her finger and touched it to his cheek. 'You are a really nice person, Lee.'

'But you are still hungry.' Then, as she had to smile, he exclaimed, 'There! When you came in you looked kinda preoccupied; now you look happy and hungry. That I recognise. That I can cope with.'

He took her to a small but fashionable restaurant in the Western Addition and revelled in the ripple of attention their entrance received. 'You can have something French if you order it,' he grinned with no apology in his tone.

'Hey, I'm just a staked plains Texan!' she laughed. 'Mexican I can manage, but I doubt they serve tacos, tortillas or enchiladas in San Francisco.'

'Come again?'

Charisse put aside the menu after an initial glance. 'You order for me and then I'll tell you about a real home-style Texan *barbacoa* with a whole steer spitted over a pit of coals and logs.'

The waiter hovered. 'Monsieur?' he prompted, and Lee handed him both menus.

'Hi, Bob, how's the wife? Fourth, isn't it? Boy or girl?'

The man immediately dropped the suave French accent, whispering, 'Another girl. Seven pounds three. We're calling her Annabelle. The wife is fine. Just fine. After four what else would she be?'

'Better luck next time, Bob.'

As an aside to Charisse the waiter informed her, 'Four girls and we are still hoping for a boy.'

Charisse gave the man a twinkling look. 'Well, since you are obviously one of Lee's innumerable friends, do you think you could conjure a very rare steak out of the air? You know the kind—mooing on the inside and cremated on the outside. I haven't had real beef since I left Texas.'

The waiter flinched. 'Lee, your lady is the loveliest creature I have ever seen, but, as a friend, may I suggest—with respect—her palate needs some very minor adjustment?'

Lee grinned. 'A steak, Bob, and the usual for me.'

The waiter adopted a resigned expression. 'Why do you come here, Lee?'

'Probably because you serve the best beef stew in the city.'

'*Boeuf bourguignon*. . .sir!'

'And steak for the lady.'

Charisse gave a gurgle of laughter. 'Lee, you are definitely the best person for me today; I'm so glad I abducted you.'

'My bloodhound tendencies told me you needed someone like that.' His voice lowered and he spoke for her alone. 'You know you only have to tell me. What can I do?'

'Just be with me.'

'That's the easy part.'

'Tell me about your latest case.'

'For real?'

'Yes. Please.'

The world-weary eyes lost a fraction of their glow. 'All right, honey, maybe you need to hear me talking about a seventeen-year-old that left a certain unnamed family on Nob Hill and went to the City of the Angels with a sailor. I'll talk, baby doll, and I'll feed you, but beyond that. . .you need something I can't give.'

'And that is?'

'Instant amnesia.' A slightly more lop-sided grin than usual. 'All right. No questions and, most of all, no easy answers. Everyone has answers or they'll make them up to please you. Well, this crazy female. . .'

Charisse listened, smiled in the right places and nodded, and at the end of an excellent meal— untasted—she said gratefully, 'Thank you, Lee. Thank you more than you know. Will you take me back to the Gateway now?'

A short nod. 'Where else!'

Approaching Nob Hill, he finally forced himself to say, 'Some of us lucky ones find love twice in a lifetime and, even if the second time doesn't work out, it is still better than not having loved at all. Some, on the other hand, fall once and so hard that love never comes again. Don't let his reputation get in the way of your gut feelings, Charisse.'

Startled out of her reverie, she turned, but he was staring fixedly at the road ahead. 'It isn't just a well-earned reputation, Lee, it's the man's whole character that sees every woman as a cross between a woman of the streets and a black widow spider. He doesn't see beyond the beautiful exterior and, as far as he is concerned, I'm no different from any other. He only wants one thing and admits it. He enjoys the game, his ability against the other players, with the lady of the day as the pot.'

Lee had to smile, though his heart felt as if the vice that held it was slowly closing. 'Perhaps this is one game he'll lose. Handling a deck of cards is one thing; handling love is quite another. He won't find it at the tables or in a bottle of aged bourbon and because it's unfamiliar territory he runs from it.' He slowed and drew to a halt before the hotel and, because he loved her, still could not surrender as easily as his heart told him he should—or suffer deeper pain.

'I'm no hand with cards,' he smiled, 'though I do enjoy a good glass of bourbon. I'm a mite under six feet, and I can't give you such luxurious surroundings as you're used to, but if there is anything I *am* it's persistent.' He caught the distress in her eyes and let her off the hook—just a little. 'A bit like a faithful hound, don't you think?'

Charisse laughed aloud. 'You *are* good for me, you know.' Then, more seriously, she told him, 'And I do so wish I loved you.'

'"If wishes were horses beggars would ride,"' he quoted softly, then allowed his gaze to leave her face and move past her to the entrance of the hotel. 'But wishes never made the man and here's one who sure doesn't rely on them.'

Dace had seen them coming in, quite by accident happening to be bowing off a portly senator and his wife. He watched the barely roadworthy Ford pull up and saw Lee Rand assist Charisse down. For one split second—and quite unbidden—came the desire, again, to be left alone for five minutes with the man who had made her laugh so and touch his arm in that special, warm way. He went forward. 'Charisse, you're early!' To Lee he said, 'Thank you for delivering her so promptly for our two-thirty appointment. I didn't realise she had a business meeting this morning.'

Lee met that emerald-sharp look and smiled, feeling good inside. 'I can't think of any reason you should have, Mr LaVelle.' To Charisse he queried, 'You OK?'

'Yes, thank you, Lee.'

The honey-brown eyes went from one to the other and for her ears alone he said, 'Shoot, it weren't nuthin at all, ma'am,' then, aloud, 'Be seeing you. Take care now.'

'Thank you. Yes; I'll be in touch.' And for him alone she added, 'Thank you for being there when I needed you. . .again.'

'Always will be.' And with a brief nod to Dace he climbed back into the car.

She turned to the glowering Dace and felt the taut anger radiating from him as an almost physical force. 'I called on Lee and *asked* him to take me to lunch.' Then, realising that she had sounded defensive, she attacked, 'Dace, I am ready to accompany you around town this afternoon as arranged—but not while you are looking like a thunder-cloud—or I can write home to Poppa. Your choice.'

He stepped forward and took hold of her arm. 'You could no more write a constructive sentence than I could think of one. No, we shall do something, anything.' He calmed. 'Where did you have in mind to go? Tell me and I'll take you, or leave it to me and we'll commit the Lee Rands to Hades.'

'Dace, Lee is a friend——'

'And then some!'

'Stop it! You sound like a. . .a. . .'

'Charisse, I am sorry.' He loosed the crushing grip on her arm and took a step away, then, chameleon-like, accepted, 'Very well. Where did madam have in mind to visit?'

Recovering slowly from that devastating virility and the light of possession that had burned into her, Charisse gave a quick shake of the head. 'I don't know. I had no firm plans. Perhaps, though, since you will be with me, I could go back to Chinatown. I should like to see more of the area and thank that little man who was so kind to me. It is, after all, full daylight.'

He bowed over her hand. 'Your wish is my command.'

She wanted to ask, '*Is* it, Dace? Is it really?' but knew the answer and, holding her thoughts in check, merely smiled and allowed him to lead her inside to await the car that would be brought round.

Within minutes they had drawn up halfway along Grant Street and Dace suggested, 'It might be as well to walk from here.'

Charisse felt a sense of wonder, safe now on Dace's arm, and could absorb the sights and sounds of the area that the inhabitants called Little China, settled since the Gold Rush of forty-nine and made uniquely their own.

They turned into Washington, still known as the Street of a Thousand Lanterns, a crowded thoroughfare with shops, restaurants and open-fronted stores displaying every kind of Oriental merchandise. 'What you don't see,' said Dace grimly, 'are the opium dens and fan-tan parlours.' He did not think it fit to tell her also of the cribs into which dozens of girls were enslaved like battery hens for the sick sport of anyone who had six bits or more.

Charisse clung closely to his side, though felt little fear even though her peaches-and-cream skin and sungold hair brought envious, even avaricious stares. They reached the tiny store, but no sooner had they entered than three young Chinese appeared and crowded in behind them.

'Shop closing,' stated one, raising a hand to emphasise his point.

Charisse was about to speak when she found herself being pushed firmly behind Dace, who differed quietly, 'This is a social call, so it will not matter to Mr Wu if we stay after hours.' His tone was mild, but Charisse detected an edge to it that she could not understand.

A second Chinese stepped forward, smiling, but the smile never reached his eyes, which were as cold and black as obsidian. 'This is not your concern, sir. It is a family matter. I would be most obliged if you would return—preferably to your own part of the city.' His tones were educated and gave Dace cause to re-assess him. Young, possibly early twenties, with hair parted and sleeked back in the modern style, and wearing a heavy blue linen shirt over denims. A student by appearance, or one of the innumerable 'breakaway' youths who balked at the constriction of family tradition and found work outside Little China. Dace did not underestimate the suave looks.

At that moment the elderly Mr Wu came from the back room and the smile of welcome died as he saw the group, his pale golden skin turning the colour of aged parchment. 'Please,' he implored, coming forward to face the young Chinese. 'Please allow my friends to leave. I have the money.' And he continued in a stream of Chinese until the man before him cut off the flow with a sharp chopping gesture.

Those cold eyes raked Charisse from head to foot, then he gave a brief nod. 'Go.' And as she hesitated a knife appeared as if by magic in his hand. 'I said go!'

Charisse felt a trickle of ice down her spine. 'Who are you?'

'It does not concern you.'

One of the other two snickered and drew his own weapon, a short club.

Quietly Dace educated, 'When the Chinese settled here, Charisse, they brought with them *all* their culture, both good and bad. The greater majority are honest, hardworking people like Mr Wu here, who keep themselves to themselves. But the criminal elements which were split into small enclaves in the old country are now being gathered together by a society, cult, call it what you will, that goes by a variety of names. We call them the Triads or Tongs; they call themselves the Hung—which is exactly what they should be. If they succeed the whole structure of law and order will be threatened and, while in my book it is no concern of mine that the inhabitants of any ghetto kill themselves off, it is not so acceptable when they spread into the outside or when they threaten friends of mine.' The green eyes grew glacial as he rounded on the gang leader. 'Do I have it right? If we leave now you will take your protection money and go, perhaps mess up the store a little to make certain Mr Wu understands his position?'

The leader's smile was not pleasant. 'You are educated in our ways, sir.'

Charisse felt the heat rise in her, clouding better judgement as instinctively she moved to the old man's side. 'I am a stranger to your city,' she stated clearly, eyes flashing. 'One doesn't have to be a resident and it doesn't take education to recognise something that has slithered out from under a rock.'

'Easy, honey!' Dace warned, torn between admiration for her courage and annoyance at her stupidity in facing up to three armed and dangerous men. If only she had not been present—but then, with a flash of memory. . . 'Charisse, perhaps with a little extra these gentlemen may leave without harming anything or anyone.' As she turned scornful eyes to his he willed her to understand. 'Don't you have such an. . .incentive? You usually bring a little something in your purse or in your pocket.'

Her face lost all colour and he saw that she had understood completely, but before she could answer one of the youths strode forward and snatched the purse from her hand. Dace prayed as he had never prayed before and the fates—who were known to be on the side of drunks and fools—answered his prayer. The purse contained nothing but three dollars in change.

Charisse glared at the boy. 'Having already suffered a similar action from another of your countrymen, I no longer keep anything of value there and, since I have also been warned of pickpockets, I leave those empty, too.' She stared fixedly at Dace, the blood beginning to race in her veins. 'Lee Rand advised me that a saloon girl of his acquaintanceship kept such. . .valuables strapped to her garter.' And she almost smiled at his look of incredulity.

'That's enough talk!' the young leader snarled. 'Wu, the money. You, woman, if you have enough to satisfy us we'll take it and leave and no harm will come to any of you. Any objections and we take it from you anyway. Come on. Move!'

His companion with the club gave that ugly little snicker again. 'Maybe we should do that. It would be interesting to see what white ladies wear underneath all those fine feathers.'

Charisse faced him, but spoke for Dace's benefit alone. 'Very well, I shall give it to you personally.'

She had their attention—all of it—and Dace reacted. With a cry that for a split second froze them he leapt at the leader, one iron-hard hand closing over the knife wrist, the other curled into a fist, punching into the man's throat and then grabbing the trachea, cutting off the air supply. With a wrench he pulled the man's head down on to his raised knee, smashing the nose, following through with a grip that rolled his victim to the ground. As his man landed Dace almost gently relieved him of his weapon.

At the same moment Charisse bent, pulled up her skirt to reveal a shapely calf—and the derringer strapped to it by the special holster that Lee had purchased for her. In one smooth movement she drew, crouched and fired. A look of comic disbelief crossed her opponent's face and the club fell from suddenly nerveless fingers as he clutched at his shattered knee. With a sobbing cry he crumpled to the floor, rolling sideways in agony.

The third youth came away from the wall in a crouch, knife held low, but Dace had already moved with the lithe and deadly grace of a black panther to meet him. The boy was frightened and disorientated by the shock of the events and, as the knife swept outwards in a deadly arc, Dace caught his sleeve, kept the action following through, twisted hard in and threw the Chinese over his hip. As the boy crashed to the floor Dace kept hold of the knife arm and snapped it over his leg. With a scream his attacker went down, writhing and sobbing.

Dace straightened, his gaze sweeping over the mêlée about the floor, then up to Charisse, who had begun to tremble, the derringer still held unsteadily, pointing at the fallen man she had shot. Very gently he said, 'You can put that away now, Texas; it's all over.' She stared sightlessly at him, then dropped the gun and with a rush went into his arms. 'There, there!' he comforted, holding her quivering frame in a tight, warm embrace. 'It's all right. You can't collapse on me now.'

With a shaky laugh she managed to straighten and take a half-pace away. 'I. . .I don't do that. . .that sort of thing every day!' Then, recovering completely, she explained, 'When I go hunting vermin I usually take an old Winchester Repeater.'

Dace laughed in admiration. 'I'm glad you didn't use one here, or we would have a corpse rather than a cripple on our hands.' He turned his attention to the old Chinaman, who was leaning weakly against the counter. 'We came to thank you for your past kindness to Miss Linton. I am glad we did. Are you all right, sir?'

'Oh yes! This unworthy person very much all right. I am glad you come. I lost much money to repair shop two times already.' His face contorted in frustrated anger. 'Cannot fight all Hung, but I think these spawn of the devil not come back in a hurry. Hung is like octopus with many tentacles. They take little gang like this, train them, make like army. But an army no one leaves or escapes once in.'

'But surely the police. . .the government. . .?' Charisse asked.

Dace made a sweeping gesture. 'Are helpless. No member of the society will talk: the penalty for doing so is far more terrible than any of our laws could inflict. Few are caught and even among the whites there are Triad members now. The rewards can be as great as the punishments.'

'You sound as if you know.' Then quickly she added, 'I meant through your contacts. You said you knew people in all walks of life.'

'No need for diplomacy. I won't deny I have been approached. I'm far from a saint, Charisse, but I only play on men's greed to relieve them of their money, whether it is by poker or fan-tan. I don't harm the weak and old and, as far as I know, no woman or child has been hurt as a result of any action of mine. I make money through business deals, also where I can out-bluff the con men, and so far I have been successful at it. I run the Gateway honestly, though many doubt it. I could, however, be far wealthier if I used it as a façade for drug-running or laundering dirty money.' He gave a twisted smile. 'The Tong are a peculiarly polite bunch who never pressure a potential recruit unless he is of supreme importance to them. . .in government or playing games with the world's curren-cies, for example. I refused their generous proposition and have not been approached since. I'm that unfortu-nate individual who can't be bought off and won't be scared off.' To the old man he said, 'I can dump this carrion outside and help you clean up.'

'No. Please. Not necessary. Very grateful. I call number one son, Hsiao, and friend in restaurant next door. We deal with this mess.' He clasped his hands and made a low bow. 'This humble person in your debt all life, sir.' And to Charisse he said, 'And yours, madam. You have softness of gentle breeze in wind-chimes, but strength of hurricane. Honourable sir very lucky man.'

Charisse blushed. 'You and I are friends, Master Wu, and one helps a friend in need. I am leaving the city soon, but will take your friendship with me and leave mine with you.'

He reached across the counter and handed her a tiny envelope of pastry. 'Fortune cookie. Maybe you not leave so soon as think.' He gave a gap-toothed grin. 'You open now and see future.'

Laughingly Charisse bit into the crisp morsel and extracted the tiny slip of paper contained inside. On it, written in English for the benefit of the tourists who thronged the quarter, were the words, 'The Phoenix rises'. 'What on earth does that mean?' asked Charisse, intrigued, but the Chinaman shook his head.

'You make own meaning. Different meaning for different person. You go now and forget these insects. I see to it.' And, bowing several times more, he showed them outside.

To Charisse's amazement all was normal. No crowd had gathered at the sound of the shot, of breaking furniture and the cries of the protagonists. No one in the busy street looked askance at the white couple emerging from an obvious battleground into the early afternoon sun. 'I don't understand it. Are they so accustomed to such terrible things happening?'

'Partly,' he answered. 'But here in Chinatown one learns to make an art of minding one's own business. That's what gives the police an almost impossible task here—they are surrounded by wise monkeys! Come now, let me take you back to reality.'

And the message on the fortune cookie was forgotten—until much later.

She stopped, bringing him to a halt beside her. 'This *is* reality, Dace. For that old man and his neighbours this is the reality they live with.'

He took her troubled face between his warm hands.

'There is nothing either one of us can do, honey. I have never known a woman with such a natural bent for tackling impossible odds head-on, but you can't fight the most insidious and, for the most part, invisible enemy the world has known; not even you can do that, little tigress.' He dropped a light kiss on to the mutinously set lips. 'Come, I will take you to a place as far removed from this as one can get and make you forget everything that has happened here.'

He drew a deep breath of relief when she nodded acquiescence and took his arm. Any other woman he knew would either have collapsed into hysterics or fainted clean away at the first sight of that drawn knife. But then, as he already knew, Charisse Linton was not *like* any other woman he had known, and the thought nagged at him that she was, in all probability, unlike any woman he would ever meet in the future. It was a disquieting thought, but he was becoming accustomed to those since he had first met the oil baron's daughter with the bayou cat's eyes.

CHAPTER ELEVEN

THEY drove north for almost an hour before finding themselves in the cool depths of the five hundred and fifty acres of Muir Woods, renowned for its giant redwoods. 'It seems incredible,' murmured Dace as they left the car, 'that some of these sequoias are over a thousand years old. Do you know, they are supposed to put on a foot a year for the first hundred years? No wonder they reach to well over two hundred feet.' He looked down into her twinkling eyes and grinned. 'I guess I'm not impressing the lady. I heard a senator—one of my regular poker players—talking of it when he was saying how they planned to open the area as a National Park. You see? One *can* gain an education at the poker table!'

They strolled deep into the cool, humid interior and Charisse bent to pluck a small white flower, touching its still dew-damp petals to her lips.

'Lucky flower!' But his tone was light and held no seduction.

She threw him a sideways smile. 'As a child I would gather wild flowers in the spring and weave them with grasses into a coronet, pretending to be a great lady, but somehow the coronet invariably ended up as fodder for my pony and I never did make it to great-lady status.'

His smile warmed her. 'I wish I had known you then.' He indicated a half-hidden tree-trunk tumbled by who-knew-what force greater than itself and now covered by ivies and lichen. 'Were you the type to climb over trees like this, skinning knees and tearing dresses, or did you play sedately with your dolls on a rug in the parlour?'

'Oh, the skinned knees every time,' she laughed. 'Only it was great rocks, not trees. Ralph was the one immersed in books and his sketches in the parlour.' The memory of her brother and the good times they had shared in her childhood sobered her. It also reminded her that in a few days she would be leaving.

Dace caught her mood and led her over to a grassy hummock warmed by the sun trickling through the filigree of leaves and branches above them. Folding down on to it, he pulled her gently down beside him. 'Whatever it is that has taken you from me at this moment must be put aside. This is the here and now.' Gently he turned her face towards him. 'I don't want to see you go, Charisse, any more than you want to go.'

Charisse looked deep into the changeable eyes, now smoky jade, and felt that familiar ripple of fire that moved up from her stomach, clutched at her heart and caused her throat to go dry. 'There may be,' she conceded, voice husky, 'a moment or two when I may miss you.'

'A moment or two. . .hmm. . .a moment or two out of each day?'

'Possibly.' A secret smile tugged at her lips. 'Quite possibly.'

He held that deep, soft gaze, then nodded. 'I'll accept that.'

She knew that it would happen and the instant before his mouth touched hers, light as swansdown, she closed her eyes. Every tactile sense seemed concentrated in her lips as he savoured them, tongue teasing the curves into a smile, teeth nibbling her lower lip into a pout, tracing every curve and swell and bow as if committing it to memory.

'I want you so very much,' he murmured against her mouth. 'I don't think my life will ever be the same, but then I knew that from the first moment I saw you. Your beauty was gold-bright, but I never knew then of your courage, your sweetness, your warmth.' All the while he spoke he covered her face and neck and ears with feather-light kisses, making her senses reel.

Charisse felt the earth beneath her back, though had not been aware that he had eased her down on to it. Only when she felt his fingers at the neck of her dress did sanity burst in on her. 'No!' she cried, and she grasped his wrist, her eyes flying open.

Immediately he raised his head, smiling down into that half-fearful, half-longing gaze. 'I have never,' he stated softly, a strange wonder in his voice, 'seen eyes that drew me so completely into their depths.'

'Dace, I. . .this isn't right. I am not the kind of woman——'

'It couldn't be more right, my love, and I know exactly the kind of woman you are: a wonderful, innocent, brave wood-nymph with the fire of the plains wind in your veins, the gold of the sun in your hair, and all the mystery that is woman in those incredible eyes.'

His voice washed over her and all the time that mobile mouth was interspersing his seductive words with those tantalising, teasing kisses. Charisse felt the languor in her limbs and knew, even as her mouth finally opened beneath his, that this was all that she had ever wanted. No yesterday, no tomorrow, only the scented breeze and the lushly grassed ground, and the man—who was more male than any had a right to be—here beside her. She knew that she was a fool, that she was only a transient pleasure for the man whose warm fingers were stroking over the curves beneath the light dress, moulding gently, setting her afire as if the material never existed.

Reading her thoughts, Dace promised, 'Since the first day we met there has been no other woman, nor will there be until you leave.' He opened a button of her bodice and then another. 'And if you tell me that you will return there won't be any other until you tell

me you no longer want me. You fill my every thought,
Charisse. Let me fill yours. Let me teach you, let me
love you. You *are* mine, why deny it?'

She was unable to answer, unable to take her eyes
from his, but then those sensual fingers slipped inside
the bodice and beneath the silk camisole top to cup
one breast, and a gasp was dragged from her throat.
For a moment the fierce, burning, all-consuming possession she saw in his eyes blinded her with fear, but
then the need in her, a deep, primal instinct for the
surrender of a female to its mate, overrode the thin
veneer of civilisation and she closed her eyes and
whispered, 'Teach me, Dace.'

Dace felt that need in her and a sense of power
swept through him, yet, mingled with wonder rather
than triumph, a power that made him feel stronger
than he had ever been, and ten feet tall. His fingers
were deft on the buttons and fastenings of her clothing
and within minutes the material was cast aside. As the
cool air brushed her skin her eyes went wide and
behind the misty sheen of desire he read the panic of a
young fawn beneath the touch of the hunter. 'Don't,'
he smiled. 'I would do nothing to harm you. You can
stop me at any time if there is anything you don't want
. . .any time.'

'I'm not afraid,' she lied, then amended, 'Not very.'

Holding his own desire in check, he quickly divested
himself of his own clothing then took her gently into
his arms. 'We have time.'

Charisse's whole body seemed to vibrate as she felt
the leashed power of the man when she curled sinuously against him with an innocent seduction as old as
mankind itself. She wanted him to take her, to conquer
her doubts, dispel her fears by the very power that
even now overwhelmed her, yet at the same time she
needed this moment, this warm, comforting embrace,
to last forever.

He moved away, but then rose to kneel beside her

and bent to caress her with long, sweeping strokes. Her pulse ricocheted as his hands savoured her warm flesh, the swollen, sensitive, magnolia satin breasts, the slender waist, the very slighly convex stomach, over a hipbone, until he reached the silky soft triangle at the apex of her thighs.

His eyes followed the path of his fingers, treasuring the perfection of her. Slowly, gently, he slid his fingers into that warm, secret place, forcing himself to curb the white-hot desire that was eroding his sanity. Her tiny cry, a sound between a moan and a whimper, was not, he realised with sudden elation, caused by fear but by response. Yet he knew even now that, in her innocence, he could still frighten her, so still gently he stroked, probing with a teasingly sensual rhythm until her body arched, begging mutely for fulfilment of desires of which she was only half aware. This time he knew that there would be no holding back.

Charisse felt the rhythm of those lean, knowing fingers reaching the very core of her. A rip-tide of sensation tore through her, volcano-hot, powerful, all-consuming, and she cried out, her body arching in spasm as the explosion came, and then again as the ripples of fire possessed her, and she flung her arms backwards over her head, clutching the grass, feeling her whole body straining to meet him, then sinking, quivering to the earth again.

Dace experienced an incredulous joy at the total abandonment of her response, the release of her passion. It was an accolade to his expertise, but also a surrender, a trust, a defencelessness that humbled him. When the dazed eyes sought his he could not meet them, but drew her close, as he might a child, stroking the damp hair, her back, her temple. He had always been a man who knew how to please a woman—and had worked assiduously to perfect the art—but at no time, with any woman, had he felt this sense of wonder, this. . .gratitude. His own passion was still unreleased; why, then, did he feel that he was flying?

Charisse could only guess at his sacrifice, but tentatively raised her arms to hold him even closer. 'I want all of you, Dace,' she whispered, running light fingers down his chest and over the muscle-ridged stomach, feeling the quivering response. 'Now.'

In one smooth movement he laid her back and raised upwards over her body and, as her thighs parted, slipped inwards, feeling the slight resistance of that delicate barrier, hesitating for an instant. But Charisse twisted and thrust upward, permitting no impediment to the joy she wanted to bring him, and rejoiced in his gasp of pleasure. Clinging to the broad back, she brought her legs up to curl around his hips, drawing him even deeper inside her, crying out again, soft and ragged against his ear, as the explosion of sensation burst within each of them. The storm tide receded, leaving them gasping on the brink, then welled up again, sweeping them upwards in the maelstrom so that they cried out in unison, helpless before the ecstatic wave upon wave of incredible emotion that held them prisoner.

Then, when finally it cast them down, to drift slowly on to the beach of sanity, they lay as if unconscious, he still within her, a part of her. Her limbs still encircled him, holding him close, revelling in the weight that crushed her. Slowly he raised his head, seeing the tears shimmering on her cheeks, and bent to brush them away with his lips as he moved aside.

'You are the most incredible woman I have ever known. No one has taken my heart and body both at the same time in such a perfect way.'

She gave him a tremulous smile. 'If only I could keep both, but I know that nothing so wonderful can last.'

Dace knew it too, and was all too aware that he could make a commitment that would keep her by his side forever, but he had made such a commitment before and seen it betrayed. His heart was wary and his mind even more so.

Charisse sensed his withdrawal and guessed at the reason, but still felt a wrench of pain when he rose abruptly and began to gather their scattered clothing. 'So soon?'

Deliberately he lightened the mood and she would never know what that cost him, when all he wanted was to fall back by her side and take her again and again, to bring back the glow now lost in those eyes. 'We are corrupting the squirrels, and I'll not share you with anyone.' Scooping her up, he deposited her on her feet, still holding her hard against the lean length of him. 'Get dressed, woman, or we shall never get back today.'

Forced to accept the teasing tone, she wrinkled her nose at him. 'Then we should undoubtedly be in a sorry mess when we did return,' she said, and she raised her face to catch the fine mist of rain that had begun to fall. 'Although I have heard that rain-water and lovemaking both are good for the complexion.'

'Witch!' he laughed, relieved, and kissed her again, but then put her firmly away. 'I won't have you catching a chill. Here, put this on, and this.' Chidingly, like a nurse—or lover—he helped her to dress.

Walking back to the car, Charisse bent to pick up a piece of bark, fallen from one of the great trees. 'I shall keep this,' she declared, then, with a half-embarrassed sideways glance, 'Not that I shall ever forget this moment, but I would like to take a part of the woods with me, and a squirrel just wouldn't fit in at home.' She was glad of his laugh and it was with a companionable closeness that they returned to the Gateway.

Even so, as they drew up before the hotel, she felt the need to say, 'I never knew it could be like that— being made love to. If it never happens again I will treasure this afternoon, Dace, but that is all it was—a perfect afternoon, so you have no reason to worry: I shan't make any commitments, nor ask any of you.' But already she knew that her heart had labelled her a liar, that she was totally, completely, irrevocably in love with the handsome Creole and always would be.

The dark eyes were enigmatic. 'You didn't need to tell me that, Charisse. I suppose I should be grateful— most men in my position would be; but I'm not most men. What you gave me today was a gift so fragile, so wonderful that it took my breath away. Neither one of us can ever again be the same two people that embarked on a casual trip to the woods to forget an unpleasant incident. I didn't take your body alone, we made love, and although, yes, I admit that I had planned to do just that from the first, I never realised how it would affect me. I would be a fool to attempt to make light of such an experience, but an even greater fool to make false promises until my heart stopped ruling my head.'

Charisse laid a finger across his lips. 'No more, Dace.'

She would have said more, but a cool voice behind them cooed, 'How sweet!' and Melinda stepped from a gleaming Mercedes that had drawn up behind their own.

Magnificent in sapphire-blue lavishly embroidered in black silk and trimmed with ribbon lace, she strolled over to them with that slumberous, hip-swinging gait that turned every head within sight. One long look swept Charisse from head to toe and back again, missing nothing, and when blue eyes met grey they shot fire. 'I really must recommend my hairdresser, Miss Linton, or perhaps you *prefer* the carefully casual look.'

Charisse felt the colour rise to her cheeks, certain that there must be a dozen or more leaves scattered in her hair.

'Charisse may not, but I do,' Dace answered gallantly. 'I assume this is purely business, Melinda, so shall we go to my office?' He smiled down at Charisse and her heart turned a somersault at the expression there. 'Thank you,' he said, and the 'for everything' danced between them.

'Thank *you*.'

Melinda's smile was feral. 'Now that everyone is duly grateful may we get out of this rain? I shall be in your office, Dace.'

They followed her in and as they reached the foyer Charisse said, 'I have to write to Poppa and that always takes me an age, and then tomorrow I promised I would take Mark out.'

'And tomorrow evening?'

'I don't know.'

'Dinner, then.'

'No. . . I. . .' She averted her head, wanting to scream, 'Go to her, damn you! Tell *her* pretty lies about her hair and skin. Can't you see she will never let you go? No wonder you won't make fool promises. She is more of a woman than I could ever be and you know it. . .first hand!' Instead she prevaricated, 'I'll let you know.'

Her sudden coolness puzzled him. Surely she couldn't be jealous of Melinda when he had made his feelings so plain? 'I will pick you up at seven,' he said, but already she had turned away.

In the warmly panelled office Melinda perched becomingly on the edge of the mahogany and rosewood desk, swinging one elegantly silk-stockinged leg. She had removed her hat and the red hair blazed with life. Dace was not fooled by the deceptively casual pose. 'I hope this won't take long; I have a heavy schedule.'

'But not too heavy to spend an apparently riotous hour or so with the now-not-so-innocent Miss Linton.'

'Careful, Melinda!'

'Oh, I don't mind, darling. A beautiful animal with

your appetite must have *some* sustenance and, since I haven't been around to keep you completely satisfied, I should imagine you must have made up for it in quantity if not in quality.'

'State your business and get out.'

'Or what?' She slid gracefully off the desk and glided over to stand before him. 'Will you put me over your knee and give me a good spanking?'

Despite himself a smile tugged at his mouth. 'No, you'd enjoy it too much. Come on, Melinda, what is it you want this time? More money? I already make you a more than generous allowance and have no intention of increasing it.'

Her mind was still on one track. She had seen the look in Dace's eyes as he talked with Charisse, and Melinda knew, even if Dace himself did not, that he was more than half in love with the girl. Melinda would not allow that. 'When is the chit leaving?' she asked, and inwardly fumed as the sparkle left his eyes.

'I don't know. Now, Melinda, I have every intention of going about my business unless you come immediately to the point.'

She pouted prettily, the full lower lip pursing outward and begging to be taken between teeth and nibbled, but, seeing that his mind was still elsewhere— and not needing a great deal of imagination to guess where—she said, 'I *do* need money, Dace, really I do. Georgia Parker is going to Europe for three whole months and has asked me to accompany her.' One carmine-tipped finger came up to tease his ear. 'You would have me out of your hair for almost six months if we take a leisurely journey there and back into consideration. Now isn't that worth something?'

Pushing off the wriggling finger, he gave an exasperated shake of his head, but was smiling as he surrendered. 'You always get your own way, by fair means or foul, don't you, Melinda?'

'No, darling, not always, or we would no longer be divorced. However, I'm still working on that one.'

He crossed to a large safe in the corner and, juggling the combination lock, opened it and withdrew a cheque book. Taking it to the desk, he wrote, signed and handed a cheque to her. 'This should cover six months without you, but that's the last.'

The blue eyes gleamed at the generous amount. 'Yes, Dace,' she agreed, 'thank you so much, darling,' but both knew that it would not be.

'Now leave before I change my mind; I have work to do.'

Turning at the door to bid a final farewell and thank you, she saw that already he had forgotten her. He was staring up at a painting of Muir Woods and an almost imperceptible smile touched the firm mouth. Melinda felt the jealous fury rip through her. Never had she seen his eyes as soft. The chit had to go, she vowed, and she had to go immediately and permanently. Only then could Melinda work on bringing Dace back to his knees before *her*. Somehow Charisse Linton had to be scared out of the city, scared so completely that she would rather die than return. . . Rather. . .die. . . Melinda was smiling as she left the hotel—the smile of the snake as it contemplated a mesmerised bird.

CHAPTER TWELVE

'I REALLY like you, Charisse,' declared Mark LaVelle. 'I may even marry you when I grow up.'

They were crossing the bay to Oakland on the morning ferry to visit an acquaintance of Dace's whose retriever bitch had just produced a litter of five pups. Mark had plagued his father for a puppy for almost a year and finally Dace had surrendered with the stipulation, 'But you feed it, clean up after it and exercise it and, in a hotel, *you* keep it quiet.' Now Mark was literally jumping with excitement.

Charisse ruffled the dark hair, so like his father's. 'Don't you think I may be just a little old for you by then?'

'You will never be old,' stated Mark stoutly.

The two had formed a close bond over the past days and the very thought of leaving him wrenched at her heart, for, each in a different way, she loved both father and son intensely.

Absorbed in their conversation and plans for the puppy, neither one noticed the two men who had boarded the ferry behind them. Both wore the garb of seamen, but there the resemblance ended. The taller of the two, his flaccid gut hanging over the filthy trousers, his lank black hair falling over the low simian forehead almost veiling the hooded black eyes, was named Tovey. The other, Keach, was a weasel of a man with darting grey eyes that missed nothing: everything about him was sharp and angular. Both were typical of the wharf rats that came and went with the tide and inhabited the dives around the harbour or visited the lowest brothels on the Barbary Coast. Both had been hired by Melinda, through a contact of

'dubious reputation', to 'take Charisse Linton up into
the hills and scare the living daylights out of her, then
leave her to make her own way back'.

'Never said ought about a kid,' Keach worried.
'What do we do about him?'

Tovey's brain did not possess the capacity for doubt.
'We take him with us.' The black eyes roved over the
curves of the woman, revealed by the crisp wind
pinning her dress against her. 'Nice bit o' work there,
Keach.' And he grinned, revealing yellow and rotting
teeth.

'That wasn't in the orders,' Keach stated firmly. 'We
were to take her up in the canyons around Mount
Diablo, rough her up a bit and leave her there. The
man said there'd be a closed cab waiting t'other side of
the ferry.' He fingered the knife tucked into his trousers
beneath the navy jacket. 'She won't give us no trouble
and the brat is only a half-pint anyway—a clip round
the ear will keep him quiet.'

Charisse and Mark left the boat with the other
passengers and looked around for one of the cabs that
invariably were there to meet the ferry. Suddenly
Charisse froze as a voice behind her ordered, 'Don't
move,' and a sharp sting in her back told her that a
knife-point was pressed there. 'Now—walk over to
that hansom nice an' easy like, and get in.' A jab made
her gasp and she took a step forward but then halted.

'Let the boy go. Whatever you want from me is
nothing to do with him.'

With Keach still holding the knife on her, Tovey
came around to face her and Charisse felt sick with
fear at the mere sight of the man. 'The brat comes with
us.' He smiled and the stench of his breath assailed her
as he leaned close. 'He will keep you sweet, little lady.
You wouldn't want him to get hurt now, would you?'
With a speed that belied his size his hand shot out and
seized Mark by the upper arm, dragging him close and
up on to his toes.

Gamely Mark lashed out. 'You let me go!' he demanded but was silenced by a cuff to the side of the head that caused Charisse to cry,

'No! Let him be! I'll come with you.'

At the cab Keach gestured his victims inside, but as Tovey went to climb in after them said, 'Not you. You drive.' The big man rounded on him sharply to argue, but, with a meaningful gesture of the knife, the weasel-faced man ordered, 'Drive, Tovey. I seen the way you looked at the woman and I'll not have her harmed before we arrive. S'pose someone stops us?'

Reluctantly the other climbed up to take the reins and Keach joined Charisse and Mark in the dim interior.

'Where are you taking us and why?' Charisse demanded, hating the slight quiver in her voice. 'We have no enemies. What is this all about? Is it Dace you want to get back at? He will undoubtedly pay you more than whoever hired you. Is it a ransom you want?'

For an instant the sharp eyes flickered, but then he snarled, 'Shaddup!' He pulled a length of cord from his pockets and cut off two lengths. 'Hold out your hands; you too, boy.' Within seconds their wrists were expertly tied in front of them and a length of cord tied one ankle to the other with an eighteen-inch play between. 'Long enough to walk but too short to run off.'

For what seemed an eternity the horse was driven at a steady trot out of Oakland and east towards the foothills that rose broodingly from the coastal plain. Charisse could not see which direction they were taking, nor any landmarks, for at the first indication of interest Keach had drawn the blinds in the cab, plunging them into darkness. 'Don't reckon on calling for help either, or you'll lose some of them pearly whites. There'll be time enough for shouting where no one can hear you.' And the threat in his words made her blood run cold.

The Diablo range of mountains slashed a path south

from behind Oakland for over a hundred and fifty miles, and were ruled by the great Mount Diablo, which, according to the Indians, was the dwelling place of a powerful 'puy': an evil spirit. The mountain, it was said, was named by a Mexican missionary who, on first encountering its mysteriously dark and deep ravines and its craggy, inhospitable slopes, crossed himself with a cry of 'Diablo!'—devil. There were places where only the foolhardy would go, some of whom never re-emerged.

It was to this alien and evil place that Tovey and Keach had been ordered to take Charisse. Melinda, driven by jealous rage, had been certain that the apparently fragile and doll-like blonde who was taking her ex-husband's attention would emerge an emaciated, broken wreck from her ordeal. There was now a good road into the foothills and tourists made regular journeys there, so there was every chance that if Charisse made it out of the canyons she would be found—eventually. Melinda had planned it well, but had not known that Charisse had formed such a deep friendship with Dace's son—a son whom Dace adored and was capable of killing for.

The hansom was driven as far as the horse could go, far beyond the limit of the other visitors who picnicked there, then concealed in a thick copse. 'We walk from here,' Keach ordered as Charisse jumped awkwardly to the ground. 'I'll untie you because there's some climbing ahead, but there's no way you can outrun us and if you even think of it just take one step too fast and I cut the boy. Understand?'

Charisse had recovered from the initial shock on the journey and had been plotting with a coolness that surprised her in the circumstances. At all costs Mark must not be harmed, but it was the gargantuan Tovey she feared, not the more intelligent Keach, even though it was the latter who carried the knife. She knew that she could reason with Keach, but the pri-

meval mentality of the other was beyond her reach and
the look in his eyes nauseated her.

For the first two hours the big man needed all his
energy for the climb and the greasy striped shirt was
soaked with sweat in spite of the cool depths of the
rocky canyons they trecked into. Charisse, too, was
uncomfortable in the clinging petticoats, but thankful
that she never wore the constricting corsets dictated by
fashion, and had equally unfashionable boots beneath
the long skirts.

Only Mark, with the resilience of the young, seemed
to regard the whole thing as an adventure, keeping
well out of Tovey's reach and staying close to Charisse.
Only once did he earn a slap from Keach, when
Charisse stumbled and Keach gave her a sharp prod in
the back. Bravely Mark had shouted, 'You leave her
alone! My daddy will kill you if you hurt her!'

Casually, almost absent-mindedly, the scarecrow
figure had backhanded the boy, ordering, 'Speak when
you're spoken to.' But beyond that no words were
exchanged.

It was still early in the afternoon but the warming
rays of the sun never reached into the deep ravines and
crevasses and only the glimpses of blue sky far above
indicated that it was day. On one of their stops Charisse
had asked of Keach, 'Did you bring any food or water?
Neither Mark nor I have had anything since breakfast.'

'So go hungry,' was the curt reply. 'That's the whole
idea.'

'Whose idea? Who is paying you? Are you to hold
us for ransom? In which case it would behove you to
keep us fit and healthy.'

'You talk too much,' Keach told her, and he rose to
sharpen the gleaming knife on a rock.

Tovey came to lower himself ponderously beside
her, frowning when she turned aside. 'You'd better be
nice to me, real nice if you want to get out of here.'

'I'd sooner pet a rattlesnake!' Her head snapped

sideways with the crashing blow and lights flashed behind her eyes, but Keach's voice ordered,

'Lay off, Tovey. We're not far enough in yet and she's gotta walk.'

Those words alone turned Charisse's blood to ice. 'Where is "far enough"?' she asked Keach. 'Where are we going?'

For a second he did not answer, then gave a shrug. 'We just got the directions. I got a map here in my pocket. There's an abandoned hut we should reach afore long.'

Charisse did not want to ask the next question but *not* knowing was even worse. 'And then what?'

Again there was that brief hesitation, then, 'Look . . .this is nothing personal. We get paid and we do a job.'

Charisse coughed to clear the choking sensation in her suddenly dry throat. 'Are you going to kill us? If you are I think we deserve at least to know why.'

He met her eyes and read the courage behind the fear. Keach knew a fair amount about fighting for his life and knew of bluffing a foe with a false display of bravery, but this was no bluff; this woman had more guts than any of them had given her credit for. In his eyes that earned her the truth. 'No,' he denied and saw the sudden tears of relief. 'No, we were told to take some of the spunk out of you and leave you up here.'

'But we'll *never* get out! You're the one who has been studying the map. We've been through a maze of canyons and side-paths already.' She reached to take his arm, ignoring the instinctive recoil and gripping his sleeve. 'Take Mark back with you. You can't want to harm him, he's only a baby. Do what you will with me, but take the boy, I beg you.'

'Sorry,' Keach said, and he was. 'We go back, get paid off, and we're booked out on a boat going to Australia the day after tomorrow. If we haul the kid back we might not get paid. No. Forget it. Go on. Get going. We've wasted enough time already.'

The hut, when eventually they reached it, filled her with dismay. There was little left of the roof, several holes in the walls where the rotting planks had fallen away and, inside, only a filthy palliasse on the wooden floor. 'That'll do me,' stated Tovey and pushed her forward.

'Just a minute, Tovey,' objected Keach. 'We weren't to do more'n rough her up a bit and get out.'

The rotting teeth were bared in a wolfish grin. 'You rough her up your way and I'll do it mine.'

'Wait!' Charisse went quickly to face Keach. 'I don't expect mercy, nor do I think you have any control over this animal or what he intends.' She swallowed and her eyes were dark with the horror of her nightmare imaginings. 'You must know that when he is finished with me I may not even be alive. I won't beg for *my* life, Mr Keach, but I *do* beg you to take Mark out of here. Take him half a mile down the canyon. Don't let him hear or see anything of this, I implore you. You *know* what it would do to him. It would stay with him for the rest of his life. . .assuming he *has* a life. Please. For his sake, not mine.'

For one terrible moment she thought he would refuse—when all of her plans depended on having the two men well separated—but then he nodded.

'I want nothing to do with this. I'm going back.'

Tovey licked his lips with a thick tongue. 'Fine by me.'

Keach took Mark's arm in a firm grip. 'You come with me, boy, and if you know what's good for you keep your mouth shut or I'll leave you here with Tovey.' To Tovey he ordered, 'Give us a bit to clear the area. I'll take the brat back down the trail and wait fifteen minutes only. Fifteen minutes, you hear?'

Tovey's simian forehead wrinkled and the black

brows drew together in a deep frown. 'Take more'n that for what I got in mind. Could take all night.'

'Fifteen minutes, you scum-bag, and *I've* got the map. You want to try and find your way out in the dark without a map, you go ahead. . .if she's worth it.' And, when the giant's brain could not assimilate all the ramifications of that, he elucidated, 'We been going up and down and round for nigh on three hours now, and that in the light—such as it was—with a map. You try to make it alone in the dark and you could still be going in circles a week from now—if the snakes don't get you or the wild pig, and if you don't die of thirst. Come, boy.' And, turning, he walked out, dragging a protesting Mark with him.

Immediately Tovey swung back to Charisse, but, backing to the wall, she begged, 'Let them get clear, Tovey. Let Keach get Mark down the canyon.'

'I don't care about no kid.'

'Wait, then!' She held out her hands, warding him off, praying as she had never prayed before. The timing had to be just right, or all of the past hours' planning and re-planning would be lost. . .with both her life and Mark's. 'You want me, Tovey, don't you?' It was a statement, not a question.

'Gonna have you, too.'

'Yes. Yes, I know. But, Tovey. . .' she forced her voice into a dulcet purr '. . .wouldn't you rather have me all sweet for you? You are a big man, Tovey: more man than any I've seen. That Keach, now, he's only a runt. I had to get rid of him, but you are a real man, Tovey. I just bet you really know how to please a girl.' She saw him grow an inch and the barrel-chest swell.

'Sure don't get many complaints,' he grinned. 'But I ain't never had one o' you *ladies*, not a *real* lady.'

Slowly, keeping her eyes on his every movement, Charisse undid one of the buttons at the neck of her dress, then another. 'There's no difference but the silks and satins, Tovey. Our skin may be a little softer——'

she ran a finger over her lower lip '—and our hair a little brighter.' Slowly, very slowly, she took the pins from her high-piled *coiffure* and watched his eyes bulge as that flaxen glory tumbled to her waist. She had him now.

Seductively she bent and twitched up the hem of her skirt, revealing a slender ankle, hearing the whistle of his indrawn breath. 'You filth,' she murmured softly.

'What? What you say?'

'You scum. You slime,' she added, her whole being concentrated on that moment when he took a vengeful step forward. It came.

'You been lying to me! You ain't gonna give me nothing! You high-tone bitch!' He stepped forward, reaching for her, one fist raised.

At the same instant Charisse dragged the skirt high, wrenched up the petticoats beneath, drew the derringer and fired blindly upwards, all in one movement.

He was closer than she had anticipated. The gun barrel was rammed into his side when the explosion came. Still the force of it hurled him backwards as the forty-one slug ploughed through the thick rolls of fat, carved a fiery path through the stomach wall to exit in a mess of cauterised nerve and tissue, severing the spinal column as it did so.

Tovey made no sound at all, but the crash of his great body against the wall brought Charisse upright. She did not even glance at him but rushed blindly past and out into the dusk.

Stumbling, falling, rising and running on again, she raced down the path that she knew Keach and Mark would take. Her mind refused to acknowledge the fact that she had killed a man; later she could afford the luxury of tears. At this moment her whole *raison d'être* was to find Mark and rescue him from Keach. Beyond that there was nothing. She fell again and sprawled flat, the wind knocked out of her, the gun skittering off out of sight, but it sobered her fast. It was almost dark and she could not afford to lose her quarry. More carefully now she moved forward, using every sense to track the two ahead, and could have wept with relief when she heard voices.

Creeping forward stealthily, she rounded a giant rock at the side of the trail and came upon them—Mark sitting cross-legged on the ground, Keach standing leaning against the canyon wall. To her horror his steady gaze was on the very spot from which she had emerged, but yet he did not move nor draw the knife tucked into his belt as he saw her.

Charisse braced herself. 'I shot Tovey. I had a derringer under my skirt, but I fell and it went off into the rocks somewhere back there.'

'Figures. *You* wouldn't be alive if *he* was.' He straightened. 'Can't take you back and can't let them catch me, but I'm not from under the same rock as Tovey. Don't mind messing up a woman, but ain't never raped or killed one yet. Gotta leave you here and make sure you don't follow until I'm clear, so I reckon I just gotta tie you up. By the time the kid gets them seamen's knots undone I'll be long gone.' He read her expression and shook his head. 'Don't even think of it. I mayn't be so big, but I got the knife and I got the boy.'

Despairingly Charisse nodded and sat down, allowing him to tie her wrists and ankles securely. 'You said you were no killer.' Her eyes willed him to show mercy. 'When you reach the city give that map to someone, anyone. Tell them to take it to the Gateway Hotel. At least give them a chance to find us. You will be on your way to Australia. They won't find you.'

His bony fingers paused in his task, but the only concession he would make was, 'I'll think on it,' and he soon had her hands captive before her.

Mark came to kneel at her side and put an arm about her shoulders. 'I am glad you found us, Charisse.'

Keach rose and for a moment stood looking down at

them. Musingly he said, 'Wouldn't of minded a plucky kid like that. And you, girly, you got pure steel in your craw. I mighta been a different man if I had known someone like you a while back.' But then, regretting the admission, he said, 'No good you thinking of shouting. No one for miles and all the tourists gone home from the foothills even if the sound did carry. Save your energy for the walk out.' And, so saying, he turned and disappeared down the dark trail.

For a long moment after he had gone Charisse leaned back against the rock, eyes closed, fighting the threatening tears, but then, hearing Mark's subdued sniffles, she pulled herself together. 'Don't cry, love. We will get out of here. When we don't get back on time your father will come after us. He will find us, even if we *do* lose our way.' She prayed that Mark was too young to see the total illogicality behind her argument: that, even if Dace was concerned, his enquiries would first start within the city itself, and there was absolutely no reason, even if all else failed, why he should think of searching the Palo Duro area. The sniffles died and she breathed a quick prayer of thanks. 'Now, Mark, you must be very strong and very brave and try to undo these knots.'

Half an hour later Mark was again in tears and Charisse had to admit that the fingers of a seven-year-old were no match for a seaman's expertise, and whether Keach had tied such knots unthinkingly or deliberately, she would never know. 'It's all right, Mark. Don't cry. You did your best. I'll find a sharp piece of rock, but it's too dark to try now. Come over here and put your head on my lap. We'll try to get some sleep and it will all seem better in the morning.'

Exhausted by the fear and the strain and the long walk, the boy gladly complied and within minutes had fallen into a deep sleep. Gently Charisse stroked the dark curls and a smile touched her mouth. 'There's my brave lad,' she murmured. 'Didn't the bard say some-

thing about sleep unravelling the threads of care? I
hope so, my little puppy, for you have a long day
tomorrow.'

But it was many hours before Charisse herself was
able to fall into an exhausted and oft-disturbed sleep.

Dawn rose over the canyon rim and Charisse awoke,
not immediately realising her situation until she
attempted to stretch and the cords about her wrists and
ankles bit in, causing her to cry out. Mark yawned,
stretched, and sat up. 'Daddy?'

'No, honey; he hasn't come yet. First we must get
these cords off. I need a really sharp rock—you know,
like an Indian's tomahawk.' His blank expression told
her that, as he was a city child born and bred, no one
had thought to educate him along those lines, so she
made a shape with her fingers. 'Like so, with at least
one really sharp edge.'

Glad for something to occupy his mind, he leapt to
his feet, but pulled up as she called, 'Wait! Now stay
where I can see you. Try over there, and there.' It
seemed an eternity before he found the right stone and
longer still before the cords on her wrists parted
beneath the constant sawing and she could rub at the
chafed skin before eventually freeing her ankles.

'I am hungry *and* thirsty, Charisse.' There was no
whine in his voice, only a statement of fact, and she
sent up a silent prayer for his resilient and trusting
character and the strength of one far beyond his years.

'I know. Me too. Water is a priority and then I'll set
some traps. That's why I kept the cord from my ankles;
it will help with the traps, but we must also find edible
berries and roots.' Beneath her breath she finished,
'Just in case. . .'

Mark paled. 'I. . .don't think. . .we should.' And
she caught the fear of memory in the wide eyes that
sought her face.

'It's all right. I promise. I won't let you eat anything

that I don't know about. I've stayed out in the plains back home for days at a time, living off the land. I know quite a bit about such things; I really do. You must trust me.' And she took him by the arms, pulling him into a close hug, willing him to believe. 'I love you, Mark. I wouldn't let anything hurt you. I love you.' Cheek against the raven curls, she realised that she did, more than she had believed possible. How ever was she going to leave him and return to Texas? How could she leave either one, him *or* his father?

'I love you, too,' he assured her in a muffled voice. 'I do trust you. You made me better and you brought Daddy to me. Of course I trust you.' And he smiled up at her, widening the crack in her heart.

'Come on, then,' she decided. 'No time like the present. After last night my legs are stiff and need the exercise.'

Determining the direction from the sun's shadows on the rocks, she led them downward to the west and thanked the gods who, within the first mile, revealed an icy cold stream breaking from a fissure in the rock. They drank greedily, and washed and soaked one of Charisse's petticoats. The other petticoat had the lace trim torn from it, which was then ripped into short lengths that Charisse tied to bushes in plain view of any search party—or themselves, should they end up walking in circles!

Following the stream downwards, Charisse was disappointed when it ended in a small pool to one side of a sparsely grassed clearing. It had been a vain hope that it might flow out into the foothills, but at least, she reasoned, they had water. 'If only we could carry it.'

'I'm still hungry,' a small voice reminded her.

'Of course you are. Here, help me set some traps,' she suggested to take his mind off his grumbling stomach—and her own. Using a flat rock and branches from a tree growing almost horizontally from the canyon side, she constructed a dead-fall trap. Weaving

more branches, she formed a rough cage and, with the
cord, made a noose.

Mark's eyes grew wide. 'Where did you learn that?'

'Oh, an old Indian whom we have at the house. We
will stay here tonight, which is when the animals will
come down to drink.'

'I haven't even seen a bird.'

'There were hoofprints in the wet mud by the water.
I'm not clever enough to know whether it was a wild
pig or deer, but *something* certainly visits here. Now,
we must find somewhere to sleep, out of sight of the
clearing, and construct a shelter. Then we'll find some
food, berries or whatever, to take us through the day.
That should keep us well occupied.' The thought of the
weasel-faced Keach crossed her mind. Had he disappeared on to the high seas without a qualm, or had he
passed on the map and, if so, had it reached Dace or
been tossed aside? Please find us, Dace, she prayed
silently, but aloud said, 'Come on, Mark, this could be
a real adventure. Just think what your friends will say
when you tell them!'

CHAPTER THIRTEEN

THE man facing Melinda Marsh almost pitied her as the lovely face drained of colour, leaving it alabaster-white and resembling a death mask. But he had known her for over two years now and a small, secret part of him rejoiced to see her brought to quaking fear—she who had brought so much misery to others.

'A boy?' she repeated, though her lips could hardly form the words. 'About six or seven? With black hair, you say?'

He nodded, drawing a crumpled sheet of paper from his pocket and dropping it on to the table against which she leant. 'One of the men I hired—who of course must be nameless—returned the map to me when I paid him off, but made me promise to wait until his ship had sailed before taking it to the Gateway Hotel. He said the woman had a derringer hidden on her and had killed his partner. You never said anything about a gun; she was supposed to be some spoilt oil man's daughter, cosseted and pampered all her life. This man said she had spunk, and so did the kid, but he left them up there anyway as ordered, with her well tied.'

'And. . .that. . .was?'

'The day before yesterday. I figured, since you are the one who's paying me and not your ex, you'd earned the map; do with it what you will. LaVelle would probably have paid me well for this, but on the other hand he might simply have taken the map, beaten hell out of me and kicked me out. You, on the other hand, will pay me because you need my kind to do your dirty work for you.'

Melinda hardly heard him. Charisse, yes, *she* could be mourned and forgotten in time—with all the induce-

172

ments and comforting that Melinda had planned. But Mark! Dace was capable of killing the man—or woman—who caused the death of his son. Melinda's first blinding thought had been, I must run, must escape! Then, God, what a mess!

'Well?' demanded the man before her. 'I'd prefer cash, but jewellery will do, though I'll only get twenty per cent of its value.'

'Europe,' Melinda murmured. 'I'm going to Europe at the end of the month. I must stay out of sight until then. He mustn't find me.'

'Lady!' the man interrupted. 'I don't have all day!'

'No. . .yes. . .of course.' She went into the bedroom, moving with the jerky motion of a puppet on a string, and returned with a string of pearls and gold bracelet. 'Here.' Ignoring them, the man brushed her aside and went to the jewel-box, opened it, scanned the contents, nodded and extracted a diamond choker with matching bracelet, gold watch and ruby pendant.

'This'll do.' His smile was not pleasant. 'Say you had a break-in and claim them back off insurance, but leave it until you come back from your vacation. They will be off the market by then.'

'Those are worth thousands!' she protested.

'So is your pretty neck if I talk to LaVelle. Keep your peace, Melinda, and I'll keep mine.'

He left, and a long, lost, screaming silence fell. Melinda's mind fell into crystalline shards, each one stiletto-sharp yet isolated, not whole, not gathered together, and she was unable to form one coherent thought. Pushing the map into her bag, she left the room and made her way outside, walking blindly, colliding with passers-by and unaware of their stares and comments. For hours she traversed the city streets, crossing intersections randomly, until dusk fell and her exhausted body was at a state of collapse. Only then did she return to her hotel suite, fall, fully dressed, on to her bed and lose consciousness. The Melinda Marsh

who was accustomed to spending a full hour in luxurious, sybaritic preparation for bed was no more, and it
was a frightened child who cried out in the night with
dreams of a pursuing horseman on a fire-breathing
black stallion.

Late in the afternoon of the following day a tiny,
overcrowded ground-floor apartment in the Mission
District received an unexpected visitor—one the inhabitants had thought never to see again. 'Mrs LaVelle!'

Melinda stood poised in the doorway as if ready to
take flight. 'Mrs Verucci, I need help and. . .and you
are the only one I can ask.'

The dark-haired woman immediately opened the
door wide. 'Come in. Come in. Frank is still at work,
but will be home soon. Some tea? Coffee?'

Melinda followed the other into an immaculately
tidy living-room in which the edges of poverty had
been smoothed by the addition of bright, hand-
embroidered cushion-covers and fresh wild flowers.
Nevertheless, the scrubbed floorboards were bare of
carpets and there were no ornaments or pictures vis-
ible. 'Just a glass of water, please.'

The woman's eyes were bright with curiosity, but she
waited patiently until Melinda was seated in the one
good armchair and had sipped at the glass of water.
Then she asked, 'What can we do for you, Mrs
LaVelle? Since you returned from New York alone we
have heard nothing from either yourself or Tonio,
although of course we have seen your face in the
society papers on the news-stands. . .' She trailed off
delicately.

'I won't offer you meaningless apologies or worn-out
explanations,' Melinda smiled tiredly. 'Your brother
and I ran away together before we got to know one
another. I left Dace and should never have done so; it
is as simple as that. I am not here to re-write history.
You and I once could have been friends——'

'No, probably not, Mrs LaVelle——'

'Please call me Melinda. Dace divorced me. For
what I need to ask we can't stand on formalities.' She
closed her eyes momentarily before admitting, 'I desperately need your help.'

'What can I do?'

'I can't tell you all the details, but I have done
something that in Dace's eyes is not only unforgivable,
but bad enough to have him hunt me down and
probably beat me to within an inch of my life. He
knows my own circle of friends. . .acquaintances.' She
gave a wry smile. 'I have no friends, but then never
needed any. The shallow compliment, the casual
pleasure of the moment always sufficed—until now. I
need a bolt-hole, Mrs Verucci. . .Rosa. I need a hiding
place until the end of the month when I am leaving for
Europe.' A slight frown pulled at the delicately arched
brows. 'Though Dace will of course stop the cheque. I
shall have to find another. . .matters not. . .'

'You wish to stay here?' The dark brown eyes
compared the mustard and gold-trimmed walking dress
beneath the red fox stole to her own drab linen skirt
and cotton blouse. 'We could not give you anything
that you are accustomed to. We eat simply—a stew of
marrow bones and potatoes, some rice and a little
fish. . .' Again she came to a halt, not ashamed of their
poverty, for her husband worked as hard as any man
on the wharf, but only accepting and pointing out the
insurmountable difference between her family and the
vision of easy wealth before her.

'I would gladly pay you,' offered Melinda quickly.
She opened her purse and took out a handful of coins
and the few notes there. 'This is all the change I have
at this moment, but there is some jewellery I can sell
and more money in the safe at my hotel. Please allow
me to stay.' And Melinda, who had never begged for
anything in her life but always demanded—and
received—felt the tears pricking her eyes.

Rosa Verucci glanced down at the money on the

table and reflected that this 'change' alone would keep her family in food for a week. In the short silence came a child's whimper and the woman's head came up, tilted a little, listening, but then as silence fell once more she relaxed and slowly nodded. 'Lucy has consumption. The doctor says she should be in warm dry air, but Frank only knows the sea and we couldn't afford to move south. I can't say your money won't be manna from heaven. We haven't even been able to pay the doctor for his medicine, not to mention his time spent on visits. Very well, Mrs. . .Melinda. We do have a small back room that at present we keep as a storeroom, but Frank can move the stuff into our room and you can sleep there until the end of the month.'

'Thank you, Rosa; you have undoubtedly saved my life. I will go straight back to the hotel and pack.' She hesitated. 'There *is* one more thing, only a small favour, but one that may save another life and possibly redress the balance a little.' She took the crumpled sheet of paper from her purse and smoothed it on to the scrubbed wooden table. 'Do you know someone you can trust implicitly? Someone who will give this map into the hands of Dace at the Gateway and, no matter what, will not reveal where it came from? No matter what!'

Rosa accorded her a long look. 'You call this a small favour? Your tone tells me there is cause for much fear in this map, but if it is to save a life. . .and I do not even ask what it is you have done. . .but if it will save a life I shall go myself. I do not think your husband will hurt a woman, and he never met the sister of the man who made him wear the cuckold's horns.'

Impulsively Melinda gave her a hug—she who had never willingly touched another woman in her life and regarded her sex as little more than contemptible pawns in a man's world. 'Thank you. I shall never forget this.'

Rosa, however, was a woman who also knew her

own sex. 'Sure!' she acknowledged drily. 'Go now and I will settle Lucy. I shall see you later this evening.'

'At least tonight I shall sleep,' breathed Melinda. 'Last night lasted forever.'

On a ledge behind a screen of woven branches Mark gave a sigh. 'I can't sleep, Charisse, I'm cold.'

The woman pulled him close. 'At least we have food and water, but, yes, we do need a better shelter and more wood for a real fire.'

It was their second night in the wilderness, almost dawn, and Charisse was fighting both tiredness and despair. That first night they had caught a small rabbit, but the even smaller fire Charisse had finally managed to kindle left it almost raw and neither of them could bring themselves to eat more than a few mouthfuls. They had set out walking that morning but with the turns and twists in the trail knew that by noon they were completely lost and when, an hour later, Charisse had seen one of her own ribbon 'flags' it was almost a relief. Eventually they had found their way back to the clearing and the shelter they had first made, and that night a baby pig fell prey to the dead-fall trap.

'We must stay here now,' decided Charisse, comforting the tearful Mark, who had hated the sight of the battered head of the piglet, 'and wait for the search party that is bound to come. I'll climb as high as I can and light a fire, but we need wood and plenty of it. It also takes forever to get a spark. I have a mirror in my bag. . .' she gave an involuntary shudder '. . .which is in the hut. There was also a broken bottle there we can use. We must go back. The hut itself will provide enough wood for a fire to cook the pig and the bed will burn with a fair amount of smoke. During the day it will be seen for miles.'

The thought of passing Tovey's by now more than a little unsavoury body to reach her purse and the glass from the bottle to catch the sun's rays brought the bile to her throat, but she knew that she had no choice. She could survive indefinitely with food, water and warmth, but Mark was showing the strain and, as a child raised to comfort and luxury, was feeling both the heat of the day and the crippling cold of the nights more than she. She would not chance leaving him alone, even for a moment, so when the hut came in sight she made him promise to 'stay by this bush and not move an inch'.

'All right, but please hurry up. I'm hungry.' With the resilience of youth he had by now relegated the piglet to the status of pork and could not wait to see it roasted.

The hut was as she had left it and, deliberately avoiding looking at the body—which did not smell much worse in death than it had in life—she reached down for her purse. Something—a mere whisper of sound—froze her in the action as she crouched, one hand extended. Slowly, against all will, she looked over her shoulder and gave a shudder. Tovey's eyes were open and it was, to her taut imaginings, as if he was looking directly at her. One eyelid flickered. He *was* looking directly at her!

Pure terror did not make you scream. To scream you first had to draw a breath. Pure, unadulterated terror froze every muscle in the body. Only the mind was screaming. And the eyes. Tovey's eyes were not screaming. The screaming had passed when the slug from the derringer had severed that small section of nerve and bone in the spinal column, paralysing him from the neck down, but, incredibly, passing at such an angle as to leave him alive—almost, for the thing it had left was a cruel travesty of the word.

Now, his eyes glittered with hatred and—a new emotion for him—fear, as his intended victim finally rose to her feet.

Unable to take her eyes from that terrible masklike face, Charisse stumbled backwards until brought up short by the wall. For several terrible seconds she

expected to see him stagger upwards and fall on to her,
but then, as sanity slowly returned, she realised that he
had not moved since she had raced past him to freedom. Her throat worked and she swallowed hard to
overcome the constriction. 'You're. . .alive!'

Again that horrible gargling whisper of sound that
had first alerted her. The eyes flickered shut and then
opened again, staring.

'You can't move! Oh, sweet lord, what have I done?'
As blindly as she had fired at the man who had been
about to rape her, so now she moved to help a creature
who could not harm anything. What she had done had
not been through hatred but an atavistic instinct for
survival and the protection of a child, but it was quite
beyond her to leave a paralysed man unattended, as
frightened as she still was of him, remembering that
great hulk bending over her and the evil, salivating
smile. 'I don't know what I can do,' she told him. 'I
dare not move you.'

The lips parted a fraction and the tip of a swollen,
blackening tongue came out. Mutely the eyes begged.

'Water. You have been three days without water
since we left the ferry.' At last able to take some
constructive action, she ran outside. 'Mark, Tovey is
alive, but terribly wounded. He can't move and we
must not move him until help comes. I must get some
water for him.' He shook his head, the fear stark in his
eyes. 'It is all right, love, he can't hurt us; he can't hurt
anyone. Literally he can't move off the floor. We're
safe from him, but if we don't give him some water he
will die of thirst and that would be deliberate murder.
You must be brave and you must help me. I have to go
back to the stream and I can go faster alone. We have
nothing yet to carry the water in so, as before, I must
soak my petticoat that's in the shelter. That will hold
enough to squeeze into his mouth. Stay here. Don't
move. Promise me, Mark, that you won't move.'

'I'm frightened.'

'I know.' She bent to hug him close. 'Me too, but you must be brave and stay put until I get back. I will run all the way.' And with that she had to leave him.

When she returned to the hut with the dripping material and squeezed a little of the cool spring water into the fallen man's mouth he closed his eyes, swallowing painfully. Charisse wiped the filthy face and neck, bringing instant relief. 'I dare not move you; I don't know enough. You can obviously swallow. I trapped a piglet and with those pieces of glass can light a fire, so we won't starve to death. I must believe that they have sent out a search party for us. I must believe that.' She did not know why she was talking to the very enemy who had brought her to this, only that he was another human being and, in the lonely desolation of this wilderness, *any* human contact was preferable to solitude.

By mid-afternoon the aromatic scent of roasting pork wafted on to the cool breeze, and the fire, well constructed in a well of rocks, burned steadily. During the time it had taken the piglet to cook, speared on a green branch and supported over the fire by other crossed and tied branches, Charisse and Mark had cleaned out the hut. Mark's initial fear of Tovey had abated, but he still sidled quickly around the man for the few occasions it was necessary for him to pass.

A second fire had been constructed on the rocks high over the hut, a fire of green branches and leaves and the remnants of the filthy straw palliasse from the hut. In the afternoon sunlight this slow-burning signal fire emitted a thin stream of grey smoke that curled upwards; by night it would become a beacon that, Charisse prayed, would be picked up by anyone scanning with a telescope. They had also made a pole from one of the broken planks of the hut and to this Charisse had tied a length of her petticoat, a snowy white banner of hope.

'Your daddy will come, Mark, I know he will,' she

promised, and some inexplicable faith within believed it. More, it was a certainty that she could not, *would* not die before telling Dace that she loved him!

'I don't want to sleep in there,' Mark stated adamantly as night fell.

'It will afford us some protection from the night air, though not much,' admitted Charisse, in all truth not wishing, herself, to spend the night with Tovey's black eyes boring into her as they had done each time she was within his range of vision.

'Can't we go back to the shelter? It's nearer to the stream and we could set more traps.'

'This piglet will last us a couple of days or more. I'll hang it up on that corner of the hut so that no passing critters can get to it. However, you're probably right: we shall sleep more soundly down by the clearing. Tovey will be well enough alone and the signal fire is well banked. Very well, let's go down. Maybe Dace will come tomorrow.' And silently she prayed, *Please* let Dace come tomorrow!

'Will this night never end?' Melinda stood in the doorway of young Lucy's room, afraid to enter for fear of contamination, while Rosa comforted the restless child.

'Go back to bed,' Rosa advised over her shoulder. 'Frank has gone for the doctor. There is nothing you can do.' And quietly, heart breaking, she added, 'There is little anyone can do but wait.'

'What kind of doctor would come out at one o'clock in the morning?'

The Italian woman smiled. 'A good one.' And, at a noise outside, she said, 'He may not be a true saint but he is the nearest to one *I* am likely to see.'

Melinda moved aside as the young doctor entered, passing her with barely a glance and going directly to the bed. Melinda was unaccustomed to handsome young men ignoring her: perhaps he had not seen her in the dimly lit room. 'I am Melinda Marsh,' she said. 'Is there anything I can do?'

The man took his attention from his patient for a few seconds to accord the beautiful stranger a long, assessing look, then shook his head, returning to Lucy. 'With respect, you don't look nursing material and there is little in that field that Rosa can't do.' He gave the mother a warm, personal smile. 'I wish I had a dozen Rosas at my side.'

Melinda frowned. Not only had she been dismissed as useless, but the man's brilliant sapphire eyes had given the drab, plain Rosa Verucci the look that would normally be accorded her. Something about the young doctor nagged at her as she watched him coax a glass of medicine down Lucy's throat and settle her more comfortably on the high-piled pillows. Something about that white-gold hair and fine features, the high cheekbones and, above all, the slightly elongated eyes. . . He had risen to go and, not wanting to break that tenuous thread of thought, she asked, 'Have you been in San Francisco for long, Doctor? Someone who attends his patients at such uncivilised hours could make his fortune in my part of town, yet I have not heard of you before.'

There was a disquieting directness in that piercing gaze. 'I go where I am most needed, ma'am. Those on Nob Hill don't need a doctor at midnight, they need a soporific for boredom. I am not that kind of physician—at any price.' He smiled then and Melinda almost gasped at the radiance, the beauty that shone from that ascetically handsome face. 'I came to San Francisco from Texas eight years ago and have never regretted one moment of it, nor do I regret the poor and dark places I serve in, but I must admit that, very occasionally, I see a vision as lovely as yourself and it enables me to continue for a few months more. Goodnight, ma'am, and thank you.' He moved past her again, almost touching, and she felt the loss of that instant of non-contact.

'Your name, Doctor?' She blushed—she, the coolly sophisticated Melinda Marsh who reduced men to jelly with one raised eyebrow. 'Just in case I *really* need help one dark night.'

He paused briefly at the front door. 'Ralph. Ralph Leonard. Rosa knows where to find me. . .if you *really* need me.'

CHAPTER FOURTEEN

ROSA faced the man in the dark grey double-breasted business suit and attempted in vain to keep her hands from shaking as the whole of her insides were. 'I am Rosa. Just Rosa,' she repeated for the third time. 'I was given the map and told to hand it to you personally.' She could not remember a moment in her life when she had been so afraid as those glittering eyes again swung to her face.

'Why?' The word hung in the icy air between them. 'Why my son? Ransom? Vendetta? Yes, even though not Italian I know that word. Why?'

'I have told you,' she pleaded, 'I know nothing.'

'You lie.'

Although the words emerged softly she took an involuntary step backwards, even though there was the width of the desk between them. Mutely she shook her head, unable to voice the lie that they both knew she would tell.

Not since that first moment when she had been shown into Dace LaVelle's office, placed the map before him and seen the colour drain from his face; not since the fingers about the wine glass he held tightened, splintering the delicate stem to send the contents over the papers on the desk; not since then had he raised his voice. At that time he had looked up, heard her say, 'They have your son and your woman,' and given one incoherent cry of denial, sweeping the papers, glass and map on to the floor.

Then he had demanded, very quietly, 'Who is responsible? Who will I kill at the end? Who are you? What part do you play? If you want to leave this office alive you would do well to answer me,' and the tone held the sibilant softness of a side-winder moving across the desert floor.

'I am Rosa. Just Rosa,' she said as had been planned. 'I know nothing. I was given this by someone who paid me well to hand it to the owner of the Gateway Hotel. That is all I know. The. . .person told me your son and the woman were alive when left. That was three days ago.'

'Three days?' One hand clenched spasmodically, the other went to claw roughly through the sable hair. 'Do you know what it's like up there?' He rose from behind the desk and came to stand over her, not touching her, but by his very stance terrifying as he searched her face. 'Why you? Are you an accomplice? This has been well planned. A woman like you doesn't just happen to be strolling up Nob Hill on a weekday afternoon. Who hired you from the first? Who are you protecting?' His hand raised and she flinched, expecting the blow, but he lowered it again.

'No,' he denied in that controlled, vibrant voice that held all of the leashed violence in the broad frame. 'No. If I touched you I should kill you.' He spun away, walked half a dozen paces to the far wall, slammed his palm against it with a crash, pivoted and strode to the window, staring blindly out as his fist crumpled the velvet curtain into a ball, unaware of the scattered papers beneath his feet. Again he asked, 'Who are you? How much did they pay you? I can double it, whatever amount it is.'

Seeing the agony in the dark eyes that swung to her face, Rosa was tempted, not by the money, but by an understanding of his pain. She did not know this man, but in that moment almost betrayed the woman to whom she had promised sanctuary and protection. 'I'm Rosa,' she said for the third time, and felt the tears start in her eyes.

When his further questioning elicited no further response Dace went again to sink into the burgundy

leather wing-back behind the desk, his great forearms
on the desk-top as he leaned forward, pinning her with
his regard. 'Very well, I'll let you go back to whomever
paid you enough, or scared you enough, to purchase
your soul. Tell them I *will* find my son and Charisse
and then I will find the person who sent them there. If
Mark and Charisse are harmed I will inflict twice their
suffering on the person you are protecting. If. . .' He
choked down the fiery ball in his throat that threatened
to cut off his air. 'If they are dead then their murderer
will take as many days to die. This is no threat, Just
Rosa. I do not make threats. This is a statement of
fact. Now go.'

Still she hung there, barely able to see through her
tears. 'Mr LaVelle. . .I pray they are safe. I *cannot* tell
you who it is who has done this terrible thing, only
that. . .I myself am not being paid for my secrecy. It
was a promise I made.'

His eyes widened. 'A promise? A promise worth the
life of my son? What in mercy's name is worth that?'

'It was not *meant* to be Mark,' she blurted out, then
clapped her hand over her mouth, realising her error.
As he surged upwards, she cried, 'I cannot! I cannot
tell you!' and raced for the door before he had cleared
the desk, running out and slamming it behind her. For
a moment she thought he would come after her and
beat the information out of her. Heart pounding, she
rushed down the corridor, down the flight of stairs to
the foyer, across and out into the street.

Dace had reached the door before his senses pulled
him up sharp. There was no point in pursuing Rosa, he
knew, for the only way he would obtain further information would be by violence and he had never raised
his hand to a woman in his life, though Melinda had
sorely tempted him on a number of occasions. He
returned to his desk and dropped his head into his
hands, mind racing. Not Mark. No ransom demand.
Not Mark. Charisse. Why? Why a stranger? Hardly

anyone knew of her existence in the city. No one knew of her connection with him and why would anyone resent that association enough to——? Realisation crashed in on him like a lightning bolt.

'Damn her eyes! Melinda!' he cried.

Instantly he was up and racing for his car, then embarked on an almost suicidal drive to the hotel where he knew she last stayed. An officious clerk attempted to tell him that, as the occupant of suite two hundred and twenty-three was out, he could not hand over the key. When Dace seized him by the shirt front, hauled him across the counter and demanded, 'The key. Now,' before hurling him back against the key-and-letter rack, the key was immediately handed over.

The suite was empty. It was more than empty, with the kind of emptiness that came only with hurried and complete departure. No clothes hung in the closets, no lacy frilled underwear drifted from chest drawers yanked out and thrown aside. The dressing-table was clear, only clean marks in the powder traces to show where pots and boxes had once stood. The bed was unmade, sheets and blankets in a crumpled heap that bespoke a tossed, sleepless night. 'Damn her eyes!' he reiterated, hands clenching and unclenching at his sides. He caught his image in the mirror, saw a monster with glaring eyes and wild, unkempt hair—and forced himself to slow down. Revenge was a dish best eaten cold. Melinda could wait.

At Reception he threw the key on to the shining counter-top. 'Suite two-two-three had checked out,' he told the still quivering clerk, and went out into the street, finally thinking logically. 'A posse,' he decided and a grim smile touched his mouth at the image of an old-time band of sworn-in marshals galloping across the plains after the outlaw gang. Only this time the pursuers would be businessmen and card-sharps and their quarry a very frightened little boy and a woman who, Dace had to admit, was an unknown quantity.

Her courage had been proved, but it would take more than guts alone to survive three days and more in the wilderness. He put down the rip-tide of despair that threatened to drag him under. There was work to be done—and fast.

Bill Johnson opened the door to his spacious penthouse apartment on Russian Hill and gave a wide, welcoming smile. 'Dace LaVelle in the flesh! Why, it must be over a year! How *are* you, man? Come on in and confess all!'

Dace followed the stocky, sandy-haired man into the homely, cluttered living-room and nodded to the slim young brunette draped over the couch, saying to the man, 'I don't know what they see in you, Bill, but I can't fault your taste.'

A low, husky laugh came from the woman as she uncoiled and went to link both arms through Bill's. 'I see a lost cause, Mr LaVelle, but thank you for the compliment. My husband has told me a great deal about you.'

Dace raised a placatory hand. 'I sincerely apologise, Mrs Johnson. I never believed that Bill *could* reform, but if anyone could do it, having met you, I believe you are the first capable of the miracle. Whether he is *worth* salvation I'm not so sure. That he is totally unworthy of you, ma'am, I have no doubts at all.'

Again that husky laugh. 'He's right, you *are* a charmer. However, I'm sure you didn't come here after so long away just to hear of this old reprobate's hard-learned conversion to monogamy. I have a million things to do; in fact I was going to meet an old friend whom I also have neglected.' With a smile she held out a slender hand. 'It has been a pleasure, Mr LaVelle. I shall be about two and a half, three hours, and if you are still here when I get back you are more than welcome to stay to dinner. I can actually cook too!' She turned, twined her arms about her husband's neck and kissed him in a way that caused Dace's toes to curl and steam to pump from his ears just watching her. Then, with a twinkling look, she said, 'Be good now!' and left.

A silence fell. Finally Dace said, 'I think I had better leave this to another time.'

'But you've only just got here! Hey! What's up, buddy? You've sure changed in the two seconds since Ruthy left.'

'Yes, I guess so. I came to ask a favour of you, but it isn't the kind of favour I would ask of a married man.'

Bill took Dace's arm and firmly drew him into the room. 'Look, Dace,' he said seriously, 'Ruthy is an angel in disguise, but I have known her three months; we have been married ten days. You and me, we go back to a week after you arrived in town. You literally saved my hide when those card-sharps set me up for a fall. I knew they were cheating and, instead of quitting, called them out. They would have killed me for sure if you hadn't stood beside me.'

Dace had to smile. 'And that was just the first time. You've an Irish temper, Bill, even if you aren't one.'

'So what is this favour? It's about time I started to pay you back for all the unasked favours you've done me. You know you've only to say the word.' As Dace weighed all odds he persuaded, 'A glass of bourbon-and-bourbon does wonders for loosening the tongue and tightening the resolve.'

'That I will accept, favour or no favour.' And when the drink was poured—a lethal half-tumblerful—Dace took a long draught, put it aside and began, 'I need men to ride with me to the Palo Duro area, possibly tonight.'

Bill sat down hard on the couch, but all he said was, 'You've got it.'

Dace felt the warmth deep inside. 'You haven't asked why.'

'Wanted you to know you have at least one man,

whatever the reason. *Now* you can tell me the why.'
And, at the end of it, the usual easygoing smile wiped
from his face. Dace had omitted Melinda's part in the
kidnapping—only spoke of 'someone who wants
revenge over a past incident'—and Bill asked only,
'When do we leave?'

'When I have four more: you were the first.'

'Thanks for that, old buddy. All right. I shall be
ready when you call back. Go see Mike Costas. The
crazy Greek is happier strumming on that bouzouki of
his than running his restaurant, so he'll be glad of a
hunting trip. Apart from which, he owes you, just as I
do.'

Dace frowned. 'I don't call in such debts. I was in
the right place at the right time, that's all.'

'Not just once either. After seeing those guys off
who were convincing him his restaurant needed protection, you went back again and again just to make sure
they got the message.'

A smile. 'I needed the exercise, but then, so does
that fat Greek. Very well. I'll call on him next.' They
shook hands strongly. 'I'll be back.'

From his meeting with Michael Costas, a meeting
loud with curses against 'the animals—worse than
animals' who had committed the crime, Dace left in a
more positive mood. 'Two,' he said quietly to himself.
'And two of the best.' For, in spite of his joking
reference to Michael's size, that great frame was
packed with the solid muscle of a one-time longshore-
man and the brilliant seascape eyes had a longer vision
than most. 'Now who?'

Cal, or Calico to most, had no surname that anyone
knew of; neither did he have a past before his arrival
in the City of Hills the previous spring, and anyone
looking into the dead, onyx-black eyes soon lost
interest in the question. Not only did Dace have no
interest in the man's past—he had the personal experience of one who wished for convenient anonymity in

his own—but he held a healthy respect for the way the man handled a deck of cards and throwing-knife—usually in that order.

At the door of the room on Geary Street Dace smiled as his soft double knock was followed by the rattle of a door chain being applied, then bolts drawn back top and bottom before the door opened a bare three inches. 'Nervous, Calico?'

The door closed, the chain was withdrawn, then the door opened wide. 'Just careful, Dace. What can I do for you?'

'It could be a social call.'

'You and me?' The white eyebrows rose a fraction in the alabaster-white face beneath the snow-white hair. Calico was not a true albino—hence the dark eyes—but all else ran true and the name Calico had been given to him by an irate poker player who had snarled, 'I don't cotton to losing, and I purely hate to lose to a damned calico cat.' The player had left the city, but the name remained, since Calico offered no other.

Dace entered that spartan room that held no ornaments, nor wall pictures, no personal memorabilia usual to a man who had been resident in the same city, in the same room, for almost two years, no touch of any luxury at all. If the man left it could be done by his simply walking out—with one exception. On the bedside table sat a black leather case. Inside were a pair of the finest Sheffield steel throwing-knives.

Dace's eyes swept the room, and the case, before meeting that emotionless regard. 'I need you and your toys both. My son and a woman I. . .think highly of have been taken into the Palo Duro wilderness. I don't know by whom or by how many. I have a map, but I don't know why I was given it unless the person I suspect had them taken there had last-minute misgivings or regrets, though it would be somewhat out of character. I have Bill Johnson, whom I believe you have played against, and another, a Greek named Costas. If I can, I will leave tonight, but I need at least another man after you.'

Neither man doubted Calico would be a part of the expedition and he accepted that by recommending, 'Johnny Rainwater is the best tracker in or out of the city. . .any city.'

'I don't know him.'

'I'll find him. He is part-Comanche, part-cougar, and part-hawk——' his lip curled '—and all mine! You might say we are blood brothers!'

'How?'

A flicker of a smile at the poor joke. 'We are both outcasts of society who were born fifty years too late. I pulled him out of a bar in Amarillo; he pulled me out of a knife fight that started out three to one in the City of the Angels—only I've never met one there—and we have been wary sidekicks ever since.'

'Like us?'

Again Dace witnessed that half-imagined lift of the mouth that was the most anyone had ever seen of Calico's rare humour. 'I would not equate nursing a man in almost indecent luxury for a full two months quite the same as rescuing one from a brawl, especially when that man's one idea was to die.'

'I had a spare room at the Gateway,' Dace shrugged, 'and don't figure an accident of birth warrants a man being kept beaten and drugged in a cage in a Barbary Coast cathouse for the amusement of the customers.' He turned to the door. 'Which reminds me of one other member of the party, and the last. I will leave your tame Comanche to you and we will all meet at my office at, say, eight-thirty.'

The last person to be called arrived first in the luxuriously carpeted office at the Gateway, his black suit and snowy shirt with its immaculately folded stock accentuating the rapier-thin frame that had earned him his nickname. Dr Samuel 'Slim' Parker was a once-prominent Washington surgeon who had suffered from that unforgivable vice—pity. The young, frightened girls who had come to him after an innocent surrender to an older man's seduction, or as the equally innocent victims of a cruel rape, had been received with gentle understanding. The unwanted fruits of that unwanted union had been gently, cleanly, competently and completely harvested. Such men made mistakes. Samuel's mistake was a senator's daughter who, under pressure, had revealed all. Dr Samuel Parker had been struck off and run out of town. Now he was reduced to serving as mentor, advisor, surrogate father and 'clean-up man' to the higher-class whorehouses in the city. But officially he did not exist and if caught plying his vocation would have found himself facing an impossibly high fine or a prison sentence.

Now he faced the man who had earned his respect as well as affection and accepted a proffered cheroot.

'I am no mountain man, Dace. I would be as lost in the Palo Duro as your boy and Miss Linton.'

For a second Dace's features appeared to age ten years and he did not attempt to hide the agony of mind reflected in the eyes that met the doctor's level regard. 'You are still the best doctor I know and the only one who could face. . .what might be up there. Even if we start tonight we won't reach the hut until late morning—their fourth day. After we find them, and I have to believe they are alive, every minute may count. Your presence may make the difference, literally, between life and death. I know you are a city man, Slim, but I am asking you to be there with me.'

'You know I'll come, Dace. I just pray I won't be needed.'

CHAPTER FIFTEEN

It was the fourth day and Tovey was near to death. Charisse had been forced to strip and cleanse that bloated frame through the sheer necessity of retaining her own sanity. He had eaten the pork and drank of the clear spring water and the gross body had done the rest by its natural function. When the stench became too much to bear Charisse had knotted a length of petticoat rubbed with sweet-smelling grasses over her mouth and gone to work. She could not know whether he felt pain but at the end of it at least he was clean. Twice she had stumbled from the shack to be physically sick, and now, as the weak morning sun penetrated the clearing, she sank to the ground, knees drawn up to her chin, arms clasped about her to stop the reactive trembling. She had done all that was possible; no human being deserved less.

Mark, too, was ill, his delicate constitution unable to fight the furnace-heat of the day and the icy cold nights. He did not want to eat and was running a fever. The large blue eyes implored her to 'magic' his father out of the air, but no word of complaint passed his lips and his courage tore at Charisse's heart. More than once she had been tempted to walk out again, carrying Mark or dragging him on a travois—the litter made of poles and branches that the Indians used to convey their belongings and the sick, or the pregnant women, across the plains.

She would have left Tovey, having done all that was possible, having to put Mark first, but then Mark's weakened condition and her own uncertainty of finding the right track in time left her confused and at odds with herself. Had she been alone there would have

194

been no problem: she would have prepared for weeks if necessary with the knowledge that she had the ability to survive, but Mark's presence complicated that choice.

The end of her strength came late that morning when, with a suddenness characteristic of the region, the sky clouded over and a torrential storm hit the rocky range. It passed as suddenly as it had begun, but the signal fire had been washed out and all the wood and brush within a five-mile radius was soaked and unuseable. Standing on that high peak, staring down at the steaming fire, Charisse felt the impotent fury and despair rise within her, coursing up through her stomach, shooting adrenalin through her veins, ripping a scream of rage against all of the gods, old and new, who had caused this, to tear out of her mouth in one long-drawn-out, 'No!'

And it was heard.

The six men in the high foothills less than an hour's ride away heard that one high, animal-like, yet human scream and it froze them in their tracks. Then quietly Dace said, 'She's alive!' and in his voice was the ragged knife-edge of agony. That cry had held a keening wail that was in its essence a primal rejection of all that was. To the man on the exhausted buckskin gelding it meant only one thing—his son was dead.

The man beside him gave a non-committal grunt. His leathery skin, shoulder-length hair and deep-set eyes told of his Indian blood. His white name was Johnny Rainwater. 'Coulda been a cat. You are hearing what you want to hear.'

'No.' But there was not the same certainty in his voice as Dace again studied the crumpled map. 'We will follow this until we reach the hut. If she. . .they aren't there, you'll take Bill and Mike, and you, Slim, and Cal will come with me. We'll quarter the area until we find them.' The gold-flecked jade eyes challenged each and every one of them to question a time limit or the possibility of failure.

Since the previous day, when Rosa had brought the map to Dace, he had neither rested nor eaten nor slept. He would have left that night but the Indian advised patience. Then, two hours out, after having abandoned the two cars and taken to hired horses, one of the animals had gone lame. Rather than slow down by riding double, or losing one man entirely, they had returned for another. And then that cry.

Dace drove his animal far past the point where any horse should have been capable of going, but, animal lover that he was, he would have killed the creature rather than lost another minute of time. He turned with a snarl as the Indian seized the reins, dragging both mounts to a halt, and for a second Dace's powerful hand clenched. No word was spoken, but, with a momentary tight closing of the eyes, Dace acknowledged, 'You're right. We'll go on foot from here.'

In the small clearing by the stream Charisse pulled off several small pieces of cold pork and set them down on the flat stone that served as a table. 'We will have to set more traps tonight: that's the end of him, or at least I don't think he'll be entirely fresh tomorrow, and I won't take the slightest chance. We're in enough trouble as it is.'

Mark sipped from the 'cup' of woven twigs lined with flat leaves that he had made under her instruction in one of her efforts to keep him amused, and nodded, but his fever-bright eyes showed no enthusiasm for the task. 'I don't think I'm very hungry.'

Putting down the dread that clutched at her heart, she forced a smile. 'You don't want to miss out on raiding the cage, do you? I tell you what; if we find a rabbit in it we will keep him alive this time.'

A spark of interest lit his face as obediently he

swallowed the morsel of meat she held to his lips.
'Why?'

No mention had been made that day, or the previous
one, of leaving the area and now Charisse put an end
to it. 'We are going home, Mark. I don't know how
long it will take, I don't know what food we will find
on the way, and I don't even know if we will succeed,
but tomorrow morning we will move out. If anything is
alive in the traps, well, live meat lasts longer than
dead, and if it *is* a rabbit and we can take it out without
having to kill it, then you can keep it as a pet. How
about that?'

He gave a dry chuckle which lifted her heart. 'Daddy
will be surprised. I go out for a puppy and come back
with a wild rabbit!'

He would have said more, but Charisse suddenly
clapped a hand over his mouth. 'Hush!' There it was
again. The faintest rattle of dislodged stones. 'Don't
move.' Slowly, warily, she rose to her feet, taking up a
sharp-edged rock in one hand—then felt all of the
strength drain out of her at the sound of human voices,
and one that commanded,

'Get moving, dammit! We're nearly there!'

He came around the bend of the trail and she could
not stir, nor make any sound. His bulk filled her world.
The five men crowding up behind him did not exist.

Mark raised himself on one elbow, struggling to rise.
'Daddy! Daddy!'

And Dace, unable to believe, afraid of breaking that
ephemeral dream that came from all longing and
therefore, surely, could not be real, just stood there
looking at them.

Her very life in her eyes, Charisse asked, 'Won't you
. . .stay to lunch?' And then, in a rush, was in his arms,
the breath crushed out of her, no tears, no laughter,
no joy, all emotion suspended, too deep for release.

Of the long journey back little would ever be said.
Tovey did not survive the rough trail down, even

though the four men it took to carry the great bulk on the makeshift stretcher did their best, against all better judgement or desire. Charisse had insisted and even *she* was not sure why she did so, only that she had suffered so much in keeping the man alive that he had become, in a strange way, a reason for keeping up her own strength. They buried him beneath a pile of rocks, but not one had the inclination to speak a Christian word over him, and no one looked back as they continued towards the setting sun.

Only later, much later, in her suite at the Gateway, with Mark warm and dry, sleeping deeply in the top-floor rooms overlooked by a nurse, did Charisse ask, 'If we had not been there?'

'I would have kept looking!'

'Until you found us?'

'If it took the rest of my life.'

She would not, dared not, take Dace's words literally, for that would challenge the very rules which had been lain down when—it seemed a lifetime ago—she had decreed, 'No commitments.' Instead she got up stiffly from the couch and stretched, then drew the silk dressing-gown tightly about her. 'I never realised how much these past days have taken out of me. Dace, I know it's all over, but. . .' She bit back the threatening tears, hating any weakness. 'I am afraid I'm really not up to playing pioneer woman, Indian-fighter, and society hostess all rolled into one. . .at least not tonight. If I don't cry quits on today I think I shall have the greatest difficulty in facing tomorrow. My mind and body are about to come out on strike in spite of all the efforts of the management.'

He came to stand before her and the backs of his fingers brushed her cheek. 'Leave that to me,' he said, and before she could protest he swept her up into his arms and carried her into the bedroom.

'No, Dace. Please, no,' she protested, but tiredly, no fight left in her. 'Not tonight!'

'Hush, woman! Trust me.' Gently he lowered her on to the turned-back sheets then pulled back the remainder. 'Now take that dressing-robe off and lie face down on the bed.'

'Dace!'

'You are as stiff as a board, every muscle is screaming, and there is no way that you'll be able to sleep if I leave you now.' And he disappeared into the bathroom.

Charisse obligingly lay on her stomach but only because it seemed the safest position and certainly the most comfortable. Her muscles tensed as she felt his weight beside her.

'Relax. Just relax.'

To her surprise she felt him take hold of one foot, his hands smooth and cool with the scented bath oil from her cabinet. Slowly, firmly, he massaged the foot and ankle, then moved to her calf with long, firm strokes, kneading and manipulating each until, in spite of her initial resistance, she found herself relaxing. 'Four days in the same clothes, wearing heavy boots, negotiating rocks—no wonder your muscles are tight. Come, now, Texas, give your body a chance; surrender it into my hands; let me help you.'

Her robe was whisked off and more oil was applied to his palms, then she felt those strong, supple fingers on the backs of her thighs, then over the soft mounds of her buttocks to her waist, and back to her knees, and up again, kneading and stroking, easing the taut muscles into bone-deep relaxation, soothing the tender flesh.

Charisse gave a sigh, unable to resist the insidious spell of those knowing hands. 'I feel as if I could sleep for a week.'

He gave a chuckle. 'Not exactly what I had in mind, but at least the time and the place is right.' He shifted, straddling her, and with a gasp she realised that he had removed his trousers, but already his fingers were moving strongly over her spine, manipulating, massaging, moving upwards to her shoulders and the tight neck muscles, stimulating, yet at the same time almost impersonal. Feeling more relaxed than at any time since her arrival in the city, she murmured, 'Thank you.'

'Don't thank me yet.' His weight left her briefly and when he returned, the scent telling her that he had replenished the jasmine oil on his hands, he commanded, 'Roll over.'

'But. . .'

His hand on her shoulder took the decision from her and she was turned on to her back, looking up into that pagan face. It was a small shock to realise that he was quite naked. A half-smile, then he moved to her feet, massaging as he had done before, working up to her knees. She watched him through half-closed eyes— the bronze torso, the broad shoulders and muscular, tanned arms. His features were remote, yet Charisse knew the very instant his touch changed from the soothing to the sensual, and found that she no longer wanted to resist.

The strong fingers rubbed gently at the taut thigh muscles, moving in almost mesmeric patterns on her skin. Without warning he looked up. Their eyes met. Slowly, yet with no hesitation, he eased apart the silken thighs. No words. No waste of his total absorption of her body. He moved forward in one fluid motion, covering her, his mouth coming down on hers. Those magic hands created a maelstrom of sensation and her hips arched to meet the following, driving thrust that she knew would come. Glorying in the unquestioned possession of her body, she allowed her mind to burst free of its chains and soar with all eagles beyond the clouds.

* * *

When Charisse awoke she stretched beneath the sheet with the total abandon and tiny smile of a satiated kitten. She did not expect him to be there but he had at least thought to leave her a note.

Mark had a nightmare and, as instructed, I was called. I have a busy day today, but will see you for a champagne breakfast tomorrow—Wednesday. D. P.S. You sleep beautifully.

Charisse's smile deepened. She had not been in the wilderness too long to have forgotten the days as they passed and she knew that tomorrow was Wednesday the eighteenth of April—exactly one month since her arrival in San Francisco and their first meeting. 'Happy almost anniversary,' she said softly. But the thought that she had spent so long away from home and, apart from the typically brief note from her father two weeks ago which demanded, 'I am still around, why aren't you?', had heard nothing made her realise how quickly the time had passed.

'Ralph *must* have returned by now, so why has he not contacted me?' she worried aloud.

Quickly she dressed in a linen tailored jacket over a soft, high-necked lace blouse, and a modern pleated skirt in a creamy beige that matched the jacket. Few men liked these new tailored suits, saying they reflected the masculine fashion adopted by the suffragettes, but in Charisse's eyes the suit was far more practical than a flowing, trained walking dress, especially in the area into which she intended going. If she was to have the entire day to herself she intended calling on Lee Rand to take her to the Mission District and again track down her elusive brother.

Lee had not attempted to contact Charisse during the past few days, assuming, as she had, that Ralph would make contact on arrival. George Davis had given Lee a more than substantial payment for his services before leaving for Australia so, in effect, Lee's job was done. Backing off, leaving the field, going on to another contract, made a great deal of sense, but, Lee reflected, he had never been long on brains. He had an outdated belief that, if one wanted something enough, somehow, somewhere, some time the goal would be achieved, the prayer answered. His mother had once told him, 'God always answers our prayers, son, but he doesn't always say yes.' And now Lee had to acknowledge that a very firm no had been given. Nevertheless, looking at the vision that smilingly stepped into his car late that morning, he could not help but reject that answer.

'I thought I wouldn't see you again,' he said.

Charisse lightly touched his arm, sending ripples of fire to his brain. 'I would never have left without saying goodbye; you've done so much for me.'

'All part of the job,' he lied.

'No, Lee, you have gone far beyond that and you know it. I have, to say the least, had a rough few days.' She felt very tired, as she had since her ordeal, the stress of her days in the canyon telling on her, eroding her natural resilience, and she leaned back against the leather seat.

'Want to tell me?'

'I think I must, since, in a way, it affects us all. . .my leaving the city, Dace's feelings for me and Melinda's jealousy.'

'Slow down, honey,' he ordered, eyes worried. 'Suppose you start at the beginning. The last time I saw you, you were flying high after having found Ralph. Now you look as if you haven't eaten or slept since. Is it LaVelle? Has he——?'

'No,' she answered quickly, seeing the whitening of his fists over the steering-wheel. 'It was Melinda and her insane jealousy, and the awful thing about it is that in all probability she had no cause. Dace has, after all, made love to other women and still returned to her.'

Lee felt the blow to his stomach as if he had been hit

by a freight train, but nothing of his personal agony was reflected in the gently probing voice that suggested, 'Suppose you tell me, baby doll? Tell me everything, slowly, from the top.'

And she did, omitting nothing. . .almost nothing. She did not tell him of the previous night, but knew that she did not have to. 'So I *must* leave, don't you see?' she finished. 'I can't take any more. I *won't*! I must go home to a place I can cope with, to people I understand. But, Lee, I do still need your help one more time. Ralph never answered my note and I'm certain he must have returned by now. Would you take me back to his apartment and, if he isn't there, perhaps we could look around a little?'

'My pleasure.' Any moment in her company was pure masochism, but he could not tell her that, and he was almost relieved when they found the apartment empty, though the landlord advised them,

'Doc Leonard *was* here. Got back three days ago. Guess he was just too busy to answer your note, ma'am.'

Charisse frowned. 'No, he wouldn't do that. . .at least. . .not the Ralph I knew.' She turned to the detective with a misty, hard-won smile that constricted his throat. 'Surely he has forgiven Father after all these years? Surely he wouldn't choose *not* to meet me?'

Lee curled a reassuring hand over her shoulder. 'We'll know when we find him. Come on, we'll take a drive around and return here later this afternoon. The man must eat some time and, from the little I know of him and the evidence here, he doesn't go to fancy restaurants.'

'Thank you, Lee. Thanks for your faith, too. I have come to rely so much on you.'

'Nice thought. Wish it were habit-forming.' Then, seeing her face, he added, 'Sorry. Let's go.'

They left the dilapidated tenement and drove around the streets until past lunchtime, when Lee called a halt.

'We aren't even seeing straight. I am taking you to lunch and we can continue later.'

Driving a few blocks north to Union Square, they found a tiny, immaculately presented restaurant where the food, though plain, was delectable and the atmosphere intimate. 'Relax,' ordered Lee gently. 'Put the ordeal you have been through behind you and, if it will make you feel better, tell me what you will do when you get home. . .if it *is* home now.'

Over the main course of succulent minted lamb— 'Not pork, please!'—crispy baked potatoes and fresh peas, Charisse told him of the life she once had and would have again at home, now a home that seemed an alien world, a million miles away.

'I knew that I could survive out there, thanks to my *past* life,' she told him, 'but I don't know whether I want that for my *future* life. I love this city, Lee. I love it, yet I *must* return home.'

'It loves you.' Both knew what he meant.

She touched his hand with one finger. 'You have been a good friend.' Both knew what she meant.

'Let's go back and find that brother of yours.'

Ralph, however, was still as elusive as the Scarlet Pimpernel, and as dusk fell Charisse brought their wanderings to a halt. 'I'm going to stay at the apartment until he *does* arrive. There is a bed there if he doesn't get in until morning, but I *will* see him, Lee. I *have* to. He has to change and wash some time. If he doesn't come to me, I must go to him. We have been apart for too long.' Belatedly she remembered the champagne breakfast. 'One more favour, Lee, and I hate to ask this of you, but there's no other way. Will you tell Dace—or send someone to do so—that I may not be able to keep our appointment? If you tell him where I am and what I am doing he will understand, I know.' She read the hurt in his eyes. 'I am sorry.'

He forced a smile. 'Me too, but of course I will tell him.' Then, to ease her discomfort, he said lightly,

'Hey, I'm not jealous. . . . I just hate the guy!' and saw her answering smile.

At Ralph's apartment Charisse bade Lee goodnight with, 'You know where I am. I'll call you in the morning, I promise,' and settled in the armchair to wait. 'Where are you, brother mine?' she asked, then, musingly, '*Who* are you now? Will we even *know* each other, or will we be strangers when we meet?' Sudden tears pricked her eyes. Home seemed so very far away.

CHAPTER SIXTEEN

HALFWAY between dreaming and waking a distant rumble, like thunder rolling across the bay from the north-west, teased at Charisse's senses. She frowned, burrowing deeper into the armchair with a murmur of objection, then, as that strange, almost imagined noise gathered in intensity, came awake with a start. Initially disorientated, still half asleep, she wondered aloud, 'Where am I?' then, as she regained full consciousness, 'Ralph! Of course. Not back yet?' and glanced at the clock on the mantelshelf. 'Twelve past five? What an uncivilised——'

Suddenly the floor rocked beneath her feet so violently that she was thrown out of the chair. The mantelclock slid sideways and fell to the floor, the round dining table tipped, spilling its books and papers, as well as the cup, saucer and jug which she had used to make coffee. Then, just as suddenly, the tremor passed, leaving an eerie silence behind. Charisse pulled herself to her feet and bent to pick up the broken cup and replace the clock, drawing a deep, shaky breath, remembering, Lee said I would have to get used to these, but this could become expensive and——

The crash that next hit the building came without warning, as if a cannon-ball had smashed through the outside wall, driving her to her knees. This time the roar was deafening—as of a hundred hungry lions— overriding the screams and cries from the other apartments and the terrified barks and howls from dogs in the street below and the distant whinnying of panic-stricken horses. The table rolled across the floor as the room tilted, its contents swept sideways as if with a giant hand, littering the floor with smashed china and

206

glass, books and papers—and Charisse. A crack appeared over the fireplace and, as she threw herself sideways in terror, scrabbling crablike for safety, that wall buckled and the chimney-breast crashed inwards, leaving a gaping hole.

On and on it went, the shock waves heaving her back and forth, while strike waves dragged her sideways, helpless as a toy beneath the onslaught. She seized a chair. It was dragged from her grasp, only to be hurled back, dealing a numbing blow to her shoulder. Half conscious, she was only aware that somehow she must get out, traverse the two flights of stairs down, reach the front door and—and with a crash of glass the bay window imploded, splintering into a thousand tiny, lethal shards. 'Dace!'

The Gateway rocked on its foundations, bringing people upright in their beds, crying out, only half convinced that this was not a nightmare. Dace knew it was not. Within a minute of that initial thirty-second tremor he was half dressed and out of his room, on his way to the still sleeping Mark. Gathering the sleepily protesting child up, he ordered quietly, 'Come on, son; we have to get dressed and out of here.'

He kept his own fear out of his voice and, even when the boy objected, 'It's only a silly shaker! I'm tired!' he could still retain his calm and patience.

'I don't think so, Mark; not this time.'

And then that second blow slammed into the hotel and both were thrown across the room to end up in a heap by the massive oak wardrobe. Dace saw it tip sideways, backwards, and sideways again, and just in time dragged Mark clear as it was hurled forward to crash inches from them. Covering Mark with his body, Dace crawled into the space between the fallen wardrobe and wall, where the wooden base had jammed across a corner. For the moment they were safe.

The crazy gyrations of the room ceased. The lamps,

toys, chairs, clothing littered the floor and as they
stepped clear and Dace swung a trembling Mark into
his arms, carrying him into the living-room, they saw
that the same chaos reigned there. The chandelier had
fallen on to the beautiful onyx table, smashing both
beyond repair. 'But at least we are alive and
unharmed,' Dace observed quietly and it emerged as a
prayer. 'Now, let's get dressed and downstairs.'

He went to the window as Mark scrabbled into his
clothing and looked out to the east towards Chinatown
and then across to Market Street. His face greyed. 'Oh,
dear God!' In long strides he reached Mark, swept him
up and ran for the door.

Taking the stairs two at a time—unable, unwilling to
help those screaming in elevators trapped between
floors—they reached the crowded confusion of the
foyer before he *heard* the evidence his eyes had already
fed him. A man cried, 'Fire!'

'Where are we going, Daddy?' panicked Mark,
catching the terror of those about him, clinging to his
father's neck in a stranglehold as Dace pushed through
the crowd to find the manager.

'We are going to Charisse, but first I must issue
orders for the evacuation and rescue work.'

They found the manager, bruised but otherwise
unhurt, attempting to calm a woman and child, both
covered in blood from splintered glass, and Dace issued
brief, succinct orders before turning away.

Mark had been put down and, as he saw his father
turn, cried, 'Don't leave me!'

Dace took time to quell his own agony of mind and
bent to hug the boy close for a moment. 'I wouldn't
leave you, son. Now let's find Charisse.'

'But the hotel, Daddy. I saw smoke.'

Dace paused to throw a long, sweeping look about
him. 'I must take a gamble on it being here when we
get back,' he decided. But this time Lady Luck was not
at his shoulder and the Gateway, won by an ace in the

hole, was to be lost by a hole in the ground—or, more precisely, a two-hundred-and-seventy-mile-long crack in the earth called the San Andreas Fault.

A spark from a downed electric cable, a lighted candelabrum overturned, a student burning the midnight oil, people returning from the theatre or from hearing Caruso sing and lighting gas lamps or candles for a late, late supper, gas from fractured gas mains—in the Gateway, staff already up and preparing for an early morning breakfast, coals from the huge range falling on to hot spilled fat. That was all it took. That one candle, that one spark—repeated a hundred times throughout a city still staggering beneath the great quake.

Within two hours the fireball had ripped through the scene like a monster of the Last Holocaust, feeding on the wooden buildings of Chinatown, gulping in the smaller fires, fanned by the stiff morning breeze into a single inferno. It engulfed Market Street, already shaken to pieces by the quake, and swept on to the devastated mean streets south of Market and the Mission District. It was no respecter of wealth, gutting the great villas of Stanford and Hopkins on Nob Hill, finishing off the imposing City Hall—now a monstrous pile of rubble even before completion—and the Gateway.

The thirty-eight strong horse-drawn fire-engines never stood a chance, even had the quake not fractured the water-mains, leaving them only the sea and a few artesian wells. They tried dynamiting concrete corridors, but, laid by inexperienced laymen, they exploded outwards and caused more fires. They threw up barriers of steel and sandbags. It melted them as if they had never been. Before noon the monster was out of control.

'Will we find her, Daddy?' Mark questioned, clutching tightly at his father's arm, fighting back tears.

'We'll find her,' Dace promised him, but with an assurance he himself was far from feeling, and, for one of the very few occasions in his life, found himself praying, 'Lord, don't let it be. Let me see her one more time, walking down any street, framed in any doorway with the light making a halo of her hair. Let me see those eyes—those rare, catlike, wonderful eyes, softer even than bayou mist—let me see them smiling again for me alone.'

A man stumbled against him, breaking the vision, and another pushed past, staggering beneath the weight of a huge over-filled box, snarling, 'Out of my way!'

Dace swallowed hard and squared his shoulders; this was no time for either regrets or prayers. She must have gone to find her brother, he decided. Either that or she was with Rand at some all-night club, or coming back from *Carmen* at the Opera House on Mission. No, she wouldn't do that. Oh, why was I out last night? She might have left me a note. I didn't even bother to check my mail or ask at the desk. Why should I? We were meeting for breakfast!

Indecision halted him in his tracks. In a city of forty-nine square miles, inhabited by over three hundred and forty thousand people, where did one begin to look for one woman? She had spent a month, with professional help, looking for her brother, and the city had been whole then. Now, out of this devastation, with fires raging over a third of the city and wiping out landmarks as if they had never been, he had to find someone who might possibly be hurt—or even buried beneath a pile of rubble like that which they were passing. 'No!' he denied aloud. 'No, I won't believe she isn't safe! Somewhere out there she is safe and unharmed. She *has* to be!'

Long before, Charisse had clambered down the broken staircase and, with the other tenants, some still in nightwear, crying or grim-faced, spilled on to the street. There, a scene of total devastation greeted her: people milling around confusedly, from a neighbouring building a woman screaming to passers-by to help her dig her child out of the ruins. Charisse ran to help, but then, moments later when the child was discovered—a pitiful, battered corpse—her mind screamed, Mark! Stumbling and falling down the pitted, crumpled street, over piles of masonry and twisted girders, she headed towards Nob Hill.

Then, as if by a miracle, she heard her name called and spun about. 'Lee!'

'Charisse! Oh, thank the Lord! You're alive!' He crushed her to him, kissing her frantically, then pulled away, eyes holding all the horrors of his search. 'I couldn't sleep for thinking of you. I went to the office and tried to work, then when that failed I tried to lose myself in a bottle in a bar on Sacramento. I was there when all hell broke loose.'

'I must get to the hotel, Lee.'

His jaw tightened. 'The Gateway is in flames.' Then, at her cry, he reassured her, 'No, they're OK. The manager was helping some people trapped in there. He said Dace and Mark left before the fire got under way. All he heard Dace say when denying him help was "I've got to find her", so I guess, like me, Dace had only one person on his mind. I left Ralph's address at Reception since he was out yesterday, so I guess he is on his way.'

Charisse leaned weakly against him. 'Oh, Lee, I was so scared. Ralph didn't return. We must find him, Lee. Now that I know Dace and Mark are all right I must find Ralph. I had already told Dace where Ralph lived after we first came here, so, yes, he may well be coming for me, but I can't take a chance on missing Ralph.'

'He'll have his hands full, that's for sure. Look, why don't I look for Ralph and you wait here in case Dace turns up? Otherwise you stand a chance of missing both of them.' He turned away from the gratitude in

her eyes. 'Do what you can in the immediate area—
heaven knows, there's enough!'

Charisse looked about her. Already the inhabitants
of the ruined tenements were gathering their lives
together. Some still dug in the wreckage of the three
collapsed buildings in that block and one group fought
a fire at the end house, forming a bucket chain. Others,
even exchanging a joke or two, had begun to cook
their breakfast over makeshift stoves in the street,
sharing what little they had with others.

'I'll report back in an hour,' Lee said. 'Don't stray
far.' He went to turn away but she stopped him.

'Lee. . .'

'Yes?'

'I am glad you found me.' She walked up to him
and, with only the slightest hesitation, kissed him full
on the mouth, then stepped back.

He gave that familiar lop-sided smile. 'That felt like
goodbye.'

'I am sorry.'

'Me, too, believe me.' His hand came up and with
one thumb he traced her lower lip. 'You know, when
this is all over, I figure I'll start up a missing persons
bureau. I could make a fortune.'

'Not you. If the client couldn't pay, you would do it
for love anyway.'

Both knew they were wasting precious moments.
Both knew that they might never get another chance.
Finally it was Lee who said, 'Take care. I'll be back.'
He took her face between his hands and kissed her,
hard, a heartbroken kiss out of time, then released her
and deliberately turned away, striding purposefully
down the street.

'Oh, Lee, I *am* sorry!' But then, drawing a deep,
shaky breath, Charisse looked about her. Where to
start? She approached a group pulling masonry from
an overturned car, but spun away, stomach heaving,
from the objects—surely not human—revealed there.

A distant cry for help took her into a side-street and she found herself alone. Little damage had been done here and most of the rescue and fire-fighting efforts were being concentrated on the main street behind her. Her eyes scanned the dusty dimness and near the end she saw a hansom cab on its side. Everything in her told her to flee, but then again came that cry, fainter now, a woman sobbing, 'Help me! Is anyone there? Help me, please!' Quickly, before her rubbery limbs refused to obey orders, Charisse hurried forward.

The horse was dead, a broken neck by all appearances, and the driver, too, his body thrown clear and crumpled against the near wall. One side of the roadway had heaved a foot higher than the other and an open-fronted shop had been torn apart, its provisions scattered over the street. All this registered only fleetingly as Charisse clambered over the wreckage and peered down into the depths of the vehicle, then pulled back with a start of disbelief. 'Melinda!'

The woman's eyes were glazed with shock and pain, the contorted features chalky white, yet, when recognition washed over her, the full lips twisted into the parody of a smile. 'Of all the people in the city, it had to be you.'

For one terrible split second Charisse was tempted to turn away and Melinda saw that in her eyes.

Again that ghastly twist of the lips. 'I wouldn't blame you,' she said, pain lacing her dry tones. 'Poetic justice. I hire two thugs to leave you on Palo Duro; you leave me trapped here.' A spasm constricted her face, but then those brilliant sky-blue eyes were clear again. 'We both lose, Charisse. I never knew Mark was with you. Sending the map back to Dace only salved my conscience over the boy; I never had any regarding you. There! Does that make it easier for you to walk away, or don't you have the guts to commit murder?'

There had never really been any decision to make.

'Shut up, Melinda, and tell me where you're hurt. Can I get you out, or will I need help?'

Something akin to respect flickered in the woman's eyes. 'You *are* a fool! No, you can't get me out alone. My right leg is trapped below the knee.' She bit her lip. 'It's certainly broken and I don't want to think how badly.'

'Damn!' Charisse cursed, muttering to herself. 'Oh, Ralph, where are you now?'

'A block and a half away,' provided Melinda and, at the other's wide-eyed stare, 'I was on my way to see you when the quake hit. I have been staying with the sister of the man I left Dace for—fool that I was—and your brother is tending their little girl. He was with her when I left, and had been for most of the night. I never told him I knew. I was going to the Gateway before anyone was about. . .before Dace was up.'

Charisse could hardly assimilate all that she was being told, hardly believe. 'Why?' That at least she could fasten on to.

Melinda again bit into her lip, drawing blood, as the knife-like agony shot through her. 'You survived the canyons. If you had your brother you would leave. . . leave Dace to me.'

Seeing the perspiration break out on the ghost-white features, Charisse put all else aside. 'Where is my brother? He can bring something for the pain and we will both get you out.'

Unable to fight any longer, Melinda gave her the address, saying only, 'If you change your mind it would just make us quits.' But already the other had left and with a sigh she rested her head against the carriage-side. For the very first time in her life Melinda prayed—and meant it.

The devastation grew and, as Charisse rounded the corner, she gave a cry. The house to which Melinda had directed her did not exist and the ground floor of the one next to it was on fire, though being brought under control by the local inhabitants with shovels and blankets beating at it. 'No!' she denied, refusing to surrender to the ball of black despair that clutched at her throat. The scream of denial welled up in her as it had in the wilderness. 'Ralph!' Heads turned. Suddenly, a voice cried, 'Charley!'

Only one person in the whole world had ever called her Charley. She spun in the willing suspension of disbelief, heart pounding, then disbelieving no more. How could she ever have doubted she would recognise him? He was bone-tired, gaunt with tiredness, hollow-eyed, cavernous-featured, but that ascetic beauty radiated from him like a beacon fire. 'You look awful!'

He laughed and the sound was pure music. 'What in heaven's name are you doing in San Francisco?'

'Didn't you. . .? My note!' But by this time she had reached him and only then realised that the bundled blanket he carried so tenderly was a child of around four or five with wide, frightened eyes and long black hair tangled about her shoulders. 'It will keep. Who is she?'

'Her name is Lucy Verucci.' He glanced back at the house from which he had just emerged. 'Both parents are gone. I've been fighting to save the mother. They were friends more than patients.' His face registered the pain of parting. 'Lucy is all right, a few minor lacerations and bruises. She is my responsibility now.'

'Ours. But Ralph, I need you desperately. There is a woman trapped in a cab a block and a half from here. She doesn't think I'll be back. Her leg is broken, possibly crushed. Please hurry.' She took his arm, urging him to follow her. 'I should hate her, I have every reason to, but I can't, even though she tried to kill me. Oh, I know I'm not making sense, but I will tell you everything later.'

He recognised the underlying hysteria and soothed, 'It will be all right, Charley. I promise you I'll do all I can. Don't worry.' He knew that after such a traumatic experience—the loss of a loved one, a disaster, an accident that one had survived—the survivors wanted to talk. Usually it was senseless, a repetition of how they had escaped, re-living each second and spreading it into hours—as it had seemed at the time. Always it was necessary: only the stoics collapsed at a later date.

They reached the cab to find Melinda unconscious, but as soon as Ralph began climbing in she cried out in pain and awoke. Recognition was mutual. 'Mrs LaVelle!'

'Hello, Dr Ralph.'

The child Lucy had been handed to Charisse. 'Keep her warm and calm, especially calm. She has consumption and I don't want her to cough.' His eyes had met hers. 'It's lethally contagious, Charley, even though it's still in its earliest stages.'

'*You* have been treating her.'

'I am different.'

'So am I, Ralph,' she said, and his smile warmed her. 'I will take her back to your apartment, or at least where it was. There is a man, Lee Rand, a detective I hired to find you. He is looking for you now, but said he would check back to the apartment every hour.'

'We could use him.'

Lee was already combing the area when Charisse returned and the moment he saw her ran to take Lucy from her arms. 'I thought I had lost you. Who do we have here?'

Charisse stroked back the dark, curly hair from the little girl's forehead. 'I don't think she can speak, but it could just be that she's in shock. Her name is Lucy. Both parents are gone. She is mine now, mine and Ralph's. I have found him, Lee.' The tears started but she blinked them back quickly. 'Right now we need you. I'll explain as we go.'

Lee hefted the girl to lie across his chest and over one shoulder. She gave a little cough and immediately Charisse pulled the blanket over her mouth. 'Oh,

please don't cough, love, not now.' She realised that
she had handed the child to Lee without thinking and
said, 'I'll take her, Lee. She isn't all that heavy. You
can hurry ahead; it's just down that street. I'll follow
on.'

Without relinquishing his burden, he gave her a
searching look. 'How sick *is* she?'

For the first time since Ralph had appeared with the
child, Lucy spoke, her voice heavily accented with a
soft Italian lisp. 'I am five years old and Dr Ralph
promised I am not going to die if I try not to cough.'

'Consumption?'

Charisse nodded, seeing the flicker of fear bravely
quenched. 'Ralph said that it was in its earliest stages.
I can take her now.' To the girl she said, 'You aren't
going to die, Lucy, not if Dr Ralph promised you. I
have known him for all of my life and have never
known him to break a promise.'

'The faster we get her somewhere warm and dry, the
better. Let's not waste time.' And, gently shifting Lucy
to a more comfortable position that would put no strain
on her lungs, he purposefully strode ahead.

When they reached the cab Ralph was already inside
and at work, with Melinda under heavy sedation, the
lovely features composed. The skirt of her dress had
been ripped apart to expose the trapped leg and even
as Lee climbed into the cab Ralph began issuing quiet,
confident orders.

'Multiple fractures. Don't know whether we can save
it. I need a box-splint, the whole thing encased, but
first we get her out. Lee, pull there. Right. Easy. Lift.
So. Good man!'

Nevertheless, it took almost twenty minutes before
the unconscious woman lay on the pavement, wrapped
in a blanket that had covered Lucy, her leg stiffly
wrapped. Only once had she briefly regained consciousness, when, with a final pull, Ralph had slid the
shattered limb clear; then her eyes had flown open and

she had given a piercing shriek of agony, before immediately losing consciousness again.

Lee's lips tightened. 'There was an improvised hospital unit I passed over on Fifth and Mint. The Old Mint has survived. We can take her there. She may not make it further.'

Ralph nodded agreement. 'It's at times like this I wish I was a qualified surgeon. I will stay with her for as long as possible, but there's little I can do but assist.' He hesitated. 'It would be best if Lucy——'

'She will stay with me, Ralph,' Charisse had already decided to keep the child for as long as she was allowed to. 'There must be hundreds of lost and orphaned children wandering the city; Lucy isn't going to be one of them.'

Lee bestowed one of his lop-sided grins on the little girl, almost bringing a response. 'We should call her Lucky, not Lucy.'

'So be it,' laughed Ralph. 'She is indeed. All right; let's go. Careful how you lift her, Lee, you've got the heavier end.'

Lee curled both hands around the cocoon-like blanket at Melinda's head and took up the strain, even by that movement eliciting a whimper from the still half-conscious woman. 'I would sooner drop the heavy end than the already broken end,' he muttered.

The journey to the large hall, once a mission hall dispensing soup and bread to the poor and now converted to an improvised medical centre, seemed interminable, but finally they joined the throng awaiting attention. Leaving them for a moment, Ralph went immediately to speak urgently to the doctor who was obviously in charge, a tall, spare-framed man with tired eyes and the front of his white coat daubed with blood. At once the surgeon left the deep gash he had been stitching, handing the task to his assistant, and accompanied Ralph back.

One look at the leg and he shook his head. 'I can

patch it, Doctor, but, as good a surgeon as I am, this
will need specialist attention if she isn't to lose it.
Either way, I'm going to have to remove a fair amount
of that splintered bone and she will always have one
leg shorter by some, even replacing where we can.
Frankly the best I can advise is that we take it off
straight away. It will be a lot simpler and faster and a
durn sight less painful in the long run, and she may end
up having to have it off anyway.'

'No!' Charisse cried, coming forward. 'You mustn't!
It would kill her!'

'Now, now, miss,' he smiled. 'This isn't the Dark
Ages. Amputations, even in these God-awful circum-
stances, aren't the Russian roulette they used to be.
She will live, I guarantee it.'

Charisse looked down at her arch-enemy, at the
beautiful, sultry features, the full mouth, and down
over the ripe breasts, tiny waist, and wide, curvacious
hips to the mess beneath. It would be so easy! But
could she live with herself, knowing?

'No, sir,' she denied firmly. 'Melinda is not the kind
of woman who could stand being a cripple with one
leg; she would sooner be dead. Do what you have to
to save both her life *and* the leg and when this horror
is over she can be sent to whatever specialist is necessary.' She drew in a deep breath. 'Her. . .ex-husband
will pay all expenses.'

Lee put a hand on her arm. 'Do you think so,
Charisse. . .knowing what you know? Do you really
think so?'

'I know so. She has won, Lee. He loved her once
and now she will need him for the rest of her life.'

For a moment there was silence—save for the sound
of a heart cracking, just a little—then the surgeon
agreed, 'Very well. Doctor, I shall need you,' and the
step was taken.

'I must go back, Lee,' Charisse decided, not wanting

to stay to see the mutilation, however constructive, of that lovely body. 'Dace will still be looking for me.'

'I'll come with you.'

'No, it's all right. You can be of far more use here.'

'I'm no doctor, nor have I the stomach for this. I've seen my fair share of blood in my day, but never like this carnage.' He took her arm and they went back to the devastation of the streets.

There was no conversation between them, the bravery and resilience of those about them filling their hearts too full for words. A rescue squad, one of many, worked to lift a giant steel girder from a pile of masonry under which cries could be heard. One man called, 'Hey, fella, give a hand here!'

Lee hesitated, but Charisse gave him a quick smile. 'You have to, Lee. You're needed far more here than by my side. Stay with them. I know the way back. Don't worry about me.'

'I shall always worry about you. Are you certain?'

'Go ahead. I will see you later, but I must be where Dace expects me to be.'

A half-smile. 'Of course.' He turned towards the group, then halted and said over his shoulder, 'One day I will stop walking away from you.'

She raised a smile. 'Maybe one day we'll both get to where we're going. Take care,' she told him, softly finishing, 'dearest friend.'

CHAPTER SEVENTEEN

CHARISSE knew that Dace would come. Lee had told her he was looking for her. It was simply a matter of time. As it had been at the hut. As it had been for all of her life, it seemed. Waiting for Dace. Certain that he would come. And then, once again, he was there. There was the width of the street between them, but Charisse felt that it could have been a hundred miles, for now there was Melinda.

Again it was Mark who cried out, 'There she is! Charisse!' and ran forward, flinging his arms about her waist.

For a long moment she allowed herself the joy of that contact, only realising at that instant just how very much he meant to her. She had put Lucy down several minutes before, unable to take the child's weight any longer, and it was only when Lucy pulled back on Charisse's hand that it broke the spell.

Dace saw the white-gold head bend to kiss his son's dark hair, light against dark, and felt a catch in his throat. He had always been a man who had taken what he wanted from life—from women. If it did not come easy—though generally it did—then the challenge made it all the more interesting. It had been that way with Charisse at first, he admitted over the pounding of his heart, but no longer. Somehow, even though she had given herself so completely, it was not enough. *You are a fool, LaVelle!* he remonstrated within himself, unable to take that first step towards her. *What do you want? Body* and *soul?*

It came to him then like a physical blow to the abdomen. That was exactly what he *did* want, what he had wanted since Muir Woods, and never acknowledged. Something akin to fear washed over him. He had walked wide circles around love and now it had hit him square between the eyes. His heart, stomach, lungs, every nerve and fibre in his body, felt as if it had been steamrollered.

'Dace?'

Slowly he adjusted his vision. Those slightly elongated cat's eyes, bayou mist, filled now with concern, two feet away—and he had not even been aware of her crossing the street! 'Your. . .eyes will always. . .be much too large for your face.'

'Oh, Dace!' She had forgotten to breathe, looking up at him, but knew that this was neither the time nor the place to fling herself into his arms—arms that still hung helplessly at his sides. Blinking back threatening tears, she pulled Lucy forward. 'This is Lucy Verucci, Dace,' she said, and saw the slight frown draw in his brows as the change of mood and the name disorientated him. 'We call her Lucky. She is going to stay with me, with Father and me, until we can track down one of her family who wants her. Ralph is her doctor. She needs a warm and dry place and may get well in Texas. She no longer has any parents.' She spoke softly, but quickly, forcing that strange, dazed look from his eyes. 'We found Melinda, too. She is badly hurt. Her leg. Ralph is with her now at the medical unit near the Mint.'

Dace shook the cobwebs from his mind and came instantly awake. 'Melinda? Hurt? How?'

Charisse swallowed hard. So that was what it took to bring life into those strangely remote features that had not even reacted to the sight of her! 'Ralph will explain when you get there.' She swayed a little, the events of the morning taking their toll, and silently prayed, Don't let me faint now! and with an effort steadied herself. 'I must get these children to a hotel. I'm sorry, so very sorry about the Gateway, Dace. Lee told me. He passed it on his way to meet me. But I must rest. We must all rest. Take stock.' Somehow the bone-deep weariness that was far more mental than physical prevented her stringing coherent sentences together and the tears were not too far distant.

'Charisse——'

'No. I'm fine.' From the deep recesses of her mind she remembered her father quoting from Rudyard Kipling's 'If', a poem she had been raised on. Two pieces seemed entirely appropriate to the occasion. 'If you can force your heart and nerve and sinew To serve your turn long after they are gone. . .' and 'Or watch the things you gave your life to, broken, And stoop and build 'em up with worn-out tools. . .' 'I'm fine,' she repeated.

Dace saw the courage and the battle for strength in that slender frame and wanted to sweep her up in a crushing embrace, but knew that she might well collapse completely if he did so, and instead reached out to take her firmly by the upper arm. 'You are not fine, far from it, and I should guess that any hotel not caved-in or gutted would be filled to overflowing. We'll go to George Davis's old place and if that has gone then I will find another, but I am not leaving you alone, not again.' And with a half-smile he added, 'You can't be trusted out in the streets alone: things happen around you. And now look what you've done to a perfectly respectable city!'

Charisse gave a dry laugh, tempted beyond belief. Every muscle was screaming, every nerve shredded, but still she would have refused had not Lucy given a little cough and those frightened eyes swung up to her face in mute plea. 'No, don't cough, baby. Try to stay calm. Breathe lightly now. Light as air.' Without looking up at Dace, she said, 'It's the dust from the rubble, and the smoke. Very well; if you think the new owner will take us in we will gladly try it, but it's such a long walk for the children, especially Lucy. Is there any way we can find a conveyance—even an old

wheelbarrow?' She managed a smile. 'I'm afraid I'm
not half as good surviving in a city as in the wild.'

Mark gave her hand a reassuring squeeze. 'At least
you don't have to trap rabbits here; you just go into a
shop and buy one.'

The tinkle of breaking glass at the end of the street,
followed by shouts and laughter, strengthened Dace's
resolve to get them to safety with all speed. 'Some just
take what they want,' he stated grimly. 'Let's get out
of here. The army will put the city under martial law,
but the looting is only the beginning when law and
order breaks down. You will all be a lot safer inside.
I'll see what I can do about some transport on the way,
but I think our first priority is to get clear of this
particular area: you don't find the *crème de la crème* of
society here.'

'And Melinda?' Immediately Charisse regretted the
question as his face took on a carefully neutral
expression.

'She is being taken care of. Our meeting can wait.'
Bending, he asked Lucy, 'Would you like a piggyback?'
and, at her shy nod, said, 'Well, jump aboard, then.'

Although only two years younger than Mark, she
weighed half as much and Dace reflected that there
must be hundreds like her, raised in virtual poverty
with inadequate diet and no chance of improving their
lot. Thanks to a cruel twist of fate Lucy Verucci had
been given that chance. He remembered the name
now. Tonio Verucci, the piano player, uncle to this
sick, dying scrap of humanity clinging to his back.
What a small world! He gave a mirthless laugh and, at
Charisse's enquiring glance, said, 'I could probably
make your Lee Rand a very wealthy man in tracking
down Lucy's only relative, Tonio Verucci, who, as you
undoubtedly know by now, is her uncle, and last heard
of in New York with my ex-wife. But I'm not going to.
If a month or two in Texas cures her then she can come

back here. She is a pretty scrap and quieter than most. Mark needs a companion.'

Mark looked doubtful. 'I would sooner have a puppy.'

Dace laughed, shifting Lucy's weight so that he could reach to rumple his son's hair. 'You'll have your puppy; I promised, didn't I? But if. . .*when* Lucky gets better I'm sure she wouldn't mind helping you to take care of him.'

In his ear Lucy whispered, 'Yes, please!'

'All right,' decided Mark magnanimously. 'But I shall be in charge!'

Charisse stared up at the man beside her. 'You are a strange one, Dace LaVelle. I don't think anyone, however long they knew you, could anticipate what you are going to do next.'

The deep eyes gleamed. 'That's what makes me a good poker player.' They had reached the end of the block and, turning into the next street, were confronted by a sight that caused Charisse to clutch at Dace's arm, her blood running cold. Dace let out a soft curse beneath his breath.

Four youths were terrorising a grocer who had attempted to load what merchandise was left from his collapsed shop on to a small cart. The pony between the shafts was standing in quivering terror, a coat thrown over its head and the teenager hanging from the reins preventing all movement, while the other three rocked the cart, laughing and taunting as they threw the contents at the man cowering against the wall.

'Dace?' To her astonishment he was smiling, a smile of fiendish delight.

'We have just found our transport. There's just a minor impediment to overcome. Take Lucky, will you?' And, without awaiting her reply, he slipped the child off his back and strode forward, that catlike gait seemingly more pronounced, more lethally smooth, as he approached the group.

For a moment the boys paused in their torment of the grocer, but, seeing that the newcomer was only one man, with a woman and two children in the background, labelled him a 'soft' family man, and resumed their game. One shouted, 'Back off, mister!' and tossed an orange at Dace, too contemptuously for accuracy.

Dace's smile never wavered, but as the adrenalin raced through his veins his eyes swept from one face to another, assessing, deciding. Finally, ten feet from them he stopped, addressing the one he had reasoned was the leader. 'You know,' he said pleasantly, 'I was beginning to get bored with the day—my hotel burned to the ground, all the best poker players leaving town— I was wondering what to do for amusement.'

The boy at the pony's head remained, but the other three ranged alongside each other. The two either side of the leader were grinning and nudging, but the eldest boy was still and watchful. All had been raised in the gutters, but this one had a gin-soaked mother, a violent alcoholic for a father, and four younger brothers to support. He had learned from the School of Hard Knocks not to underestimate his opponent. It was to him that Dace spoke again. 'If you leave now I won't take the price of the merchandise from your hides and, as disappointed as I shall be, I really do advise you to leave.'

The leader noted the breadth of shoulder beneath the suit and the board-hard stomach. He noted—and disbelieved—the amusement, the spark of pure joy in the green eyes. He reasoned that, the odds being four to one in his favour, however dangerous, his opponent was hardly worth counting. He made a serious error of judgement. He did not immediately withdraw.

'Leave the nag, Joe,' he ordered. 'This toff thinks he's going to give us trouble.'

Ignoring him, Dace crossed to the plump Italian

grocer leaning, still trembling, against the wall, and removed his jacket. 'Would you be kind enough to hold this for me, sir?'

'I thank the Holy Virgin for you, mister, but. . .but I think you are still one crazy fool!'

'My. . .family and I have to get to Franklin Street. The little girl is ill and needs transport and I should be most grateful if you could make a short diversion and take us there, but before I can ask such a favour it appears I must first rid you of this inconvenience. Excuse me.' And, spinning on one foot, he slammed a fist into the jaw of the one they called Joe, who had drawn close to overhear the exchange. The boy travelled two feet in the air and was unconscious before he hit the ground.

Dace smiled at the others. 'Three to one,' he stated gently, stepping clear of the grocer and encouraging, 'Why don't you all charge at once? You *might* just do some *damage*.'

This time the leader made his second error in judgement by doing precisely as requested. With a shout of, 'Let's get him!' he led the other two forward. . .and continued forward as Dace caught hold, pivoted, assisted him over an iron-hard calf and threw. The bully had never learned to break-fall and landed badly on his side and shoulder. He cried out as his collarbone cracked a fraction before his head hit the pavement and night fell.

Dace continued his lightning movement round and, driving his left elbow into one boy's face, lashed out at the other with his right foot, catching him in the knee and dislocating it. With a cry the boy crumpled to the ground, eyes bulging in terror, pain and disbelief.

Ignoring the carnage he had wreaked, Dace crossed to the gaping man and relieved him of the jacket. 'Now,' he said gently, not even breathing hard, 'may I ask you to drive us over to Franklin? I can assure you no harm will come to you on the way.'

With an effort the man closed his mouth and nodded. 'I. . .I don't doubt it, sir! It will. . .will be my pleasure to take you.' And quickly he cleared a place in the cart for the children. 'You and your wife will find enough room up on the seat with me. It will be a bit of a squeeze, but the cart is too dirty for a lady and gent such as yourselves.'

When Dace conveyed the message to Charisse she glanced ruefully down at her torn and filthy dress. 'Do you think he was joking?' she asked, then, 'Are you going to leave those boys there? They could be badly hurt. You demolished them, Dace!'

'They got what they deserved. I have no sympathy for pariahs like that. There are bound to be more; a disaster like this brings everything out of the shadows that wouldn't normally see the light of day. No, let them be tended to by their own, or rot for all I care. I'll be happier when you and the children are safe.' He led them over to the cart, lifted Mark and Lucy up among the boxes of fruit and vegetables, and Charisse up on to the seat, springing up beside her.

The grocer was already mounted and turned to Charisse with a smile. 'Your husband one hella guy, you know?' She opened her mouth to answer that Dace was not her husband but the man was continuing, 'Sorry for the tight squeeze, but anyone with a wife as pretty as you should be so lucky for such an excuse to squeeze.' Chuckling, he slapped the reins over the pony's back and with a jerk they started off.

The motion threw Charisse sideways and she heard Dace's low laugh as his arm came around her waist to steady her, drawing her close. Attempting to hold herself rigid was like trying to fight the constricting coils of a python and his murmured, 'Relax!' made her aware that he was enjoying her discomfort.

The grocer, whether through relief or natural verbosity, kept up a continuous patter until they reached their destination, allowing Charisse to lose herself in thought, marvelling at the camaraderie and courage of the citizenry. The streets they traversed were relatively untouched, though two large fires raged in one block and the evacuees were assembled in apparently organised groups, sharing their salvaged food and blankets with a generosity that only such a disaster could have brought to the surface.

One man shouted to Dace, 'If you are going to Tent City could you take my wife and me?'

'We're not,' replied Dace, 'but we can give you a lift to Franklin.'

'It's OK. We'll call another cab,' came the laughing rejoinder.

'Tent City?' queried Charisse.

'The parks and spaces where the fires and quake haven't touched will be used as temporary camp grounds for those who are homeless. They will have help there and probably doctors in a medical tent. They will find loved ones who have become separated and organise search and salvage parties. Vast areas like Golden Gate Park will be a centre of operations for re-building, literally a city within a city. Ah, here we are!'

They had reached their destination and he lifted them down, first the children then Charisse, who asked anxiously, 'Dace, are you certain the new owner won't mind? Do you know him? I know it won't be for long, but. . .' And she trailed off before his wide smile.

'I think we might have played this scenario before.'

'You mean. . .'

'George Davis left the house in the hands of a realtor with his lawyer having signatory. The original purchaser changed his mind, going for a smaller place when his wife objected to keeping Davis's staff on—a prerequisite of the sale.'

'And you bought it? Whatever for, when you had the Gateway rooms?'

He turned to face her and again there was that warmth, that searching in his eyes reminiscent of Muir

Woods. 'I decided you were right. A hotel isn't permanent, not a real home to raise a family in. You once mentioned changing values; I never thought I would, never wanted to, so I guess you might say this is all thanks to a slip of a thing that drifted into my life and is soon to drift out again. . .isn't she?'

Charisse wanted to cry out, 'No, I want to stay! I want to build that home with you, beside you, for you—for us,' and she bit her lips as she remembered his eyes when she told him that Melinda was hurt. Whether he loved both women—as only a man could— or desired her and loved Melinda, it was not enough. Charisse could not settle for half a love when hers was so complete. Quietly, chokingly, she answered, 'Yes,' then, 'Shall we go in?' and turned away, not seeing the bleakness in his eyes or the tightening of the fine mouth.

Little had changed and at Charisse's question he explained, 'Apart from one or two sentimental *objets d'art*, Davis wanted to begin again; new world, new life, new home.'

The butler, Pendleton, appeared as they entered, and with a short bow said, 'Welcome, Mr LaVelle, Miss Linton.'

Dace nodded. 'Thank you. We should like some coffee and some milk for the children now, and perhaps some light refreshment later, whatever Cook can concoct fairly speedily. We all need to bathe and change, and the little girl needs a bed and some attention.'

'Mrs Frobisher will see to that and I shall arrange for some luncheon—er—dinner.' For a fraction of a second the perfect composure slipped. It was certainly too late for one and somewhat too early for the other, and only a disaster of such epic proportions as had occurred could have made him serve a meal out of the socially correct hours.

Dace sympathised, and said, 'Do what you can. The Gateway was gutted, Miss Linton and young Lucy here have narrowly escaped death when their surroundings collapsed about them, and none of us has eaten since yesterday afternoon.'

The man's face paled. 'Forgive me, sir. I am most terribly sorry. I shall see to it immediately and personally.'

Sinking into a chair, Charisse drew Lucy into her lap and leaned back, closing her eyes. 'Poor Pendleton. He was probably Caesar's handservant in an earlier life, serving a dish of immaculately polished grapes and a perfectly chilled goblet of wine while Rome burned. The perfect butler.'

'People *are* strange,' Dace remarked. 'If there is a shower of rain that cuts short a picnic they will moan all the following week about the weather. If the mail is late or a boat docks early they are ready for a lynching. Yet here we are with the city in ruins, thousands homeless, and they all pull together with not one word of complaint. Why must it take a war or disaster before one human volunteers to help another?'

'Or help himself,' Charisse said grimly, thinking of the hooligans whom they had recently encountered.

Dace caught her thought and smiled. 'They are fortunately a very small minority.'

She gave a shudder. 'I'm glad you were there.'

Seeing the remembered fear in that involuntary shudder, he attempted to lighten it. 'It *did* offer a diversion. I quite enjoyed it.'

The grey eyes looked up at him speculatively. 'I really believe you did—just as you showed no fear with that gang in Chinatown. What kind of man are you, Dace? Sometimes I think you are gentle and caring, then I see you in action and there's a deeply inherent violence in you that frightens me.' She would have said more, but caught Mark's wide-eyed gaze, so lowered her eyes, stroking back Lucy's hair.

Dace came to drop on one knee beside her chair and caught at her hand, stilling it. 'Nothing,' he said quietly but with a force that caused her heart to skip a beat, 'nothing I do will ever harm you, and there is nothing I would *not* do to protect what is mine.' Grey eyes met smoked jade and lightning flashed, but——

'Your coffee, sir,' declared Pendleton from the doorway.

CHAPTER EIGHTEEN

THAT night, with the city still in flames, five hundred and fourteen blocks of twenty-eight thousand buildings reduced to rubble, and seven hundred lives lost, Charisse slept as deeply as the two children in the adjoining rooms. The mental and physical exhaustion of all that had gone before, combined with the sudden rescue and present feeling of total safety, proved to be an overwhelming opiate. Dace, on the other hand, slept not at all.

'A brandy, sir?' Pendleton asked at just before eleven, longing for his own bed but unable to retire until dismissed, and was relieved to hear,

'I can help myself. Get some sleep; there will be much to do tomorrow.' The tone was remote, the features that stared into space were brooding in the candle-light, causing the butler to persist.

'If there is anything at all, sir, you know I am here to serve. Mr Davis often felt the need to unburden himself at the end of a long and difficult day. I am known, sir, for my broad shoulders, large ears, and exceedingly short memory.'

At last he received a smile. 'How revolting! Go to bed; I am fine.'

Dace sat there a further half an hour, the brandy he had poured untouched in the cut-crystal goblet. Over dinner Charisse had announced her intention of leaving with Ralph and Lucy as soon as transport could be arranged. By the afternoon, the ferry building being untouched, Dace had learned that refugees from the city were being ferried across to Oakland in their hundreds and he knew that with such incentive the buckled rail line to out of state would be repaired

233

within a day or two. He had three choices. He could let her go. He could beg her to stay. He could go with her. All options at that moment, in the soft glow of candle-light, seemed too fraught with complications. With each one he stood a chance of losing—and Dace was not a loser by nature; nor was he a man to show his hand until he had all other hands counted—but then, never had the stakes been so high.

He rose and, as was his nightly ritual over the past four years, went up to check on Mark. The boy was characteristically sprawled face down, half in and half out of the bed with the covers in a heap on the floor. With a smiling shake of the head Dace went to re-arrange both limbs and bedding, then, on impulse, moved to the other room to where Lucy slept. For a full minute he stared down at the child, noting the gauntness, the pallor, the hollowed eyes and, last of all but most telling, the defensive foetal ball she was curled into and the hand clutching the sheet to her mouth, even in sleep afraid to cough. 'Poor scrap,' he murmured, but did not disturb her and left.

In the room between slept Charisse and for several seconds Dace stood outside that door, everything in him crying out that he was on the wrong side. He felt an almost uncontrollable urge to fling open the door, sweep her into his arms and savour the delights of that body which had nightly haunted his dreams. Worse, he knew that she would not resist. It was not enough.

Dace the gambler was, for the first time in his rich and varied life, unwilling to take a chance on Lady Luck. Dace the adventurer was uncertain of a terrain unknown—that of the heart. Dace the victor, the conqueror, the possessor, found himself possessed. Half angrily he slammed a fist against the wall and welcomed the pain. Action, that was what he needed—hard work, a challenge that would empty his mind. Outside there was a city that needed rebuilding; that should suffice—for now.

Charisse stirred, the thud outside her door part of her restless dreaming. Slowly, reluctantly, she came awake, then sat up and swung her legs out of the bed as she heard the front door slam. From the window she saw the red glow lighting the night sky and, below, Dace cross the street and stride purposefully down the hill. 'It's none of my business,' she stated, but there was a huskiness, a tightness in her throat that had little to do with her still sleepy state. In that direction lay the Mission District—and Melinda. 'None of my business at all,' she reiterated, returning to her bed, staring up at the shadows on the ceiling. 'If he had wanted me to stay he would have asked me over dinner, or even after the children were abed and we talked, so very carefully, of nothing at all.' Then, that tightness becoming a ball of fire, 'If he loved me he would have told me so!'

In a fight-or-flight situation, when every instinct told her otherwise, Charisse usually chose the former course of action. This time she knew only that she was hopelessly in love with a man who could not forget his beautiful and now heartbreakingly crippled ex-wife. 'I *have* to leave,' she decided, 'even if only to salvage my pride.'

Sleep did return, but fitfully and filled with dreams, and waking at seven was almost a relief. Making her way downstairs, still in her only and much tattered dress, she went into the kitchen and approached the cook, who was already preparing vegetables for a thick and appetising lunchtime soup. 'I wonder if you could help me Mrs—er—Miss. . .?'

'Emma, Miss Linton. Just call me Emma. What can I do for you?'

Relieved at the dumpy little woman's open friendliness, Charisse hesitantly asked, 'Well, it's about my clothing. My entire wardrobe was destroyed at Mr LaVelle's hotel and I can't remain in this one dress. I wondered. . .well. . .'

'Of course, miss. If you wouldn't be offended, our tweenie is much of your size. Her dresses aren't quality, you understand, but Mr Davis, he was real good to us and we never went short. I am sure she'd be only too pleased to let you have her best dress until you can call a seamstress or find a ready-made.' The crackling brown eyes creased at the corners and she glanced toward the outer wall from behind which one could hear the fire bells and clamour. 'That's if there is a fashion house left. I haven't been out myself, but it looked terrible from the window. We were shook about a bit, but no damage, praise the Lord.'

Gratefully Charisse thanked her and an hour later had changed, forced down some scrambled egg and gathered the children together. 'I'm going out so you must play quietly and give no trouble until I get back. Mark, your daddy went out late last night and, since he hasn't returned, I must assume he is helping with the salvage operations.' Silently she finished, Or comforting Melinda! 'I am going over to the Gateway to see whether there is anything salvageable, and on the way I will try to find a seamstress for *all* of us.'

Mark had completely recovered after a good night's sleep and gave a self-assured nod. 'Don't worry; I'll take charge. I can look after Lucky and explore the house. It's really quite exciting, isn't it?'

Charisse laughed. 'I'm glad you think so.'

'You know I have had more adventures since you came than I have *ever* had before. You won't go, *ever*, will you?'

A fiery fist punched into her abdomen. 'I. . .I have to go back with Dr Ralph to see our father. I told you that.'

'But you will come back.'

Unable to meet that trusting gaze, she turned away, prevaricating, 'Come on now; I *must* go or the morning will be gone,' and left quickly before her heart made her sweep him into a fierce embrace and promise to keep him forever.

Once more in the streets of the city, Charisse was staggered at the devastation, and, the further she walked, the more the horror grew. Fires still raged out of control and both police and the newly arrived army patrolled the streets, the occasional burst of gunfire coming over the babble of shouted commands, signifying that law and order was being strictly enforced. Looters were not let off with a warning, few were arrested: they were simply shot and the numbers dropped drastically within hours as the word got out.

The city itself still reeled under the disaster, whole city blocks—a total of four square miles—annihilated, but the citizenry, though bowed, were far from broken. Already soup kitchens had been set up and makeshift 'post boxes' on various corners held not mail for delivery, but cards, scraps of paper, letters and messages for loved ones. Charisse paused at one and felt an ache in her heart as she read, 'Mary—Billy's dead. I will be in G. G. Pk. Tom' and 'Where are you, Toby? Be here tomorrow at noon' and 'I'm sorry I yelled at you, Jack. If you're alive write me here.' There were a score of similar messages from the heart and Charisse sent up a silent prayer that she and hers had been spared.

Eventually, with many diversions, since landmarks had virtually disappeared, she reached the Gateway Hotel and stopped dead. 'Oh, no!' She had not realised. What once had been an imposing edifice was now reduced to a blackened ruin. The buildings on both sides had also been destroyed, as had the Hopkins Villa at number 999, and the Stanford Villa at 905, as, too, was the lovely Fairmont Hotel even before its opening, and Charisse's heart went out to Dace in his loss. Men were still working on the site and a white-coated doctor bent over a little girl only just brought from the rubble.

He looked up with a frown as he became aware of

Charisse's presence. 'You a relative or just an onlooker?'

'No, I——'

'Well, we don't need morbid curiosity; we need help.' His tone was belligerent as he turned away, the exhaustion as taut as a wire behind his words, ready to snap.

Immediately, all else forgotten, Charisse went to kneel at his side. 'Tell me what to do.' She shuddered at the deep gash in the child's leg, but at his impatient glance stated, 'I'm not the fainting type, Doctor.'

'Right. Put pressure here, then, and here while I bind it. There is little I can do; she needs a hospital. Dammit, they *all* need a hospital! The whole city is a casualty area!' He finished binding the leg and called another man over. 'Take this one to the wagon. She'll live.' He rose, one hand on his aching back. 'Thanks,' he said, and went to walk away.

'Wait!'

Reluctantly he turned, chaffing at the delay. 'Well?'

'Let me go with you. I'm no nurse, but I know a little.' And as he still hesitated she urged, 'You've got to take me, Doctor: who else is available and willing?'

He looked her up and down slowly, then gave a half-smile. 'Very well, but I'm going to work your rump off, so don't say you weren't warned.'

'I'm used to that, I'm a rancher's daughter.'

'Do you always have the last word?'

'Generally. Now who is next?'

And work she did, uncaring of the dust and discomfort, unaware of the hours passing, seeing only the broken limb before her, the shock-dazed eyes, the blood—and more blood—until,

'Charisse! I've been out of my mind looking for you!' and she was lifted bodily from the ground and crushed in an all-enveloping embrace. 'Why didn't you tell anyone where you were going?' Dace growled against her hair. '*No* female has given me *half* the trouble you have!'

As she looked up he swept her face with kisses, oblivious of a smiling doctor until the man said, 'If you insist on practising mouth-to-mouth resuscitation so zealously, would you please do it elsewhere?'

Finally the grip loosened and Charisse pulled back, breathless, eyes shining, reading the worry in that intense stare and reassuring him, 'I came to see the Gateway, but found the doctor here and stayed to help.'

'And a great help she has been,' the doctor praised. 'Quite something, this little lady of yours. However, I'm afraid, as promised, I have worked her into the ground and if you've a mind to take her home—if you still have a home—I'll not object overmuch.'

Retaining one arm about her waist, Dace nodded. 'Exactly what I had in mind and, yes, we do have a home to go to.'

'Excellent! A hot drink and bed; that's what I prescribe.'

Charisse flushed crimson as those deep-jade eyes gleamed. 'That, too, is what I had in mind. Come. . . my dear. . .let's go home.'

Charisse pulled free as he escorted her away, and straightened her hair and clothing. 'You enjoyed that, didn't you?'

'I always enjoy the sight of that rose tint to your cheeks, but not half as much as the thought of carrying out the doctor's orders. . .purely for your health's sake, of course!'

'Rat!' She brushed at her skirt, desperately seeking to divert him. 'I shall never get this clean. It was the tweenie's best dress too.'

Allowing the change of subject, he promised, 'I will buy her another. I have a seamstress already at the house as well as an architect. Both will be rarer than gold tomorrow. It pays to have contacts and I have invited Ralph to stay with us, since his place was demolished.'

'That's good of you. Thank you.'

He gave her a quick sideways glance. 'The rail track won't be repaired for another two or three days, I am told—Saturday at the very earliest—so you'll all stay at least until then.'

A silence fell; a taut, painful silence in which each waited for the other to continue that thread of thought, but neither was able to take that first irrevocable step. Then, following the path that cut across that commitment, Charisse said, 'So you saw Melinda, then. How is she?'

'Still heavily sedated but conscious enough to fear me. Ralph told me that it was thanks to your vehement orders that her leg was saved. Why?'

Only the first sentence caught at her like a hand clutching her throat. 'Why should she fear you?' She halted, turning to face him, forcing him to look at her, forcing herself to say, 'Why, when it's so obvious that you are still in love with her?' and saw the pure shock widen his eyes.

'Love her? If I'd got my hands on the bitch when you and Mark came off Palo Duro I'd have near killed her! That's why she went into hiding.'

Charisse swayed, joy mingling with disbelief. 'But——'

'It was her insane jealousy that caused you such an ordeal in the first place. Like a dog guarding a dry and inedible bone, she could not, would not accept that it was finished, dead, dried up.' Calming, he gave a wry smile. 'I guess I've been all kinds of a fool. She saw it even before I did.'

Even then, looking down into the perfect curves and planes of her face in which the huge grey cat's eyes seemed to eclipse all else, even then he could not trust what he saw there. Drawing a deep, shuddering breath, he finished, 'Anyway, Melinda is no longer worth my

retribution. The quake did far more to her than I ever
contemplated. Ralph says it will be a miracle if she
even walks again, though thanks to you she at least has
a chance. I still don't understand why you, who had
every reason to hate her, first saved her life when you
could simply have walked away, and then her leg when
it would have been more logical to accede to the
surgeon's judgement.'

Charisse sighed and turned to walk on. 'You still
don't know me very well, do you? I never did hate
Melinda: I understood her too well. I could never
voluntarily let anything die that could be saved,
especially a creature as hurt as she was. As for her leg,
well, again I empathised. A woman as beautiful as
Melinda, one for whom her beauty was her whole
raison d'être, would, I felt sure, sooner lose her life
than stump around on a false leg.'

Dace shook his head. 'You are an incredible person.'

'No. On equal terms I might have let battle com-
mence, but the price was too high. I hope she recovers,
for both your sakes. You will take care of her now of
course.'

'Not at all.' At her surprised glance, the hope quickly
veiled, his lips tightened. 'Whatever feeling I might
have had for Melinda in the past she has quite effectively killed. She will go to a surgeon in New York,
one who will see that mess of bone, nerve and tissue as
a challenge. Ralph met the man at a convention here
in the city and says the work he does is nothing short
of miraculous. Of course her parents may well forgive
her too and take her back home. I don't hate her,
though there was a moment back there. . .but I shan't
lose sleep over her future, wherever and with whomever it lies.'

His words washed over her, bringing a confused
torrent of emotion, and she felt as if she were drowning
in some deep, dark whirlpool. Melinda leaving the city.
Dace appearing not to care. All so completely opposite

to her own reckoning that it disorientated her, so that she clung to the only thread of sanity in her reckoning. 'The children will be wondering what has happened.'

'Charisse——'

'No. Not now. The children!' And, almost running, she headed back to the house, leaving him to follow.

Only later, much later, when the seamstress had finished fussing over measurements and the architect over sketches, and both had departed, and Mark and Lucy were in bed, and Ralph come and gone again to toil through his second night—only then was Dace able to force Charisse into standing still and facing him. Even then, seeing the panic deep in her eyes, he knew that still he could lose the greatest gamble of his life. He wanted to seize her by the arms and shake her, shouting, 'I love you, you stubborn, proud, troublesome, worrisome, wonderful woman! Can't you see that?' But instead he asked quietly, 'What did you think of Paul Andrews' sketches?' and saw the flare of relief.

'Innovative,' she ventured, looking aside to the pile of scattered sheets of paper, each covered with daring sweeps and soaring pinnacles. 'Nothing like the old Gateway.'

'Nothing at all,' he agreed. 'I *will* build again, Charisse. I doubted it yesterday, but not now, not seeing these. I'll *build*, not *re*-build and my new hotel will rise as this city will rise, like a phoenix from the ashes, stronger and more beautiful than ever before.' His eyes were alight with visions. 'I'll call it the Phoenix. . .' His hand came up to touch her hair and his voice was liquid fire. 'No. The *Golden* Phoenix. We'll make a new beginning, a new life. We *won't* fail. Together we *can't* fail.'

Charisse stopped breathing. 'Together?'

His hands closed over her upper arms and only then did she realise that he was trembling. 'I won't let you go, not now, not ever. Run from me and I'll follow you, hide and I'll find you, if it takes me to the end of nowhere and the rest of my life. You belong to me. From the first moment I set eyes on you you belonged to me. I *won't* let you go!' His mouth descended crushingly, possessively on hers as he pulled her hard against him, taking her breath away, forcing her to believe.

Charisse's senses reeled, her heart repeating, Together, together, as a litany, her mind fighting for control, but then surrendering as the kiss deepened, his tongue finding the damp sweetness of her inner mouth, swirling over the tongue that came tentatively to meet it. She felt consciousness slipping from her as her ribcage constricted, but then his grip shifted and with a gasp she sucked air into her tortured lungs. 'Dace!'

The fierce light left his eyes, but the carved-granite features remained unyielding. Grey eyes met jade-green. Then, with something akin to a groan, he swept her up into his arms and carried her, as if she weighed no more than a feather, out into the hall and up the stairs. Pausing at the master bedroom, he kicked open the door, crossed the threshold and heeled it shut after him, only then setting her on her feet.

She had seen his gentleness, his caring tenderness, but now he was all the powers of primeval darkness— pagan, life at the beginning of life, fire even before tamed by primitive man, unquenchable, all-consuming. For one blind second she knew fear, not of him but of herself. She wanted him in that instant with the pure, unadulterated lust of a female seeking a mate—the most powerful male creature of the herd, the leader of the pack. Something rose in her that swept away all civilisation and her fingers rose of their own volition to tear back the shirt from his shoulders as she surged upwards against him. Her teeth found his throat, found the strong pulse, licked at it, moved to his shoulder, caught the scent of him and the sky began to fall in on her.

'If you don't take me here and now, Dace, I think I'll lose my mind!'

Her words destroyed the last vestige of hard-won control and within seconds their clothing was scattered about them as they fell on to the bed, clutching, entwining, rolling, arching, moulding breast to chest, thigh to thigh, gasping out incomprehensible words in which love held no dominion. She had not commanded 'love me' but 'take me'. And he did so, magnificently, almost brutally, but yet, even as the firmament crashed about them, that great strength was held in check. Charisse, however, was too innocent for such control and her nails raked long weals into his back as the multiple spasms engulfed her.

Only when the storm had passed and, almost as violently as their coming together, they rolled apart did she see the havoc she had wrought by the crimson stripes on the sheet. Her blood ran as cold as it had run volcano-hot a moment before and her voice emerged a horrified whisper. 'What have I done?'

Recovering his breath, Dace laughed huskily, triumphantly. 'You, kitten, have just emerged a full-blooded she-cat, claws and all. I have never experienced such a wondrous metamorphosis in my life. No one has taken my breath, my heart, my very soul so completely.'

Her panic faded before the laughter in his eyes and she ran light nails down his chest. 'No one?'

His smile died and he brought strong fingers to curl into her hair. 'No one, Charisse,' he stated, and the ghost of Melinda dissolved into the ether forever. 'You know, I find I have the most outdated feudal streak,' he smiled, the curve of his lips belying the searching of his eyes as he brought his breathing under control. 'I used to dream of begetting a dynasty, but right now I'd settle for a pint-sized adult who'd resemble either one of us.'

Charisse found her heart pounding. 'I. . . . I think we . . .might have made a fair start.'

His fingers brushed the glaze of perspiration from her brow as he murmured, 'One has to be quite certain,' and she wondered whether it was a child he was speaking of or something far more important to this moment.

Answering both, she met his deep regard proudly. 'Love me, Dace,' she said.

This time it was different—different from any time that had gone before—as his lips brushed feather-light over hers, caressing, clinging, then retreating, and she felt the loss of that touch. Then, as he lowered his mouth again to cover hers, she felt the passion, held in check, and the joy and wanting and needing rose within her. His tongue slipped between her parted teeth, probing and exploring, teasing at the tongue that evaded then advanced towards his. A wave of pleasure washed over her as the kiss went on, deepening, provocative, taking the taste of her as communion.

Gently now he pulled her to him so that the length of their bodies became one. 'Sweeter by far than the sweetest honey,' he murmured against her mouth. Slowly he moved his lips down, across her chin in tiny kisses, over the smooth column of her throat and down to one breast. 'Softer than all roses.' Swirling his tongue over the peak, he teased it into hardness, leaving her gasping as he took it into his mouth.

As he continued to kiss first one breast then the other, his free hand travelled over her, sweeping across her ribcage, moulding the slender waist, brushing over the soft curve of her stomach, ever downwards until he reached the mound at the apex of her thighs.

Charisse drew in a quick rasping breath at the contact and a low cry of pleasure was torn from her as those knowledgeable fingers moved inwards, exploring deeply. She felt the rising excitement as her body arched against his hand, writhing helplessly as wave upon wave of liquid fire rippled through her. A slow spiral of ecstasy built within her, a hunger that caused her to cry out his name, begging for fulfilment.

Dace's mouth returned to hers, taking that cry deep within him as he reared over her, and her legs opened to allow him access to quench the fire that threatened to consume her as surely as the inferno that had consumed the city. She felt the weight of him, felt the throbbing length of his manhood where a moment before his fingers had been, then the strong, deep surge inwards, and she cried out as her very soul melted before the heat of the sword sheathed in the velvet scabbard, and again cried out softly, in wonder, as she experienced feelings she had never before dreamed of.

Charisse felt herself totally possessed, yet in being possessed knew that she, too, was the possessor and it was this that made the difference—no distance but a fusing of mind and body. Instinctively she moved in counterpoint to his deep strokes as he reached the depths of her. She felt his fingers again creating a rising frenzy to match that within, and she clung to him, curving her legs round to draw him even deeper, her hands clinging to his shoulders.

When the spasm she had waited for ripped through her like a forest fire she moaned deep in her throat. Another, and her hips arched high beneath him in quivering response.

'Come, my love,' Dace commanded softly. 'Come fly with me. Come now.'

She gave herself up to the sensations, surrendered completely, feeling him shudder, crying her name harshly as the world crashed about them. Again and again the orgasmic quakes joined them, tossed them upwards in soaring ecstasy, before allowing them to tumble, then drift, then softly come to rest.

Dace felt her tears against his skin and tenderly he brushed them away, smiling into her dazed eyes. 'My golden phoenix,' he said in wonder. 'My perfect woman, my lover. . .my life.'

'My husband,' she answered, and knew beyond any doubt that it was so, for this moment—forever.

EPILOGUE

APRIL 1909. A third of the city had been rebuilt, stronger, more resilient, more beautiful than ever before. Into its crest San Francisco had incorporated a phoenix rising from the flames, but nowhere was it so perfectly symbolised—in spirit, in design, in fact— than in the great golden bird that soared proudly over the portals of the Golden Phoenix Hotel on Nob Hill.

The daring design defied all preconceived presumptions. It appeared to float above the pavement, its space-defying angles rippling upwards in a sweep of glass and marble a full century before its time. No gargoyles nor floral façade broke the almost stark symmetry. No artfully wrought cupolas, no stained-glass bays marred the purity of line. There was only the phoenix, blinding in gold leaf—the phoenix and the great gold dome; for Dace had found in Charisse's collection the poem which spelled out the dream:

'In Xanadu did Kubla Khan
A stately pleasure-dome decree. . .'

The time was right. The time was now.

In the elegant oyster and gold foyer were packed the dreamers, the adventurers, the rich and the would-be-rich, from all over San Francisco. Anyone who was, and many who hoped to be, flocked into the great hall for the much-publicised opening.

Mark, now a strikingly handsome ten-year-old, stood with the exquisitely beautiful, porcelain-fragile Lucy at the foot of the great curved staircase. Behind them, gentle hands curved over their shoulders, stood Ralph, one of San Francisco's most eminent and affluent doctors—yet one who would still disappear for days at

248

a time into the poor quarters to seek out bundles of rags in doorways and turn them into human beings.

'I wish Johnny could be here,' whispered Mark, and Ralph nodded.

'But then your brother is only two and needs his sleep far more than you do.'

'*I* wish Ganda John could be here,' said Lucy, thinking of the man for whom the sleeping infant had been named, but this time Ralph could not find it in him to smile.

John Linton had suffered his last heart attack within weeks of their return from San Francisco. In that time he had been a most loving mentor and guide to both Mark and the sick Lucy, but it was the latter whom he had taken into his heart and almost forced by will-power alone to recover.

'Perhaps he is looking down on us from heaven,' Ralph comforted. 'We could all have used a little extra time in our past, but none more than he.'

On the far side of the great hall stood another with similar thoughts—Lee Rand, wealthy and influential founder of Seekers, an agency specialising in missing persons. With uncountable hundreds 'going missing', voluntarily or otherwise, in the United States each year, the agency was a veritable gold-mine. Beside Lee stood his wife of a year, a petite, flaxen-haired beauty whose long-lashed smoky grey eyes constantly strayed to her husband's face in open adoration.

He turned to her and the lop-sided grin that she loved so much eradicated years from the craggy features. She would never know that something was missing from that smile and Lee would never have told her that, for all her striking resemblance to Charisse Linton, now LaVelle, she could never *be* Charisse Linton—now LaVelle. Yet his new wife loved him with every fibre of her being and sometimes, very occasionally—in the darkness of night—it was enough.

Another who had found an acceptable compromise

in life was conspicuous by her absence, for San Francisco society still remembered the vibrant personality of Melinda Marsh, who had disappeared after the quake, leaving rumours rippling for months. Not even close acquaintances had been told the name of the person who had sent the huge spray of creamy white lilies that graced a table in one corner of the hall, and only Dace himself knew of her life since the quake had torn it apart.

Perhaps it was a vestige of feeling left from the days, and nights, of the past, perhaps a gambler's desire to keep a close eye on potentially dangerous opponents, but every few months he had made discreet enquiries as to her welfare. He had learned of the agonising year of successive operations that had reconstructed her leg, and of the growing devotion of the surgeon who had made it his personal challenge.

It was therefore no surprise to learn of their engagement and a bare six months later of the wedding: not a great society affair that the old Melinda would have demanded, but a quiet occasion in a small church in New Hampshire where her husband's family lived. And so there were the lilies, and a newspaper cutting with a caption beneath the photograph.

One of New York's top surgeons—our local boy Shane Ashton—today married New York society heiress Melinda Marsh.

And there was a card from Melinda.

Be happy for me, Dace, as I am happy for you. Please forgive and, if you remember, try to remember the good times, as I do. Melinda.

At the foot of the stairs, one hand on the base column that supported the long sweep of oyster and green marble staircase, one booted foot crossed with deceptive negligence over the other, as he had a lifetime ago in another time, another place, Dace *was* thinking of the past, and how far he had come. From New Orleans riverboat gambler to millionaire, from conquering adventurer to conquered family man with responsibilities. He smiled at the thought, for the burden sat lightly on his broad shoulders and he would not have changed it for all the wealth in the world. And then he smiled no more as he caught the ripple that ran like quicksilver through the gathering and his eyes swept upwards, as his heart soared at the vision there.

Charisse stood poised at the top of the stairway, ethereal, a creature of gossamer, a butterfly about to take flight, yet a butterfly so brilliant as to tear a gasp from the throat even as it blinded the eye. The white-gold hair was piled high in a confection of loops and whorls, with one single ringlet that escaped provocatively to drape over one shoulder, the rest topped by a magnificent gold filigree tiara.

It was the dress, however, that had caused the murmur of incredulous delight. Of pale gold satin, its deeply décolletée bodice curved upwards in wired petals to barely cup the high, full breasts, with petal overlays carried on to the top of the huge bishop sleeves that began a full four inches below her bare shoulders. From the pointed waistline the magnificent bell skirt billowed outwards to be caught up at each side and held by live golden-brown, speckled orchids, revealing a petticoat of creamy Spanish lace. At the rear, more orchids were scattered in profusion over the train that rippled backwards for over eight feet. It was a creation that embodied every possible dream.

Dace took six slow steps up to meet her, but then stopped, and his arm swept outwards and upwards in a gesture of both pride and wonder. 'Ladies. Gentlemen. Friends,' he said, that vibrant, rich voice carrying to all parts of the assembly. 'I give you. . .the golden phoenix.' And as Charisse began that slow, regal descent—

spun-gold hair, sun-gold skin, pale gold dress—their
gazes met and locked.

Only yours, her eyes promised. Only for you, my
love, my lover, my husband. . .my life. And the
applause welled up in a thunderous crescendo about
them.

An irresistible offer for you

Here at Reader Service we would love you to become a regular reader of Masquerade. And to welcome you, we'd like you to have 2 books, a cuddly teddy and a mystery gift - ABSOLUTELY FREE and without obligation.

Then, every 2 months you could look forward to receiving 4 more brand-new Masquerade historical romances for just £2.25 each, delivered to your door, postage and packing free. Plus our free Newsletter featuring special offers, author news, competitions with some great prizes, and lots more!

This invitation comes with no strings attached. You may cancel or suspend your subscription at any time, and still keep your free books and gifts.

It's so easy. Send no money now. Simply fill in the coupon below at once and post it to - Reader Service, FREEPOST, PO Box 236, Croydon, Surrey CR9 9EL.

NO STAMP REQUIRED

Yes! Please rush me 2 FREE Masquerade romances and 2 FREE gifts! Please also reserve me a Reader Service subscription. If I decide to subscribe, I can look forward to receiving 4 brand new Masquerade romances every 2 months for just £9.00, delivered direct to my door, postage and packing free. If I choose not to subscribe I shall write to you within 10 days - I can keep the books and gifts whatever I decide. I may cancel or suspend my subscription at any time. I am over 18 years of age.

Mrs/Miss/Ms/Mr _____ EP30M

Address _____

_____

Postcode _____ Signature _____

ASSOCIATION OF MAIL ORDER PUBLISHERS

mps
MAILING PREFERENCE SERVICE

The other exciting

MASQUERADE
Historical

available this month is:

TEN GUINEAS ON LOVE
Alice Thornton

To Charity Mayfield's shock, she discovered a year after
her father's death that his debts could mean losing her
home. Only by marriage could she touch her inheritance
and save Hazelhurst. The only sensible candidate would
be Edward, newly come into the Earldom, and the
Mayfields' neighbour, so impetuously Charity wrote to
propose!

But she'd made a mistake, the new Earl was *Jack*
Riversleigh, and he wasn't at all disposed to help out –
which led Charity rashly to bet him that she *could* find
a husband within a month...